Alpine Falls

(MAYBE YOURS) SERIES

STILL YOURS (MAYBE) YOURS FOR CHRISTMAS
(MAYBE) FOREVER YOURS (MAYBE)

KATHRYN KALEIGH

Also by Kathryn Kaleigh

The Gravity of Us Series

(Reading Order)

Just Breathe

Just Surface

Just Melt

Standalone Suspense

Out of Ashes

CONTEMPORARY

Alpine Falls (Maybe Yours) Series

(Reading Order)

Still Yours (Maybe)

Yours for Christmas (Maybe)

Forever Yours (Maybe)

(ALPINE FALLS)

Stranded in Alpine Falls

Belonging in Alpine Falls

The Spirit of Christmas in Alpine Falls

Christmas Wishes in Alpine Falls

Finding True North in Alpine Falls

A Ghost of Christmas Magic in Alpine Falls

Secrets and Second Chances

Honeymoon with a Stranger

Not Our Wedding

(SILVER PINES)

The Way Back to You

Back to Where We Began

When We Were Us

(ONCE UPON FOREVER)

My Forever Guy

Our Forever Love

Forever Vows

Finding Forever

Accidentally Forever

(TRUE NORTH)

Borrowed Until Monday

Still Mine

The Moon and the Stars at Christmas

Perfectly Mismatched

On the Way to Forever

A Merry Little Christmas

On the Way Home to Christmas

It was Always You

(UNBREAK MY HEART)

Begin Again

Love Again

Falling Again

(FOR THE LOVE OF THE FLIGHT)

Just Stay

Just Chance

Just Believe

Just Us

Just Once

Just Happened

Just Maybe

Just Pretend

Just Because

(MAGNETIC NORTH)

Second Chance Kisses

Second Chance Secrets

First Time Charm

Three Broken Rules

Second Chance Destiny

Unexpected Vows

(FALLING FOR CHRISTMAS)

The Heart of Christmas

The Magic of Christmas

In a One Horse Open Sleigh

A Secret Royal Christmas

An Old Fashioned Christmas

(CITY SKYLINE BILLIONAIRES)

Billionaire's Unexpected Landing

Billionaire's Accidental Girlfriend

Billionaire's Fallen Angel

Billionaire's Secret Crush

Billionaire's Barefoot Bride

(TRULY, MADLY, DEEPLY)

The Lady in the Red Dress

On the Edge of Chance

Sealed with a Kiss

Kiss Me at Midnight

The Heart Knows

(STOLEN ECHOES)

When Cupid's Arrow Strikes

Chasing Fireflies

A Chance Encounter

(EDGE OF THE HORIZON)

The Forever Equation

Pretend Boyfriend

All our Tomorrows

Kissing for Keeps

Out of the Blue

The Princess and the Playboy

(RED LIPSTICK KISSES)

Red Lipstick Kisses and Small Town Wishes

Stolen Dances and Big City Chances

Chance Connections and Upside Down Plans

A Christmas Kiss on the Twenty-Fifth

Believe in the Magic of Christmas

**Vows of Inheritance Series
(Reading Order)**

Vow to Protect

Vow to Redeem

ROMANTASY

(IN THE SPIRIT OF LOVE)

Spirits of the Heart

Out of Dreams and Ashes

Etched Upon the Heart

WESTERN ROMANCE

(LONE STAR HEARTS)

Wanted by a Texas Ranger

Saved by a Texas Ranger

(WHISKEY SPRINGS)

Finding Natalie

Promising Samantha

Falling for Allyson

Saving Savannah

Claiming Charlie

Rescuing Keira

Protecting Gabriella

Courting Isabella

TIME TRAVEL

(INTO THE MIST)

Written in the Wind

Scripted in the Stars

Destined in the Twilight

Promised in the Mist

Trapped in the Melody

(DRAGON'S BLOOD)

Dragon's Blood

Lavender Blue

Champagne Silver

Twilight Frost

Mountbatten Pink

(WHEN HEARTSTRINGS BECKON)

Rescued in Time

Meet me in 1879

(WHEN HEARTSTRINGS ECHO)

Messages Across Time

Falling Through to Forever

Once Upon a Winter's Spell

(BECKONED)

Before the Storm

Twist of Fate

When the Stars Align

Once Upon a Christmas

Once in a Blue Moon

A Wish Upon a Star

(BEGUILED)

When Lightning Strikes

Storm of Time

Midnight Storm

When the Moon Falls

Stormborn Angel

(SPELLED)

Time Tempest

The Heart Remembers

A Moment in Time

Moonlight Shadows

HISTORICAL

(TAPESTRY OF BLUE AND GRAY)

Shadows Beneath Magnolia Blooms

Secrets Among Southern Roses

(IT HAPPENED BY ACCIDENT)

Accidentally Alluring

Accidentally Married

(SOUTHERN BELLE CIVIL WAR)

Beyond Enemy Lines

Love Always

Hearts Under Siege

Hearts Under Fire

Away Down South in Dixie

The Reluctant Bride

Stay with Me

Jasmine Kisses

Magnolia Kisses

Gardenia Kisses

(THE QUINNS)

Wait for Me

Take Me Home

Keep Me Safe

FATED MATES

Riley's Mate

Aiden's Mate

Brayden's Mate

STANDALONE SUSPENSE

Lost and Found

All I Want for Christmas

Serenity

Courting Alley Cat

Alpine Falls

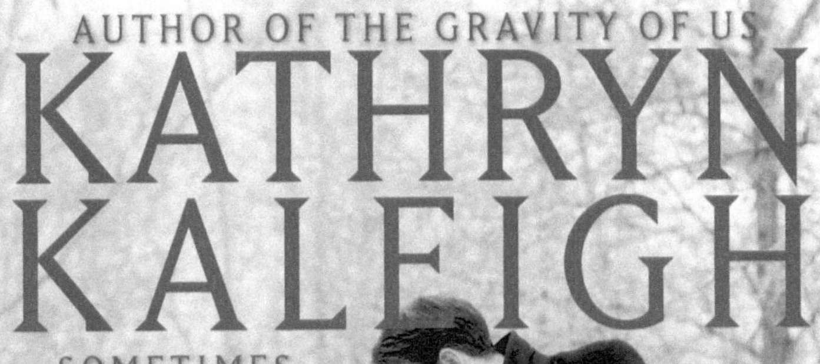

AUTHOR OF THE GRAVITY OF US
KATHRYN KALEIGH
SOMETIMES FOREVER JUST TAKES A LITTLE LONGER

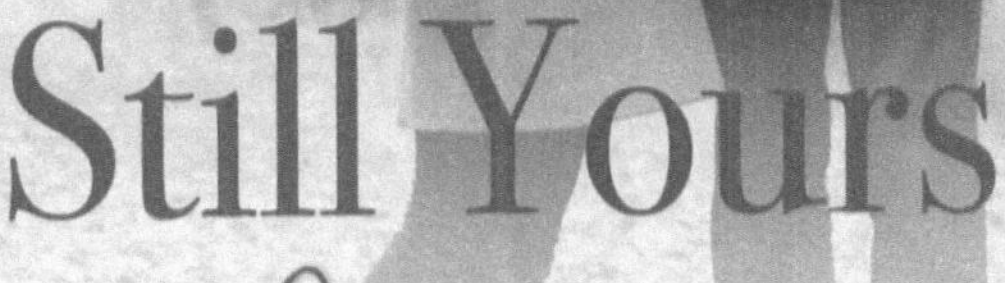

Still Yours (Maybe)
THE ALPINE FALLS (MAYBE YOURS) SERIES

Still Yours (Maybe)

She thought she was free to move on...
until the truth brought her
back to where love first began.

Chapter One

Hannah Moore

Friday Night Pizza

The Pizzeria with its fire-roasted sauce and woodfired pizza is owned and run by a second-generation family of Italians. Their parents brought their recipes with them when they moved to America from Italy, making it a unique and popular restaurant in the heart of Uptown Houston.

Italian music spills from hidden speakers blending with the sounds of the busy kitchen and the chatter of customers. Silverware and glasses clink against each other.

The tables are not those of the typical pizza parlor. The heavy tables are covered with thick white cloth tablecloths, candles in chunky white vases burning on each one.

Lush green strands of ivies wound their way up columns interspersed among the tables and over time crawled their way along the crossbeams in the ceiling, giving the indoor restaurant an almost outdoor feel.

The scent of Italian spices blends with the rich scent of pizza and the woodsmoke from the oven.

"One week from today," Olivia announces with obvious fanfare, leaning forward, her chin-length blonde-streaked hair falling forward. "You'll be married. Mrs. Theodore Smith."

Ignoring a reflexive wince, I smile brightly. Pretending a big part of that brightness isn't forced, I say the first thing that pops into my head. "I'm thinking maybe I'll keep my last name."

My two friends sitting on either side of me at the table look at me with horror in their eyes. Olivia and Madison.

Olivia is the sassy one with blonde-streaked short hair to match. Sassy is a good word to describe her. I've heard her called mouthy by a couple of people over the years. The word doesn't not fit her, but sassy is better.

Madison has long straight chestnut hair, all natural. Matches her all-business way of approaching the world. Her reading glasses do nothing to hide the beauty behind them. Serious. I'd say the best word to describe Madison is serious.

And I have shoulder-length hair in a raven-dark color, according to my stylist. If I had to sum myself up in one word, I'd have to go with complicated.

Lifting my glass of Pinot Noir with hints of cocoa, blackberry, and dark plum, I take a little sip. The red wine feels needlessly indulgent, but we're celebrating.

The three of us usually come here on Saturday nights and have a cold beer with our pizza. As Olivia sort of pointed out, I won't be here next Saturday. I'll be on my honeymoon.

Sort of honeymoon. Theo and I are combining his college football coaching conference with our honeymoon. In Tampa, Florida. What kind of fiancé would I be to say no to that? A honeymoon paid for by his college?

As he put it, that's money we can put toward a house one day. Maybe the excuse falls flat for me, but I figure it's because I'm not really a beach kind of girl. There's that and then there's the fact that his days will be spent at the conference.

I'm not for certain what I'm supposed to do all day while he's conferencing, but I'm good at figuring things out. I'll probably do some work of my own.

We use the word honeymoon loosely.

The little pizzeria in Uptown Houston is crowded as it always is. Its popularity is as much about the atmosphere as it is for the food. The food, however, is nothing to complain about. Fire roasted with handmade crust. I usually get their specialty, the margarita pizza.

The pizzeria's got that upbeat, urban vibe that people, young and old are drawn to. It's also just two blocks over from the Galleria. Far enough away that the patrons are mostly locals, but close enough that being here is still part of the happening area.

The servers may not know our names, but they recognize us. Our server tonight is John, a college student with hair too long. Claims to be a business major, but I'm not buying it. When I was a business major, and not that long ago, a guy would have been called onto the carpet for not putting forth a professional image. Maybe things are different now. Or maybe he goes to a more liberal college.

Not my problem.

"Here you go," John says. "Good hot breadsticks. Fresh out of the oven."

"Can we get some marinara sauce?" Madison asks.

"It's on its way," John says, turning just in time to see a waitress coming this way with a tray. "There it is now."

He snags the cup of marinara off her tray as she keeps walking. She says something we can't hear to John.

He just shrugs and sets the cup of marinara in front of Madison. "All good?"

"All good."

With that, he disappears into the shadows.

"I don't think that was ours," I say.

"Neither do I," Olivia agrees.

"Oh well." Madison dips her breadstick into the sauce and happily takes a bite.

The bar is currently packed, as it always is on Saturday nights. There's a line to get a table, too. And another line for takeout.

"Why would you keep your own name?" Madison asks, taking a sip of her sparkling white wine.

Just because. "Smith is such a common name," I say.

"And my MBA is in my maiden name." I shrug uncomfortably. Although keeping my name has more than crossed my mind since I agreed to marry Theo, I've never actually said it out loud.

Now, saying it out loud and getting such a negative reaction from my two best friends, I'm wondering if maybe something is wrong with the way I think.

"That's why I'm never getting married," Olivia declares definitively.

Now Madison and I look at her as though she's lost all logical thought.

"Does Dan know that?" I ask.

"Stan. His name is Stan." She bites into a crispy breadstick.

"Okay. Does Stan know that?"

"Stan doesn't need to know it," Olivia says with definite sass. "Because I'm never getting married."

Madison and I exchange a glance. That is most definitely Olivia logic at its best.

"Moving on," Olivia says. "Have you decided whether you're moving into Theo's place or if he's moving into yours?"

"We're still undecided," I say. "My place is closer to my work. His is closer to his work." I shrug. "We'll figure it out."

Madison visibly shudders. "Cutting it kind of close, don't you think? I would have needed to know this like a year ago."

"We didn't even know we were getting married a year ago."

"And that's a different topic," Madison says.

I give her a pointed look. Madison doesn't do anything that isn't on her five-ten-fifteen year spreadsheet. I've seen that spreadsheet. There is no husband on it. And yet she dates. I don't quite know why she dates when she seems to have no plan for marriage. Unlike Olivia, she just doesn't come right out and state her opposition to the institution of marriage.

The three of us had met at the Arabella, an exclusive high-rise condo building, just over three years ago. I had been a cat sitter. Olivia and Madison had been dog walkers.

We'd somehow ended up on the same elevator at the same time. Olivia and Madison had both been walking dogs and I'd been holding a cat in a carrier that I'd had to take to the vet for a client.

You would have thought that the three of us would have been fierce competitors. And yet we had too much in common to not become fast friends which soon, by way of Madison's prophetic spreadsheet, somehow morphed us into business partners.

"Are we getting the usual?" Madison asks, opening up one of the menus.

"Yes," Olivia says. "I'm up for some Hawaiian pizza."

"Hannah?"

I set my glass down. "I'm just going to have a salad."

"Since when?" Olivia asks with a vexed expression. "I thought salads were your weekday thing."

"They are," I say. "But I've got a wedding dress to fit in."

"You'll be lucky if it doesn't just drop off of you

already," Madison says. "Didn't they already tuck it in once?"

"Yes," I say. "But I can't be too careful, you know."

Olivia and Madison exchange a look.

"You're losing too much weight," Olivia says. "Order a pizza. Otherwise your dress is just going to hang there like a feed sack."

"Jitters," Madison says tell Olivia. "It's normal."

"Definitely the jitters," Olivia says.

"I don't have the jitters," I say, but it's a half-hearted protest. I've got something. I just don't think it's the jitters.

A large table nearby filled with a dozen women erupts into applause as a young lady stands up. She's wearing a white sash with the word *Bride* embroidered on it.

"Ooh," Madison says. "We should get you one of those sashes. You can wear it everywhere. All week."

"No. You should not. I wouldn't wear it."

"She's no fun," Olivia says, swirling the wine in her glass.

"We already knew that," Madison says.

I'm not even listening to them anyone.

I'm watching the activity at the front door.

Two men, handsome men, just walked in. Both of them are wearing black business suits with white button-down shirts. Nothing unusual about that.

They're striking with their suits and their expensive hair-cuts, their handsome clean-cut features (nothing unusual about that either around here), but that's not what has snagged my attention.

I know one of them. I REALLY know him.

"Hannah," Madison says, following my gaze. "Are you okay?"

I don't answer. I can't get a word out past the lump in my throat.

The man who just walked through the door is none other than Jack Thompson.

My Jack Thompson from Alpine Falls.

My husband.

Chapter Two

Hannah

Of All The Pizza Joints

Jack must have felt me staring in his direction.

It's not a small restaurant and we're not sitting near the door. We're sitting somewhere in the middle and there are people all around us. Sitting. Walking. Standing around waiting for a seat at the bar.

But he sees me.

It's like our eyes meet across the crowded room. Just like in the movies.

After saying something to his friend, a man slightly older, I don't recognize, he peels away and heads right for our table.

After my first response, freezing, my second instinct is to flee. The restroom isn't far away. I can make it before he gets here.

But being frozen in place has already won out.

Jack, his gaze never leaving mine, walks right up to our table and stops next to my chair.

"Hello Hannah," he says.

Jack is wearing a charcoal business suit with Skye Travels embroidered over the jacket pocket. His dark-colored suit and white button-down shirt are a uniform.

"Jack. What are you doing here?" I clasp my hands together in my lap.

"Of all the pizza joints, we end up in the same one. What are the odds?"

"I can't even begin to fathom."

"How are you?" he asks, his glacier blue eyes sweeping over my face. "You look well."

"I'm okay."

"I'm here with a client," he says. "So I've got to get back to it." He gaze leaves mine long enough to glance around at Madison and Olivia. "Ladies." He nods.

Then he puts a hand on my shoulder. "Good to see you Hannah."

"You too." I watch him walk away. Back to his client.

"Who was that?" Madison asks, leaning forward, her eyes wide.

"I don't know," Olivia says. "But I do know one thing. That is not Theo."

I blink and turn back to my friends as though coming out of a daze. I look from one to the other.

They both have me pinned with their gazes.

"That was Jack Thompson."

"Jack..." Olivia's eyes get huge. "THAT Jack." She turns to Madison. "Hannah was married to him."

"Get out," Madison says, looking at me now. "Married? Why didn't I know this?"

"It never came up," I say.

"It never came up," Madison says with a shake of her head. "That's the kind of thing that comes up." She looks at Olivia accusingly. "You knew."

"It came up," Olivia said in my defense.

"Well," Madison says. "As one of your two maids-of-honor. The responsible one. The one also left in the dark. I should let you know that the court is going to need a copy of your divorce papers."

"Of course," I say. "Of course they do."

"And you happen to have a copy?"

I glance at Olivia, but she's no help. Her eyes are on the menu, even though I know she knows exactly what she's going to order. "Not exactly. But I can get a copy. It's not a problem."

"Good," she says with a glance over her shoulder in Jack's direction. "Definitely not Theo."

"No," I say, shoving the hair off my face. "Definitely not Theo."

"You didn't tell me," Madison says to Olivia.

"Not mine to tell," Olivia says.

Right now I'm thinking I have one friend too many. Not that I want to ditch either one of them.

But maybe both.

Maybe I need to just ditch both of them.

But in the meantime, I've got a bigger problem.

I've got to get in touch with the clerk's office in Alpine Falls and get a copy of my divorce papers.

Maybe I thought that if I didn't tell anyone, no one would know. This is Houston. That was Colorado. It was a lifetime ago and in another world.

It was so long ago, who could possibly care about it?

I must have said that last bit out loud.

"It's all online now," Madison says. "When you go to get your license in Harris county, there's a good possibility that your social will show that you were married."

"I don't know." I hold up a hand at her expression. "But I'll get it okay? I'll get it Monday."

"Does Theo know about this?"

I slowly shake my head. "I guess he's going to find out, isn't he?"

"I don't see any way around it, Honey," Madison says.

"I'm sure it'll all be okay," Olivia says, her gaze straying over to where Jack is sitting with his client.

Of course it will.

Of course it will be.

I'm getting married one week from today.

To a perfectly nice man.

Who is most certainly not Jack.

It's been ten years since I've seen Jack Thompson.

The cute boy I'd been married to is now a handsome man. One my friends don't seem to be able to stop checking out.

Can't blame them.

I'd be the same way, but I don't dare even glance over in his direction.

Not a good idea.

Not good at all.

Chapter Three

Jack Thompson

I'd been to this Italian pizzeria once before with, actually, a different client. Very disconcerting odds since both clients, even though they don't know each other, picked the same restaurant.

That had been a few months ago, but it had not been nearly as interesting then as it is tonight.

It has the same lively urban feel to it. The same blend of Italian herbs and fire baked pizza dough filling the air.

The same Italian music mixing with the chatter of customers and the sounds of activity coming from the kitchen.

But tonight Hannah is here. Hannah, a woman I haven't seen in ten years.

The same Hannah I think about every single day.

The same Hannah I married that summer right after high school.

"I'd offer you a glass of wine," my companion, Caleb Winslow says. "But I know you won't take it."

"Bottle to throttle," I say, forcing my attention back to Caleb.

Caleb Winslow hired me to fly him from Alpine Falls to Houston. He has a meeting in the morning. Then I'm flying him back up to Alpine Falls after lunch.

I haven't been doing much flying lately. I took some time off from my job at Skye Travels to help my dad out around the ranch.

That's one of the great things about Noah Worthington, my boss. He firmly believes in both ideals and actions that family comes before all else.

When Caleb called, I jumped at the chance to get back in the cockpit. Like all pilots, at least the ones I know, I'll take any excuse for flying that I can get.

I don't mind feeding and grooming horses. Don't mind helping my dad out with any of it. I don't even mind mending fences or chopping wood or any of the other physically intensive jobs required to keep his place going.

I even rather enjoy the guided horseback tours we provide for tourists, taking them along the river and up into the back country, mostly for just a few hours at the time. Dad has always been the one leading the guided horseback rides, but with him temporarily out of commission, I've stepped in to do just about everything.

And if there's one thing I've learned over the past month or so, everything is a LOT. As a kid, working on the horse ranch, I'd known there was a lot of work involved, but since I hadn't been the one in charge, I hadn't known just how much all that work was.

Even though none of that's a problem for me, the sky still calls to me.

Sometimes I think about getting my own airplane so I can do both. Help out my dad with the family business and provide private flights.

Unless I can find someone willing to practically donate a small airplane, though, that's not something in my immediate timeline.

"So how's your dad?" Caleb asks after he orders a glass of wine for himself and I order a glass of sparkling water.

"He's still mending. The docs say he'll be out a couple of more months at best."

"But your mom is able to do some of the tours, right?"

"She can and she's quite good at it. The tourists love her. But she doesn't like leaving my dad alone. She's taking a tour in the morning, but she hired someone to come in to sit with him. Has a list of instructions a mile long."

"She's a dedicated lady. Dedicated to the business, but dedicated to your father even more. That's important."

"Hard to find," I say. My gaze is drawn back to where Hannah sits with her two friends.

I couldn't not speak to her.

I've been wanting... needing... to talk to her for years, but she vanished off the face of the earth as far as I could determine. Absolutely no social media presence. How she managed that these days, I'll never know. Seems like everybody puts their business out there for everyone to see in one form or another.

Truth is, though, I'm the same way. Other than my family's website, I don't do much on social media either. So I guess Hannah and I are kindred spirits in that way.

Unfortunately, she's having what looks like a business dinner, just as I am.

Can't very well talk to her about anything personal when she's with work associates or even friends.

At least now I have a better idea where to find her.

Houston.

Unfortunately I'm not going to be here long to find her, much less actually talk to her.

And now. Seeing her again. After all this time.

I want to talk to her all that much more.

But it's not going to happen on this trip.

Not only am I fairly certain I can't bear to go another ten years without seeing Hannah again, things have changed.

I have no choice now.

I have to find her.

Chapter Four

Hannah

Crumbling Options

"Impossible," I say, glaring at my phone.

"Meow."

Reaching down, I pick up Bandit, a little teddy bear of a cat, technically an oversized Snowshoe with thick soft fur, and hold him close against me.

I named him Bandit because of the dark patches over his eyes. He has chocolate colored ears and tail and white mittens on his feet. He has beautiful blue eyes and loves to talk. The love of talking is the Siamese in him.

"It'll be okay, right?" He purrs and rubs his face against my chin. "You're making it very hard for me to give you up, you know that, right?" He just purrs louder. "But I have to tell you, you smell like tuna."

Bandit is one of the cats I'm supposed to be putting on our website so he can be adopted. I've had him living with me for three weeks now and I still haven't posted his photo and info on the company website.

I'm surprised Madison hasn't said anything to me about it. I think she's giving me a break because of my upcoming wedding, but honestly, one has nothing to do with the other.

I just happen to like Bandit

I sit down on the sofa in my little living room and put on the brushing mitten he likes.

With papers scattered over my coffee table, it looks like a tornado came through my apartment.

Madison and Olivia are right about one thing. Theo and I have to figure out where we're going to live. Getting married in less than a week and neither one of us has made a move in either direction.

We both still have our leases and neither one of us has started packing. I'll be the first to admit, it is a bit unusual.

Right now, though, I have more important things to deal with.

While I brush Bandit, I sort through what I know.

The clerk's office in Alpine Falls doesn't have any record of my divorce. They have the marriage license. Of course. But no record of the divorce.

I called this morning. Then I called this afternoon. Got the same answer.

"I'm sorry, Mrs. Thompson. We don't see any record of

your divorce. Do you think maybe it was filed in a different county?"

What county? Seriously. Jack and I got married in Alpine Falls. We lived in Alpine Falls. We got divorced in Alpine Falls.

But Alpine Falls has not held up its end of the bargain.

Feeling my options crumpling, I Face Time Olivia.

She's at the gym running on the treadmill.

"How do you do that?" I ask.

"Do what?"

"How do you run and talk at the same time?"

"I'm in shape?" It's a statement that comes out as a question.

"Of course you are."

"What's wrong? You look vexed."

"I am vexed."

Bandit walks across my lap, turns around and walks back.

"Is that Bandit?" Olivia asks.

"No. If Madison asks you about it. No. This is definitely not Bandit."

Olivia laughs. "Don't worry. I won't tell on you."

"Good."

"Now tell me what's wrong."

"I don't know. You're in a public place."

And I can barely hear her over the roar of the treadmill and her feet pounding on the belt.

She glances left and right. Then shakes her head. "I'm wearing a headset. No one can hear you."

"Right. Well. So I called the Alpine Falls Clerk's office to get the divorce papers."

"Okay."

"They don't have them."

"What do you mean they don't have them?"

"They have no record of our divorce." I make a concerted effort to keep my voice from going full on high-pitched panic mode.

"Did you file it somewhere else?"

"That's what they suggested. No. Actually I didn't file it at all."

"Who did?"

Who did.

An innocent enough question. One I should have an answer to.

"The attorney," I say, but I've been through every piece of paper I own and I don't have a copy of it. Shouldn't I have a copy of something important like that?

"Don't panic," Olivia says. "There has to be a way to fix this."

"I've called twice now. Talked to two different people. The only two people who work there."

"You have to go there and get it yourself."

"I can't just go there and get it."

"Of course you can. It's your divorce paper. They have to give it to you."

"I don't think it's a matter of them not wanting to give it to me. I think they can't find it."

"Sometimes in those small towns like that, you have to show up to get things done."

"How do you know that?"

Olivia slows the treadmill and starts walking. It only helps me hear her a little bit better.

"I watch television. Small towns are like that."

"Well." Bandit nips at my chin. "I can't go. I can't leave Bandit."

"That's why you're not supposed to get close to the pets you're putting up for adoption."

"Try telling that to Bandit."

"You two are too far gone." She takes a drink of water from her bottle. "I think you're going to end up keeping him."

"I can't do that. I can't have a pet in my apartment."

"Oh. Right. But... Bandit's a cat... and he's in your apartment."

"Hush now. The walls might have ears."

"What about Theo's place?"

"What about it?"

"Can he have a cat?"

"I don't know." I wince. "Theo's not really into pets."

Olivia hits stop on the treadmill and picks up her phone, bringing her face closer to the phone so I can clearly see her stunned expression. "Wait. You're marrying a man who's not into pets."

I shrug.

"He does know that pet adoptions are your career, right?"

"I'm pretty sure he knows that."

"But he doesn't like pets." Oliva runs a towel over her face. "How did I not know this?"

"I guess it never came up."

"Does Madison know this?" She starts walking again.

"It's not a big deal. Theo's okay with cats as long as they're temporary."

"Oh. Well. I guess that makes it alright then." Sarcasm drips from her words.

"Maybe you can go," I say.

Olivia glares at me. "They won't give your divorce papers to me."

"Why not? It's a matter of public record."

"No. I'll be the one keeping Bandit. You need to go. They know you there. They'll give you the papers."

"You're much more intimidating."

"That is true." Using both hands, she makes a swing at her short blonde hair. "But that's not that point. You might need to sign something."

"Sign what?"

"I don't know. Maybe you'll have to get new papers."

"I don't want to talk to you anymore."

Olivia grins. "I'll shower and be over to pick up Bandit." She jabs a finger at me. "Go online and buy a plane ticket."

"With what?" I can't help thinking about my maxed out credit card.

"Get Theo to buy it."

"Have you met Theo?" I ask.

Olivia holds up her hands. "You're the one getting married to him."

"Got to go," I say. "I have things to do."

"Sometimes the truth hurts," Olivia says before she ends the call.

I hate it when Olivia is right.

But I get on my phone and start looking for a plane ticket. The first one I can afford isn't until tomorrow and it leaves at seven a.m. In the morning.

My credit card protests, but somehow goes through.

When the receipt comes in, I see why the ticket is so affordable. It's a one-way ticket to Denver.

Dropping back onto the couch, I groan.

Bandit jumps into my lap.

I wrap my arms around him. "The worst part is I have to leave you here with Olivia."

Bandit just purrs and bites at my chin.

"I'll be back before you know it."

Maybe if I say it out loud, it will manifest and come true.

Chapter Five

Jack

"You seem preoccupied," Caleb says on the flight back to Alpine Falls.

"Apologies," I say. "I guess I am. A little."

The wheels are up and I put the little jet on autopilot. It's a perfect day for flying. One of those temperate September days that promises cool fall evenings in the near future. The ones that remind me of high school football games.

Hannah and I started dating at the beginning of my sophomore year. Her freshman year.

It had been love at first sight. We'd been inseparable after that first chance meeting at the football stadium.

I'd been a quarterback and she'd been a junior varsity cheerleader.

Every memory of high school I have has Hannah in it one way or another. My freshman year either got wiped from my memory or she somehow got added in to those memories.

"Don't apologize," Caleb says. "You know you can talk to me."

"You're right." Caleb was my friend back then and we're still friends even if we don't talk. Guys are like that. We can go for years without talking. Then just pick right up where we left off. If only women were that easy.

"Well," Caleb persists.

"I saw Hannah last night."

"Hannah? Your Hannah?"

"Yes." A knot forms in my stomach. My Hannah. But not my Hannah any more.

"She's in Houston?" I nod once. "Did you know that?"

"Didn't have a clue."

He leans back, adjusting his sun glasses. "What are you going to do?"

"Nothing I can do."

"You need to talk to her."

I look over at Caleb. He's the only one who knows.

"Jack," he says. "What are you going to do?"

"Nothing," I say. Nothing has been my go-to solution when it comes to Hannah since that night.

"Okay," he says. "I guess that's worked for you so far."

"I looked for her," I say.

"Sort of."

"I did. I looked for her." We fly through a bank of white clouds making the roar of the engine seem louder somehow.

"You asked her parents where to find her." He knows good and well that I did not.

"They moved." It's been my excuse all along. No reason to change it now.

"It's been this long. Why are you so concerned about it now?"

"I've always been concerned about it," I say.

"I guess seeing her again brings up a lot of memories."

"Yeah. It does. But it's not just that."

"What then?"

I speak to the control tower in Denver and we start our initial descent.

"You're the only person who knows, right?"

"I was there," he says.

"I know you were there. I'm just asking if anyone else knows."

"Your secret is safe with me."

Caleb was there when I'd gotten the divorce papers. He'd been there as the only witness when I'd tossed them into the fire pit.

"Right." I speak to the control tower again.

"So what's different?" Caleb asks.

I look at my friend. My partner in crime. He knows enough. He might as well know the rest.

"She was wearing an engagement ring."

Chapter Six

Hannah

Winding Mountain Roads

The rental car, compliments of Madison's sky mile points is more like a go-cart in disguise than an adult car. In lime green, nonetheless.

But seeing as how I didn't have to pay for it, I'm not complaining. Not much anyway. Not out loud.

Madison scolded me for not telling her I was buying a plane ticket. Apparently she has points to share. So at least now I know how I'll be getting back to Houston.

She told me to go take care of my business, then we'll figure out how to transfer to points to a ticket for me to get home.

The drive up into mountains of Alpine Falls west of Denver is as long as I remember. I only drove this trip one time by myself and I'd been going the other direction.

The rest of the time I'd been with Jack.

Jack Thompson and I had been inseparable throughout high school.

We'd met at the first football game my freshman year and as they say, the rest is history.

We'd dated for four years and we'd gotten married in May right after my high school graduation. He'd graduated the year before me. It had been the best four years of my life.

But then Jack had left for Purdue to study aviation.

He'd put off college for a year, working on his family's horse ranch. The plan had been for us to get married, which we did, and for me to go to Purdue with him.

When that fell apart, my life had fallen apart with it. I'd had to rebuild it brick by brick.

Fortunately, my parents had moved to Denver in anticipation of my moving to Purdue. With them not living in Alpine Falls anymore, I had kept my vow to never return to Alpine Falls again.

Until now.

With every mile along the winding mountain roads, more memories come flooding back. Memories I had tucked away in the back of my mind.

Even though they're good memories, I try to keep most them at bay.

Instead, I focus on the beauty of the changing leaves. Autumn in Alpine Falls is the most beautiful time of year.

Maple trees with their red and orange leaves. Aspen trees with their golden leaves. All interspersed with a background of verdant blue spruce trees.

Winding up the hills, turning curve after curve, the forever snow-capped mountains coming closer and closer, I feel myself reconnecting with the girl I had been when I lived here.

The truth is I'm still the girl I'd left behind ten years ago.

It didn't matter that I'd gone halfway across the country and started a new life for myself. Coming back to Alpine Falls is a full on reminder of who I had been.

I'll get this thing done. Then be on my way. I glance at the time. Tomorrow. Tomorrow I'll go to the clerk's office and get a copy of the divorce papers. Then I'll head back to Denver, get on a plane, and return to Houston.

Even with the friends and family discount, my reservation at the lodge is pricey. Being part of a small start-up business, pet adoptions, is not lucrative. Especially not when I'm pretty sure I'm keeping my most profitable cat yet. Bandit. Olivia was right when she predicted that one.

I just don't know how I'm going to do it. Not with my wedding in less than a week to a man who prefers not to have a pet in the house. He knows I foster pets and he's okay with that. But a full-time cat? I don't know. I don't even know if his apartment allows pets. Mine certainly doesn't.

I pass several familiar houses telling me I'm getting closer to Alpine Falls. And apparently, over the last ten years, a lot of fancy new houses have gone up in the area. Most of them appear to hang off the side of the mountainsides. Very pretty. Very fancy.

Alpine Falls is growing.

I hadn't expected that.

I guess I expected it to always stay the small little town it always was.

Since the clerk's office is closed, I turn right and head straight to the Alpine Lodge.

The Lodge is an Alpine Falls icon. It's been here over a hundred years. Maybe one hundred fifty. And is a Christmas destination spot. People come here from all over the country at Christmastime. And, they also come here during the autumn leaf peeping season.

I pull into the little parking spot off to the side, parking as far away from the door as I can get. The little go-cart in disguise is a rental, but I still don't really want anyone to see me getting out of it.

It's a small town. People will talk. And judge. That's probably the one thing I liked least about living in a small town. The talking and the judging.

They'd talked about me and Jack getting married right after high school. I'd heard rumors that I was pregnant. I wasn't, of course, but it didn't keep people from spreading nasty rumors.

Fortunately, I'd been so blindly in love with Jack that the rumors didn't touch me. Not until they did.

But that was ancient history. I doubt anyone even remembers all that now. Enough time has passed that I'm sure they've found other people to talk about and judge.

I pull my little suitcase out of what passes for a trunk. I hadn't brought much because I'm only going to be here overnight.

Dragging it along behind me, I walk toward the lodge door.

Mr. Adams, the valet, looking decidedly older with the passing years, opens the door.

"Welcome Miss Hannah," he says, holding the door for me. "It's good to see you again."

"You too, Mr. Adams."

As I walk through the open door, he says. "I hope you're coming back to work. We missed you around here."

"Oh," I say. "I'm just here for the night."

"That's too bad. Well. Maybe you'll change your mind."

"See you later, Mr. Adams," I say, giving him a little smile.

It's a nice reminder that small towns aren't just judgy. They're friendly.

It's definitely a nice reminder.

I walk through the lobby that seems slightly smaller than it had before, back when I'd worked here as a high school senior, past the fireplace with real wood burning, open on all four sides, straight to the front desk.

"Hey Zoe," I say to the young lady, about my age, I barely recognize behind the counter.

"Oh, Hannah," she says, coming around the desk. "I saw your name on the reservation and I didn't believe it, but it really is you."

She wraps her arms around me in a big hug.

"How are you?" I ask.

She runs a hand down her stomach. "About to be a momma." She grins. "Again."

"Again?"

"My third."

"I remember when you got married."

"And I remember when you got married," she says with a big smile.

I wince.

"Oh." She puts a hand on my arm. "I'm so sorry. I still don't know what happened with you two. You were the perfect couple."

"It's complicated," I say. "And it was so very long ago. A lifetime ago."

"Not so long. Things move slower in Alpine Falls."

Great. So much for nobody remembering.

"It's good to see you," I say. "And you look happy."

"I am." She goes back behind the desk. "Let me just get you checked in."

"Right. About that. Do you think you could maybe wait until I leave to run my credit card?"

"Don't you worry about that. You used to work here. You're family. There's no charge."

"None?"

She waves a hand and keeps tapping keys. "Nope. You're all checked in. The room is available for a week, so stay as long as you like."

"Thank you, but I'm planning to leave tomorrow," I say.

"Just in case you change your mind," she says, sliding a

key across the counter. "The room is yours. Oh. And everything in the café is on the house. Just charge it to your room and it'll be comped."

"You can't do that," I say.

"I'll be in trouble if I don't."

"Thanks, Hannah. Thank you so much."

"Enjoy your stay."

I roll my suitcase toward the stairs.

Mr. Adams hurries over. "Let me take that up for you," he says.

I'd forgotten just how kind everyone in Alpine Falls is.

When the thing with Jack happened and I'd left, part of how I dealt with it was to put a negative sheen on everything.

Turns out that negative sheen was false.

Alpine Falls is one of the best places in the country a person could be from.

Chapter Seven

Jack

"Jack," Mother says just as I'm finishing up doing the after dinner dishes.

With my father out of commission and my mother taking care of him, not only does running the horses fall to me, but so does taking care of most of the household chores.

"The Lodge just called. Can you run three bales of hay out to them?"

"Hay? Tonight? Why?"

"When you go to the General Store and buy something do they ask you what you want it for?"

"Sometimes," I say. "Especially if it's at night. And it's something crazy like three bales of hay."

"They're having some kind of outdoor event and they need bales of hay."

"Okay. Fine." I straighten the dish cloth on the rack and run a hand through my hair. "I need to change back into my work clothes."

"Okay. But don't be too long. It sounded urgent."

Grumbling to myself, I head upstairs to change clothes and put on my work boots. "Who needs three bales of hay in the middle of the night?"

The grandfather clock chooses that instant to begin chiming the hour. Seven o'clock.

"Okay. Fine. Universe. Maybe it's not the middle of the night, but as far as needing hay bales, it may as well be."

I put on my work jeans, a flannel shirt, run a comb through my hair, then toss on a baseball cap. Wearing my work boots now, I head out to the two-story horse barn. Two dozen horses on the bottom floor. Hay on the top floor. Toss down three bales of hay onto the bed of the truck waiting below.

Still grumbling to myself, I climb into the old truck and head toward the lodge.

I'd been looking forward to an early night. A couple of hours in front of mindless television. A beer.

Work starts at daybreak at the ranch. That particular aspect still takes some getting used to.

It's a twenty minute ride out to the lodge. Everything in

Alpine Falls is twenty minutes apart maximum. Most things, like the lodge to Main Street is a five minute walk.

It just happens that the lodge and our ranch are on opposite sides of the town.

It's a drive I've made hundreds of times.

Hannah worked at the lodge her senior year of high school.

Being the overprotective boyfriend that I was, I drove her to work and I went back and picked her up after work. Every day she worked. Usually about four days a week.

I'd take her back to her house which usually added another twenty minutes onto the trip because I could never leave her without kissing on her for a while.

Those were the days.

Hannah and I had plans. Plans we never really got off the ground.

We were planning to live in Purdue while I got my degree, then come back and live with my parents for a year or two while we built a house of our own.

I was going to buy an airplane of my own and do private flights while helping out my parents at the ranch.

Funny how things turned out. I'm still thinking about getting an airplane of my own. But instead of coming back here to live, I got an apartment in Denver and went to work for Skye Travels.

An enviable job, for sure, and not easy to get. But living alone in an apartment was no life.

Since I was technically still married, albeit secretly, I didn't date. My fellow pilots could never quite figure out what was wrong with me. Probably wondered if I even liked women at all.

But as far as I was concerned, I was and still am a married man.

Unfortunately, my wife doesn't have a clue. Hannah thinks she's divorced and apparently she's engaged to someone else.

It's my responsibility to find her and tell her that she's still married before she goes through with it. I'm the one who caused us to still be married, so I'm the one who's responsible for getting us unmarried. In a timely manner.

I contemplate just how I'm going to go about that as I pull up to the lodge and park in the service area.

I put on my work gloves and drag out the first of the three bales of hay from the back of the truck.

Assuming they want the hay around back, where else would they want hay, I take off in that direction.

There's a fire in the fire pit going and several people are standing around it, some holding their hands to the warm flames. I can barely make out their faces in the moonlight. Just people in the shadows, but I can tell they're tourists.

This must be the occasion they were talking about. Whatever it is, someone deemed it worthy of having three bales of hay delivered.

I set down the first bale of hay, far enough away not to disturb the gathering of guests, and go back around for another.

After hauling the second bale of hay around and dropping it to the ground, someone coming out the back door catches my attention.

I stop. Blink.

Wonder if I'm hallucinating.

Drawn like a magnet, I take a step forward.

When she turns and looks at me, I know I'm not hallucinating.

Hannah.

Hannah, my Hannah, just walked out the back door of the Alpine Falls Lodge.

Chapter Eight

Hannah

After getting something from the café to eat, I spend all of an hour, maybe at most, in my room before I feel compelled to venture out.

Grabbing a novel from my bag, I head out. When I used to work here, my senior year of high school, I would imagine what it would be like to spend an evening in front of the fire just reading and enjoying the warmth of the flames.

The perfect opportunity to find out has presented itself.

Going down the stairs, I meet Zoe heading up with a load of towels in her arms.

"Hey," she says. "Some of the guests are having an impromptu campfire out back if you want to join them."

"Oh. Okay. I don't want to intrude on someone's private party."

"It's not private. It's a just a few random guests who wanted to get out and enjoy the cool night air. Sitting on hay bales. Having some hot apple cider."

"Hay bales?"

"Yes. Someone is dropping them off as we speak."

"Okay. Thanks. I might stop by. Nothing like fresh hay."

"Good," she says with a bright smile. "I'll see you out there."

I continue downstairs, noting that the best seats around the fireplace are taken. So maybe later. Fate, it seems, has other ideas.

I walk past the café, essentially a bar in the evenings. Big band music spilling out now. Seems some things haven't changed. Whichever manager, all family members, is on duty picks out the music so it changes from night to night and even sometimes hour by hour.

There are only a handful of customers sitting in the café/bar at the moment.

I push open the back door leading outside the lodge and stand there for a moment, savoring the crisp evening air. Compared to the Houston air, it's so clean, it almost hurts to breathe it in.

It smells like woodsmoke and blue spruce and remnants of the afternoon rainstorm.

And that's just on the surface.

It also smells like walks in the moonlight and lingering kisses.

And fresh hay.

I open my eyes and look around for the source of the unexpected scent of hay. Something I recognize from my time spent at Jack's horse ranch, not from my time spent here at the lodge.

The two memories collide in my head, repelling each other like the two north poles of magnets.

They most definitely do not go together.

But then I see why.

Two rectangle bales of hay are on the ground not far from where I'm standing.

My gaze shifts and I see the man standing next to them.

He's wearing work gloves, a flannel shirt, and a baseball cap. I instantly know that he had to be the one who brought in the hay.

The only person who would bring hay to the lodge.

Jack Thompson.

Our gazes meet and like two opposite magnetic poles, lock together.

He takes a step forward, but my own feet are frozen to the ground.

My senses, overwhelmed by the scent of woodsmoke and hay and memories of kisses... kisses by the man currently looking at me as though he just might like to be kissing me right now... have me turned inside out.

When I'd seen Jack in the Pizzeria in Houston, I'd seen

the pilot Jack. The man who belonged there in Houston. Business suit. Tie. Confident swagger.

But now I'm seeing the Jack that belongs in Alpine Falls. Flannel shirt. Baseball cap. Confident swagger.

The man carries his confident swagger with him wherever he goes, it seems.

"Of all the mountain lodges, we end up in the same one," he says. "What are the odds?"

"More likely than the same pizza joint in Houston," I say. "Everything considered."

"Yes," he says with a grin. "Everything considered."

"What are you doing here?" I ask.

He looks at me as though it's quite obvious what he's doing. "I'm dropping off hay bales."

I put a hand over my mouth to hide the bubble of laughter that threatens to spill out.

Hay bales indeed.

As though it's the most normal thing in the world.

Just dropping off some hay bales.

It was just days ago that I saw him in Houston fitting in there just as easily as he was fitting in here.

It's all in all, a bit disconcerting.

Especially since he's the person who's the very reason I'm here to begin with.

"There you are," Zoe says to Jack, coming through the door behind me. "If you would, just position those hay bales around the fire pit."

"Yes ma'am," Jack says with a little tip of his hat.

"He calls me ma'am," Zoe whispers as she passes me by. "It's so cute."

"I see," I say.

But the moment with Jack has passed and he's moving the hay bales, placing them around the fire as instructed.

"I'll be right back with the last one," he says.

When he glances over at me before he walks off, I feel that glance all the way down to my toes.

The magnetic attraction between us is most definitely still there.

Divorced or not.

Chapter Nine

Jack

As I head back to the truck to get the last bale of hay, my mind races, every instinct pushing me toward sweeping Hannah into my arms and kissing her senseless.

That's what the Jack of ten years ago would have done.

But the Jack of ten years ago would have had every reason to do so.

Hannah was my girl and then my wife.

Kissing was what we did best.

We probably did kissing better than we did anything else, talking included.

Maybe that was why we weren't married anymore.

My fix for every misunderstanding was kissing.

It seemed to work just fine.

Until it didn't.

Perhaps we'd needed to have a conversation instead that day.

But what can I say? I'd been young and besotted, drunk on her kisses, and I could never get enough. I mistakenly thought everything would fix itself.

I drag the bale of hay from the back of the truck and take my time walking back with it.

My mind is stunningly blank as I try to figure out what to say to her.

Hey Hannah. I've missed you. Oh. And by the way, we're still married.

No. That would go over like a ton of bricks.

I can't do that.

The first thing I need to do is to find out why she's here.

I know her well enough to know, however, that she isn't going to just spill her reasons to me.

No. The Hannah I know is still mad at me.

If I want her to talk to me, I've got to work my way around to it.

Get her to trust me again.

And that, I'm pretty sure, is the most impossible task I could have set for myself.

Good God. If I walked up to her right now and announced that we're still married, her trusting me would be the last I'd ever have to worry about.

It would not happen.

That's something to save for later. Something to tell her once I have a good way to explain to her exactly why we're still married.

As I settle the third hay bale around the far side of the firepit, I'm still coming up short on anything to say to her, much less how to tell her what I'm supposed to tell her.

Tourists find their way to the hay bales, using them as benches, just as was intended.

A quick scan tells me that Hannah is no longer outside.

Great. Gone just as quickly as I found her.

Fortunately, the lodge is small enough that know I can find her again. Maybe not tonight, but tomorrow.

I pull off my work gloves and stuff them in my back pocket.

Standing a moment, I debate whether to go inside the lodge to look for her or to just head back home and come back tomorrow.

The problem is I don't know why she's here and I don't know how long she'll be here.

But then the back door opens and she follows Zoe outside, both of them carrying trays of hot apple cider.

"Jack," Zoe says. "Come have some cider. You can't drive all this way over here and not sit for minute."

It would be rude to say no.

And I'm a gentleman.

So being a gentleman, I walk straight up to Hannah and take the tray of hot cider from her hands. "Let me get this for you," I say.

Looking into Hannah's verdant green eyes is worth all the cider in the world.

Priceless.

Chapter Ten

Hannah

Tastes Like Home

There's something about the smug look that crosses Zoe's features as Jack takes the tray of hot cider from me that has me perplexed.

But distracts me from that line of thinking when he sets the tray on the nearest hay bale and plucks up one of the cups of cider and hands it to me.

"You have to keep me company," he says.

I don't know any woman in her right mind who could refuse a cup of anything from Jack Thompson. Not when he's looking at me with that intense sky blue gaze of his.

He's looking at me as though there's no one else here.

It's the way he's always looked at me. Since the very first time we met at the football stadium right here in Alpine Falls.

"Thank you," I say, leaning against the bale of hay. I was supposed to be helping Zoe hand out these mugs of cider. That's what I had agreed to do when I went back inside the lodge with her.

But Zoe doesn't seem to even notice. She's doing a more than fine job of handing them out by herself.

She always has been a wonderful hostess.

In fact, she picks up one of the mugs and shoves it into Jack's hands. "Sit," she says.

Jack does as she says and sits next to me on the bale of hay.

This whole meeting with Jack almost seems orchestrated. Of course, that would be impossible. Who would do that?

"You brought hay," I say. I know we already covered that, but it seems like that's where it all begins.

"By request."

Okay. Maybe not impossible.

Just improbable.

"Do you often make late night hay bale deliveries?" I ask, taking a cautious sip of the hot cider.

"This would be the first."

"I see."

But not being one to look a gift horse in the mouth, I keep further comments to myself. Even if it was orchestrated, it doesn't really matter.

It's nice to see Jack again.

And, it suddenly occurs to me that he just might have copies of our divorce papers.

That would be convenient, wouldn't it?

But that's not something I can just come right out and ask him.

Not knowing what I know about Jack.

He would probably just grumble something and stalk off.

He's always been very sensitive about such things.

I can hear him now.

You haven't seen me in ten years and all you want from me is our divorce papers?

No. That's not a conversation I want to have with Jack.

I would much rather just enjoy the unexpected evening with him.

Besides, I'm going to the clerk's office in the morning and I'm not walking out without them. It will be one of those problem-solved situations.

"What's the occasion?" Jack asks.

"Occasion?" My first thought is that he's asking why I'm here. I haven't thought up a good answer to that particular question. Other than, of course, the truth, which I'm not ready to reveal.

"The hay bales. What's the occasion?"

"Oh. I honestly don't know. Zoe just said some guests wanted to enjoy the crisp evening air."

"It is a nice night," he says.

"Yes." It reminds me of a million evenings he and I had

spent together when we both lived in Alpine Falls. When our future stretched out before us in an endless landscape of happiness.

I swallow thickly and take another sip of my cider.

It's spicy and sweet and tastes like... home.

"It's good to see you," he says. "A pleasant surprise."

I glance over at him, my heart racing. "It's good to see you, too."

"I didn't get to talk you the other night," he says.

I look at him with a raised eyebrow. Talking was never what I would call his strong suit.

"You were with a client," I say.

He nods once.

"You're a pilot."

He nods again. "What gave me away?"

"The Skye Travels uniform for one."

"You noticed."

"Hard not to. Besides, being a pilot was your goal since, well, forever, right?"

"Yes. It was. I just don't remember working for Skye Travels ever being part of that particular goal."

I shrug. "No. But goals change and I'm thinking you talked about how much you admired Skye Travels."

"You have a really good memory," he says.

I smile. "Always."

How could he possibly think I could forget something so important to the man I dated for four years and eventually married?

But I keep that thought to myself. Maybe our relationship had a more lasting impression on me than it did on him.

"How's your cider?" he asks.

"It's good."

"Interesting."

"What's interesting?" I ask, looking over at him sideways.

"You used to hate apple cider. Wouldn't touch it."

"Yeah. Well." I hold up my mug. "Maybe I should have tried it."

"Maybe." He holds up his mug, too. "We live and learn."

Indeed we do.

Chapter Eleven

Jack

Sitting out in the chilly night air permeated with the scent of fresh hay from the hay bales I'd dropped off and the sweet and spicy scent of the apple cider in our mugs, brings back a lot of memories.

Being back in Alpine Falls is one thing to begin with, but being here at the lodge with Hannah, well, that's another thing entirely. Very unexpected and not unwelcome.

It's actually quite fortuitous, considering everything.

Considering that I happened across Hannah in Houston, saw that she's wearing an engagement ring, and then seeing her here again at the lodge.

I glance down at her hand, but she's not wearing the engagement ring she'd been wearing the other night when I saw her in Houston.

I have no doubt I saw a diamond on her finger. None.

It's the kind of thing a man notices. Especially when that man knows something she doesn't, specifically that he's still married to her.

"Tell me what's been going on with you," I say, opting to be vague and open-ended. Hoping she'll fill in some of the gaps.

"I'm part owner in a company now."

"Is that so? What company is that?"

"Forever Home Pet Placement."

"That sounds like a pet adoption agency."

"That's exactly what it is. We find pets that need a home, post them on our website, and charge a fee for placement."

I set my empty cider mug aside and stretch out my legs. "How's that going for you?"

She blows out a breath. "Interesting that you should ask."

I smile. "That bad?"

"I have this beautiful cat, a Snowshoe, that I'm supposed to be putting up for adoption, but I really want to keep him."

"You always did love cats. What's wrong with just keeping him? Surely you have more than one cat to put up for adoption."

"My apartment doesn't allow pets."

"Ouch."

"Exactly. Anyway. It's a little complicated. I just have to figure out how to keep him."

"Move back to Alpine Falls. Everyone loves animals here."

She blinks and stares at me.

I realize belatedly that that statement might be a little bit obvious, but I had actually meant it as a general suggestion.

"Right," she says. "I just can't see that happening. The two ladies you saw me having dinner with are co-owners in the company."

"You could always add a branch out here," I say.

There's that look again. The one that says she's wondering what's wrong with me.

Maybe there was a reason I was better off being the strong silent type.

"Maybe," she says, looking away and making a face when she takes another sip.

There. There's the Hannah I know and love. The girl who makes a face when she sips cider. Maybe she's learned to tolerate hot cider, but not cold cider.

"Can I take your mug?" I ask.

"Please. I see now why I didn't like it."

"I guess you just needed to try it hot."

"Maybe. So tell me what you're doing now? Are you living here in Alpine Falls?"

"Sort of," I say with a wince. "Temporarily. I'm helping my parents out at the ranch."

"So you don't actually live here?"

"No. I live in Denver. But I'll be here until my father is back on his feet."

"Is he okay?"

"Just a little accident. He's recovering nicely."

"And your mother? Is she good?"

"She watches him like a hawk. Only leaves him for trail rides when I'm not available."

"She's a devoted wife."

"How are your parents?"

She pushes the hair back off her face. "You know. We don't stay in touch. I assume that they're doing okay. If not, my brother will most likely let me know."

"I'm sorry you aren't talking to them."

"It's okay. It's just hard after what happened."

I know exactly what happened. I was there. "I feel somewhat responsible for that."

She looks into my eyes. "It's not your fault."

It's all a matter of perspective.

Here I am, feeling guilty all these years and she doesn't seem to harbor the least bit of resentment.

Maybe things aren't quite so bad as I thought they might be.

One thing is for certain. Things are better now that Hannah is back in town. Even if it is only for a moment.

Chapter Twelve

Hannah

Overdue Conversation about Things

"How long are you staying?" Jack asks.

Quiet conversations swirl around us. People just out for an evening.

Zoe brings out the makings for s'mores and there is a flurry of activity as people roast marshmallows. The scent of chargrilled marshmallows and melted chocolate is another one of those scents that brings back a flood of pleasant feelings. Not any specific memory in particular, just emotions. Reminding me how happy I was here.

"Just tonight," I say.

"Oh." Jack looks over at me. "It's a long way to come for just one night for most people."

"I'm guessing you make one night stop over flights all the time."

"I do. It's customary. But the typical person does not. Are you picking up a cat?"

"No. I had another piece of business come up." A topic I feel the need to steer him away from. "Do you know of any pets in need of adoption?"

I don't even know why I'm asking. Even if he did know of one, I could hardly take a pet back on the airplane with me.

"No," he says, with obvious amusement. "I don't know of any pets that need a home. Not at the moment anyway."

"Just as well," I say.

"I'll let you know if I come across any homeless pets."

"Okay."

"Do you want to take a walk?" he asks.

I look up at the moonlight streaming down. It is a beautiful night. "Okay," I say.

We both get up and as much as I dislike the idea of leaving the warm fire, a walk in the moonlight with Jack is worth it.

Leaving the others, we walk toward the trail leading to the river.

Already, with the conversations behind us, I can hear the rushing water up ahead.

"It sounds the same," I say, mostly to myself.

"Not much changes in Alpine Falls."

I look at him sideways. "I'm not so sure about that," I say.

"Oh? How so?"

"It seems there have been a lot of changes," I say. "The houses I saw coming in. Those weren't there before."

"Good point."

"And we don't live here," I say softly. I meant to say it mostly in jest, but instead it sounds wistful to my own ears.

I don't want to sound wistful. Not to Jack. Not when I was the one who left.

I'd had my reasons, but I'd been the one to leave none-theless.

Maybe if Jack and I'd had a conversation, we would still be married.

We both say the same thing at the same time.

"We need to talk."

Looking at each other, we smile.

Seems we'd both had the same thought at the same time.

"You go first," he says.

"No," I say. "you."

"Okay." He shoves his hands in his pockets as we reach the river, water tumbling noisily over the rocks. "We never got a chance to talk." He pauses. A light spray of water brushes over us, evaporating as soon as it lands. "About things."

"About the text message," I say.

"Yes." He slowly blows out a breath. "The text message."

Jack had gone to Purdue to visit the campus while I

stayed behind. I was supposed to go with him, but I'd had final exams and couldn't miss. He'd had to go before the students left for the summer.

We'd talked every day and everything had seemed normal.

It was after the wedding when I saw the text message come in. Three weeks, in fact, after the wedding.

I remembered every word.

Hey. It's Rachel. So glad we got to spend some time together while you were here. Looking forward to the day you come back. XOXO

"The girl..." he says. "I don't remember her name."

"Rachel," I supply.

His brow creased, he looks at me. "Rachel," he says slowly.

I can read his mind. I know he's wondering how I could remember this girl's name after ten years.

Because I blame her for blowing up my life. I'll never forget it.

"Rachel was an academic recruiter. A sorority girl. I told her I had a fiancé, but she insisted that it didn't matter. That my life would be different at college and I'd be letting go of old relationships and making new ones."

"Was she right?" I ask.

"You left," he says, his voice soft. Strained.

Nodding, I look away, feeling hot tears burning my eyes.

He was right. I had left. I'd gone home to my parents and told them what happened.

They'd told me all sorts of things. Things they had apparently managed to keep to themselves until that point.

"You got married too young."

"Jack isn't good enough for you."

"You shouldn't trust him."

I stayed with my parents for a week.

When I finally got up the nerve to go back to the ranch where I'd been living with Jack, he was gone.

His parents tried to talk to me, but I couldn't listen. I ran back to my own parents and stayed in my room for a week.

When I finally came out, my father presented me with divorce papers.

"Just sign them," he'd said. "We'll take care of the rest. And you can go on with your life."

Eventually when I didn't hear from Jack, my parents pressuring me relentlessly, I signed.

Since I'd been accepted into the University of Houston, I headed there. I wasn't planning on going there. It was just one of those schools I'd applied to as part of my junior capstone course, been accepted to, and never declined.

So I went.

And I stayed.

The wind rustles through the trees, sending a shower of leaves falling over us.

"When I went back to your house," I say. "you weren't there."

"Where was I?"

"I don't know. Your parents tried to talk to me, but I guess I didn't listen."

"I went to your house," Jack says. "But your parents said you didn't want to see me."

I nod and turn back to him. My heart breaks for him. Like me, he still doesn't know what happened. Neither one of us knows what happened. It was like we somehow crossed paths, missing each other at every turn. And my parents.

My parents had been the worst.

He looks so young right now standing there in the shadows. Like the boy I'd fallen in love with.

"I don't think my parents wanted me to get married," I say. I expect him to laugh at that. To say that it was more than a little obvious. He'd probably known it all along, but I hadn't. I hadn't known. I'd had blinders on. Blinders that only let me see one thing. Jack.

But he doesn't laugh. When he answers, he answers with all seriousness and compassion.

"You never told me that."

"I didn't know. I didn't know until after I went home and told them about the text message. My father took things upon himself. He saw an attorney. He finally convinced me to sign." I didn't have to say what I'd signed. I couldn't bring myself to say it out loud and he knew anyway. I didn't have to say the words.

"Did you want to sign?" he asks.

"No," I say, looking into his eyes. "I didn't want to. I resisted. But my parents convinced me that it was the right thing to do. That I didn't have a choice."

"It wasn't your idea?" he asks with something that sounds like hope in his voice.

"No. I never would have done it. My father went to the attorney. He had everything drawn up. Jack... I—"

Jack's phone chimes with a message.

He pulls his phone out and looks down.

I push away the memory of finding the text message on his phone so very long ago.

Another lifetime.

It has nothing to do with now.

We're different people.

But the involuntary punch in the gut is real. The shadow of pain that lingers even after all this time is real.

"It's my mother," he says. "She needs help getting my father into bed."

"Well then." I force myself to smile and hope it comes out right side up. "You have to go."

We start walking back toward the lodge while he sends his mother a quick reply letting her know he's on the way.

"Can I see you again tomorrow?" he asks.

"I have to do... my errand, then I was going to head out."

"Driving to Denver?"

"Yes. I don't have a ticket yet, but I need to get back. My friend is cat sitting."

"Meet you at the Pizzeria? We can have lunch before you go. You have to eat."

"Okay. Sure." The Pizzeria is practically right across the street from the clerk's office.

He leaves me at the firepit and heads off toward the front

of the lodge where he'd parked. "I'll see you tomorrow," he says, giving me a broad smile.

"Tomorrow," I say, sitting down on the bale of hay.

I sit there for two seconds before I get up and head inside. Being out here is no longer interesting. Not without Jack.

Jack took the light with him.

Chapter Thirteen

Jack

I have to stop by the General Store the next morning to pick up some supplies for the ranch. It doesn't take nearly as long as I expected it to take, so I have some time to walk downtown until it's time to meet Hannah at the Pizzeria.

Quickly bored, I stop and sit on one of the benches.

I have a lot to think about and in the twelve hours or so since I'd seen Hannah, I'd gotten absolutely nothing resolved in my head.

In fact, if anything, my thoughts are more tangled than they were last night.

Last night, things had seemed so easy. Just tell her what happened. She'll understand.

But now, the more I think about it, the more I don't think it's all that easy.

She hadn't told me that she's engaged. That's a big complication.

As much as I might find myself imagining us getting back together and living happily-after-ever, I know it's not that easy.

Ten years is a long time. A lot of water has passed under our respective bridges.

Most people in our shoes wouldn't stand a chance of sorting things out and getting back together.

She and I could have had a simple conversation all those years ago and maybe we could have gotten past the misunderstanding. What Hannah doesn't know is that I'd immediately blocked the girl's number. Rachel. I really hadn't remembered her name. And what's more, I'd never seen her again.

But then our parents had gotten involved. Apparently there was no love lost between me and her parents. I hadn't known that. It's one of those things I wish I didn't know even now.

But she's engaged now to someone and our breakup had created a rift between her and her family. That's regrettable. To me family is everything. To think about Hannah not talking to her family for all these years breaks my heart for her.

I hate it that it had anything whatsoever to do with me.

I just don't know how to fix everything.

I'd say that she and I just need some time.

But then. Engaged.

I don't know how much time we have.

As I'm sitting there torturing myself with impossible thoughts, I blink and realize that Hannah is walking up the sidewalk to the clerk of court's office.

She walks with determination and purpose.

A city girl. She looks like a city girl with her long wool coat and boots that come up to her knees. A little wool cap on her head. Very chic and stylish.

My first instinct is to catch up with her. Go with her to do whatever it is she's doing.

But then I remember that we aren't a couple anymore.

That's a really hard thing for me keep in my head for some reason.

Maybe part of it is because I know we're still married.

So technically we still are a couple.

As I sit there with the cool breeze brushing against my face, it hits me like a ton of bricks what she's doing.

She's going into the clerk's office to get a copy of our divorce papers.

But she won't get them.

She won't get them because they aren't there.

She might have signed them, but I did not.

I tossed them into a fire.

The divorce papers she's looking for don't exist.

This is a problem. This is a huge problem on so many levels.

It means she really is planning on getting married again and soon. Soon enough that needs proof that she's divorced.

And it means I've got to come clean about what I did. And I've got to tell her that she and I are still married.

I get up from the bench and pace along the sidewalk, instinctively dodging tourists ambling along the sidewalk, wandering in and out of stores.

She'll come out soon enough. She'll come out empty-handed. She can't get papers that aren't there.

I feel sorry for the clerk of court and her assistant.

Hannah is going to insist that they produce papers that do not exist.

Hannah's father had left those papers with me with specific instructions to sign them and turn them in to the clerk's office.

Well. That didn't happen. That so did not happen.

I have to tell her.

Hannah deserves to know what happened.

Chapter Fourteen

Hannah

Into the Stacks

I'd always liked Mrs. Rudolph. I remembered her as a mild-mannered older lady, but now I see that she's middle-aged. Apparently people look different through the lens of a teenager. Anyone older than thirty was ancient. She still has the same kind smile, though, that I remembered.

"It's like I told you on the phone, Dear," she says. "We have a record of your marriage, but not your divorce."

I feel like I swallowed a peach pit or something equally vile and uncomfortable.

"Can I look at the records?" I ask, still daring to hope

that Olivia was right. That if I showed up, so would my divorce papers.

"Of course. It's a matter of public record. But you won't find anything."

She continues to talk as I follow her back into the rows of books. The stacks, she calls them. "You won't find anything. Besides, I'd remember if there were divorce papers for Jack. He's my nephew, you know."

I stop, my feet frozen to the floor. "What? Jack is your nephew?"

"Yes. Twice removed and all that, but still. He's family. The Thompson family has never had a divorce." She says that with so much pride that the imaginary peach pit in my stomach feels like it's going to come up.

"I didn't know he was related to you," I say, forcing myself to taking calming breaths.

"It's okay." She stops, pulls out a poster-sized book and opens it up, then puts on her reading glasses. Carefully turning the pages, she lets me look with her.

"Here," she says, pointing to an entry. "Here's your marriage. We can use these numbers to locate the actual certificate in the files." She looks a little embarrassed. "We're online now, of course, but going back and putting all the old stuff online is a bit overwhelming."

"I understand. I have a friend who does that. She's actually quite efficient at it."

"Oh? I don't suppose she's looking for a job?"

"Madison? No. She just started her own business."

"Well. That's too bad. It's hard to find someone who's good at this sort of thing and enjoys it."

"Madison lives to organize. So how far out did you look?"

"I went out a year."

"Oh." I expected her to say three months. But if she went out a year, then there's no way she missed it.

"Here. Sit on this stool. Take your time. Go as far out as you want to."

I do as she says. Then stand up and take off my coat. This is going to take awhile.

Hopefully I'll be finished in time to meet Jack for lunch. It seems like a disconnect to me. Sitting here in the clerk's office looking for a divorce notice to the very same man I'm looking forward to having lunch with.

I also feel a little bit guilty about not wearing the engagement ring I'd taken off on the flight up here. In Alpine Falls I was always Jack's girl. I might not be his girl now, but I didn't want to have to explain anything. And I didn't feel like talking about Theo.

Turns out it takes me a lot less time to scan the giant book than I expected it to. Before the hour is up, I've gone through two years, looking for our names. Just in case. And scanned part of the next before I get to the end of the book.

After looking through the first year, I don't even recognize any of the names.

Jack said things stay the same, but as someone who didn't step foot in Alpine Falls for ten years, I can most certainly disagree with that.

People come and go. Jack, even if he wasn't living here, would have heard about that from his parents. He would have kept up.

It was sort of like watching a tree grow. The person who sees the tree every day doesn't notice it, but for the person who doesn't see it for ten years, it's more than noticeable. It's almost a little bit shocking.

I close the heavy bound book, stand up, and stretch.

"Did you find anything?" Mrs. Rudolph asks, appearing at my side.

"No. I feel like I should apologize to you for doubting you."

"You don't have to apologize, Dear. I understand."

"So." I put my coat back on and watch her return the book to the stacks. "If there's no record of my divorce, what does that mean?"

Straightening, she removes her reading glasses and looks at me.

"It can only mean one thing," she says. "You're still married to Jack."

Chapter Fifteen

Jack

I stop pacing in front of the clerk's office, my hands stuffed in my coat pockets. The urge to go inside is almost overwhelming. It isn't that I want to see what she's doing.

I just quite simply want to be near her.

It's always been that way with Hannah. Since that first night I'd met her, I'd had a singular need to be near her.

Although the sunlight is warm on top of my head, the breeze is cool. Someone leaves the coffee shop and walks past with what smells like a pumpkin latte, a reminder that the holidays will be here before we know it.

The clerk's office is up a flight of six steps. I have an aunt, sort of, who runs the clerk's office. Mrs. Rudolph. She and her husband stopped by my parents' house last Christmas. A nice lady. I'm not sure she would know me if she saw me on the street.

There's no way she'd recognize Hannah. Not only does Hannah look different now, all grown up, but it's been so very long since the wedding. Hannah certainly won't recognize Mrs. Rudolph.

My mind is going in a hundred different circles, most of them connected in one way or another, when the door opens and Hannah steps out.

She's wearing a dazed expression and she just stands there, not seeing anything in front of her.

She's stunningly beautiful, my Hannah, standing there at the top of the stairs, looked all vexed and perplexed and not a little bit flushed.

Maybe she's surprised she didn't find any record of our divorce.

I'm flooded with guilt that I haven't already told her. I could have saved her the trip up here.

But then I wouldn't have gotten the chance to see her.

The wind tousles her hair and she absently swipes it out of her face.

The movement shifts her focus and she sees me standing here.

She blinks. Then tilts her head to the side and blinks again.

"Are you okay?" I ask, stepping forward. She looks a little pale. If she's going to pass out, there's no way I can catch her from here.

"I don't know," she says.

That's enough to get me moving. In two seconds, I'm up the stairs, taking her arm. "Let me help you down," I say.

She seems steady enough as I lead her down the stairs to the sidewalk below.

"Hi," I say.

"Hi."

"You were at the clerk's office," I say, pointing out the obvious.

"I... yes... I was. I didn't know Mrs. Rudolph was your aunt."

"Twice removed or something like that."

"What does that mean?" She lifts her hair and tucks it in her coat collar, something I remember her doing back when she'd tire of fighting the wind.

"I have no idea. I think it means we see her once a year. Usually on Christmas. And my mother sends her birthday cards."

A smile tugs at the corners of Hannah's lips, but it doesn't reach her eyes or turn into a full smile.

"I think we need to talk about something," she says.

"Let's talk over lunch," I say. "I've been loitering out here for too long."

"Really, Jack. You shouldn't loiter. You know that."

"I only loiter when I'm waiting for a pretty girl."

I take her hand and tuck it in the crook of my arm.

I've waited for her so many times and being together is no natural for us, she probably doesn't even think to ask how I happened to be there waiting for her at the clerk's office.

Together we walk down the sidewalk toward the pizzeria.

We have some difficult conversations ahead of us. But for just one moment in time, I can imagine that we're back in time. Walking arm in arm along the sidewalk in Alpine Falls.

Just a couple of people in love with each other.

With a bright future.

I'll take this moment in time.

Even if it is all I get.

Chapter Sixteen

Hannah

We Need to Talk

After hanging our coats on hooks next to the booth in the pizzeria, I sit across the table from Jack. A booth by the window. The table in this booth has faded stone tiles, a mountain scene painted in shades of sunset pinks.

I'm certain we've sat together in this booth before. We've sat at every booth in every restaurant in Alpine Falls.

In fact, I can't imagine there being a path or a sidewalk that he and I haven't walked together. Being inseparable in a small town for over four years will do that. The longest we were ever apart was the long weekend when he went to Purdue.

Purdue. The beginning of the end.

"Hi Jack." The young waitress stopping at our table nods in my direction. "What can I get you to drink?"

"Water for me," I say.

"Same," Jack says. "Thanks, Abigail."

"I'll be right back to take your order," Abigail says.

"She's the daughter of the football coach," Jack says as though he owes me an explanation for how he knows her.

"It's a small town," I say. "Everyone knows everyone."

"For the most part. Except, as you mentioned, for some of the new people moving in."

"You visit a lot?" I ask. "Before your father's accident?"

"Yeah. The horse ranch is a lot of work."

"What about your brother?"

"Lucas? He comes home a lot, too."

I find it interesting that Jack still calls Alpine Falls home.

"What about Trenton?"

"Trenton." Jack leans back and sighs. "Trenton is an architect in Boulder."

"An architect. I didn't see that coming."

"None of us did."

I pick up a menu and open it, but I don't see the words.

My mind is racing.

Married.

I might be still married to Jack.

According to Mrs. Rudolph, I definitely am.

I need to talk to someone. But who?

Olivia and Madison come to mind, but they would just freak out. Remind me that I'm getting married to Theo in days. Insist I do something about it. Probably even insist that I tell Theo.

I almost feel like I need to talk to my father.

He's the one who took care of the divorce. He would know which attorney he used.

But no.

The only other person I can talk to about this is sitting right in front of me.

"Here's your water," Abigail says, setting glasses of water in front of us. "Are you ready to order?"

"We'll need a few minutes," Jack says.

"Jack," I say, speaking over the lump in my throat. "I think we might have a problem."

"What kind of problem?" he asks, leaning forward, looking compassionate.

"The divorce," I say.

"That's why you're in Alpine Falls, isn't it?" he asks softly. I'm listening for it, but I don't hear any judgement in his voice.

"Yes. I need copies of the divorce papers."

His gaze flicks to my unadorned hand. I slide it under the table.

"Hannah," he says. "Is there something you need to tell me?"

I don't want to tell Jack that I'm engaged to Theo. I don't want him to know. I want Jack to see me as available. If he knows I'm engaged to Theo, then that could change everything. It could change the way Jack looks at me.

The sudden realization of just how important that feels leaves me feeling adrift.

Maybe I don't have to tell him.

Maybe I can just let him believe that I'm still available. That there's no one else.

There really wasn't ever anyone for me but Jack.

I don't want to think about Theo right now, much less talk about him.

"When I saw you in Houston," Jack says. "I thought I saw a ring on your finger."

Chapter Seventeen

Jack

Sitting in the noisy pizzeria with Hannah is like old times. I can't count the number of times Hannah and I sat right here in this booth. She used to like this booth because of the faded pink scene painted on the marble table.

Today she doesn't seem to notice it so much. She seems preoccupied. Too preoccupied to appreciate the pink painted mountain scene on the table or the actual scenic mountains in the distance.

Big band music spills from hidden speakers. Conversation swirls. Servers dart here and there, back and forth to the kitchen.

Warmth from the stone ovens in the kitchen spills out

into the restaurant along with the scent of fresh baked pizza dough.

It's taken me years to learn to voice things on my mind. I always felt like I could tell Hannah anything, but I preferred kissing to talking.

I doubt that's changed, but since kissing isn't an option right now, I have to go with conversation.

She didn't just randomly show up in Alpine Falls. She hasn't been here for ten long years. And she didn't just happen to stop in at the clerk's office for a social visit.

I saw the ring on her finger.

Sometimes the best way to get something out in the open is to just spit it out.

"I thought I saw a ring on your finger," I say.

Hannah looks like a deer in headlights.

She doesn't say anything. She just looks at me for a moment, then looks away.

"Hannah," I say. "It's okay. You can tell me anything."

She takes a deep breath and looks at me.

"I'm engaged," she says so softly I barely hear her.

The lump in my throat is unexpected. I already knew this. And yet hearing her say it out loud is like confirming one of my worst fears.

Over the years, I'd known in my head that she would be dating other men, but in my heart, I'd secretly hoped she wasn't.

I didn't date, but I had knowledge that no one else did. Well, other than Caleb. Caleb knew, but he wasn't talking.

Just because I wasn't dating didn't mean I could expect her not to.

"Are you in love with him?" I ask, dreading the answer, but needing to know.

She looks away again, but not before I see the pain in her eyes.

Seeing that pain cross her features, unleashes a whole different chain of thoughts.

Maybe she's pregnant.

Maybe she feels like she has to get married.

"I don't know," she says.

It seems like such an odd thing for her to say, I almost smile.

"You don't know," I say, forcing myself to keep a straight face. It's hard to keep a straight face when there is such unexpected joy sweeping through my system.

If she doesn't know if she loves him, then all is not lost.

"It just sort of seemed like the thing to do," she says, looking at me now with her big emerald green eyes.

"That happens."

"But Jack," she says, leaning forward and keeping her voice at a whisper. "I can't marry him. You and I are still married."

Chapter Eighteen

Jack

Abigail stops at the table and takes our order. We order a large pepperoni pizza and breadsticks.

I ask her to bring the breadsticks out first.

I selfishly want to keep Hannah here in Alpine Falls for as long as possible. And it's not just being selfish on my part. She and I have a lot to talk about.

She apparently has just discovered that we're still married.

She has no idea that I already know.

This feels like one of those times when I don't think I can win whichever way I go.

I can't lie to her and tell her I didn't know, but can I tell her that I knew?

"I know," I say.

She blinks and sits back against the booth. "What do you mean you know?"

"I mean I know. I know we're still married."

"How could you know that?" she asks, then she puts both hands on the edge of the table, squeezing so tightly her knuckles turn white. She looks a bit like she might be sick. "You wanted to get married again."

I shake my head, but she's not looking at me. She puts a hand over her eyes and looks away, biting her lip.

"Of course," she says. "You wanted to get married again, but you couldn't find me."

"Hannah," I say.

She's looking at me again. "Why didn't you just ask my parents? They would have told you where to find me. We could have figured out why the papers didn't get filed or at least how to fix it."

I'm shaking my head again. "Hannah. No." I stretch a hand out across the table and she puts her hand in mine. "I didn't want to get married again."

"Then how—?"

Abigail shows up with our breadsticks. "Here you go," she says. "Breadsticks just out of the oven." She sets them on the table between us. "And some dipping sauce for each of you." She looks from one of us to the other. "Everything okay?"

I get the feeling she's not asking about the breadsticks. Hannah tries to slide her hand back, but I keep my hold on it. "Everything looks great, Abigail," I say with a quick glance in her direction. "Thank you."

"Okay," Abigail smiles. "I'll check back. Let me know when you're ready for me to put your pizza order in."

"Will do." My gaze is already back on Hannah. I let go of her hand now and put a breadstick on one of the plates and slide it in her direction. "See if you still like these," I say.

I keep a lightness in my voice. One that seems out of place everything considered.

She breaks off a piece of breadstick, dips it into the sauce, and takes a bite.

"How could I not?" she asks. "They have the best food here."

"I think it has something to do with the elevation."

"I think you're right."

"If you didn't want to get married again?" Hannah asks after a couple of minutes. "Then how did you know?"

"Because I didn't want to be divorced."

She takes another bite. Studies me with her head tilted to the side. A sure sign that she's confused, but working something out in her head.

"I don't understand."

I fully expect all hell to break loose. But this is Hannah and she deserves to know. It's not my fault she found out before I could tell her. I still owe her an explanation about *how* it happened.

"I never signed the divorce papers."

She grows very still. I'm not even sure she's breathing.

Then she takes a deep breath as though she suddenly remembered she needs to breathe.

"My father told me he took care of the divorce."

"He did. He brought the papers to me. Told me to sign them and take them to the courthouse to be filed."

"Okay. I signed them."

"I know. But Hannah. Did you *want* to sign them?"

"No," she says. "I didn't want to. I didn't know what I was supposed to do. My parents." She looks away. "They told me it was for the best. That you weren't who I thought you were."

"You believed them."

"No. I don't know. I didn't know what to think. I was devastated."

"It's okay. Everything was chaos. And we didn't talk. We should have talked."

"We were never all that good at talking, were we?" she asks with a little smile.

That smile is something I needed to see.

"No." I smile back. "We were better at other things."

The blush that blooms on her cheeks is one of the most lovely things I've ever seen. It so reminds me of the Hannah I knew so long ago.

"But Jack," she says, leaning forward again, her hands on the edge of the marble tabletop. "What happened? How did the papers not get filed?"

"I didn't sign them. I tossed them in the fire."

Chapter Nineteen

Hannah

The Truth

"What fire?" I search his face. "You mean like literally in a fire?"

"Yes," Jack says, finishing off a breadstick as though we're having a normal conversation. "I had a fire going in the fire pit behind the house. Caleb and I'd had a beer. Maybe two."

"Wait. Caleb knows about this?"

"He was there," Jack says, sliding another breadstick onto his plate.

"Caleb knows."

"He never told anyone."

"Wait." She holds up a hand. "So for ten years... I thought we were divorced and you... You knew that we were still married."

"That just about sums it up."

"Jack," she says. "I dated. I was going to get married to someone else. Did that ever occur to you?"

"Yes. But I hoped you wouldn't."

"You can't just..." She closes her eyes. "Do you realize how crazy that is? If I hadn't seen you in Houston, my friends wouldn't have insisted I come up here and get copies of the divorce papers. I would have gotten married." I glance around feeling like I somehow committed a crime.

"I didn't know where to find you," he says.

"You knew where to find my parents," I say. "Didn't you?"

"Maybe. I'm sure I could have figured that out. I looked for you online, but I couldn't find you."

"I hate social media. And yet it's my job to put our company out there. But that's not the point. Didn't it bother you? When you dated?"

"I didn't date."

"You didn't... Wait. Never?"

"Never. I think the guys in my class thought something was wrong with me."

"I would think so."

"I couldn't date. I'm a married man."

"This is too weird," I say, pushing my plate aside, with a half-eaten breadstick on it.

"It's not that weird," Jack says.

"It's weird, Jack. It's not normal."

"I didn't want to be divorced so I didn't sign the papers." I hear some defensiveness in his voice now. But I don't care. My face feels heated and I'm having trouble wrapping my head around all this.

That I've been married for ten years and didn't know it.

Not just married, but married to the only man I ever loved. How could he let me believe that I was divorced? "Who does that?" I murmur to myself.

"Look," he says. "I'm sorry. I'm sorry this upsets you. It was never my intent to upset you."

"What was your intent, Jack? To let me go to jail for marrying someone when I was already married?"

"I don't think you would go to jail for it," he says. "It would be an honest mistake."

"A mistake. Yes. This." I sweep a hand over the table. "This is a mistake." I raise my eyes to his. "I can't do this. I have to go."

Standing up, I grab my coat from the coat hook, but I don't bother to put it on.

I start blindly toward the door, barely able to see past the tears that well in my eyes.

"Hannah," Jack calls, following me.

He catches up to me when I reach the door.

"Hannah. Wait. Let's talk about this."

"I can't, Jack." I push the door open and turn right.

I stop. I can't remember where I parked.

I don't even remember what I'm driving. Not my car.

"Hannah. Please don't leave like this."

"I have to go."

The go-cart in disguise. I'm driving the matchbox rental. Whirling around, I start walking the other way.

By the time I see my car up ahead, I realize Jack isn't following.

My hands trembling, I press the key fob and jerk the door open.

I sit in the driver's seat and lean my head against the steering wheel.

Jack stopped. He let me go.

And that hurts more than anything else.

Chapter Twenty

Jack

I have to let her go. Hannah doesn't want me to follow her, so I stop.

But I stand on the sidewalk next to a maple tree with brightly colored falling leaves right on Main Street and watch her. I watch her get into a death trap of a car and just sit there.

Every instinct urges me to follow her. To go to her.

But she made it clear she doesn't want to be near me right now. I have to respect that.

It makes no sense. She seemed understanding when she thought I didn't know we were still married.

She'd even said we could work it out. And we can.

But once she found out I knew and purposely made no effort to tell her that I sabotaged the divorce, she was no longer okay with it.

But we can't work it out if she leaves. If she leaves, there's nothing we can do.

She's leaving without what she came here for. Divorce papers.

Does that mean she won't be getting married?

If getting married to someone else makes her happy, then that's what I want her to do. But if it doesn't... then... no. I don't want her to do it.

And deep down, I know I don't want her to marry someone else for any reason.

She's my girl. Always has been.

Even if we had gotten divorced, officially, there will never be another girl for me. I'm a one girl guy.

Maybe I was waiting for her to come back. To change her mind. I knew that the divorce hadn't been her idea. I knew it was her father's doing.

That's one of the reasons, probably the main reason, I didn't go to her parents to look for her. I was pretty sure they wouldn't have told me where to find her. Why would they? They thought she was better off without me. And as far as they were concerned, she was legally divorced and rid of me.

Finally, after several minutes, she backs out of the parking space and heads toward the highway leading to Denver where she's going to catch a plane back to Houston.

I stand there until I can't see her car anymore.

An alarm goes off on my phone. I have to get back to the ranch. There's a trail ride starting soon and I'm their guide.

With my heart shattered all over again, I walk to my truck and climb inside.

There's nothing I can do right now other than let her go.

Give her time to come to her senses.

Her wedding plans will have to be delayed. She can't get a marriage license without divorce papers and she can't get divorce papers without my signature.

So unless she decides to break all the rules and go ahead with the wedding without telling anyone about me, then there's that, at least.

I can't see Hannah doing that. Hannah isn't a rule breaker.

I don't know what she'll do, but she won't get married to someone else when she's already married. She wouldn't do it even if she could get away with it.

If she'd stayed, we could have gone together to a local attorney and gotten everything signed.

Driving in the opposite direction from her, I feel my heartstrings stretching.

I don't like being away from Hannah. Never have and never will.

But I can't hold onto her like this.

It feels too much like I'm holding onto her by force.

I'm a better man than that.

With a groan of resignation and frustration, I turn the

truck around and head toward McKenna Lawson's law office.

It's a small town. Things can happen quickly if they need to.

Chapter Twenty-One

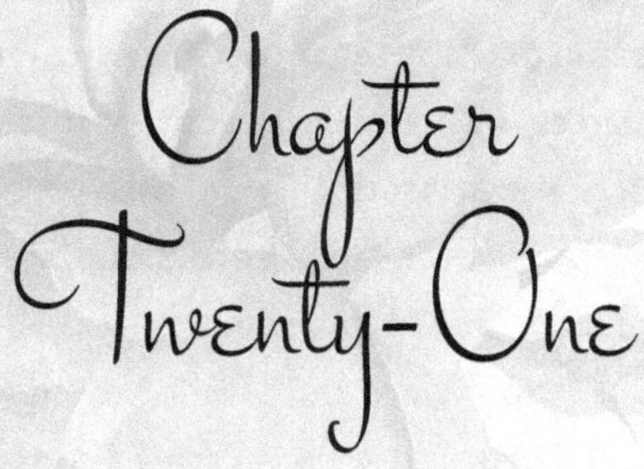

Hannah

Just Come Home

As I drive along the highway, leaving Alpine Falls, I feel like I'm leaving a part of myself behind.

Squinting against the bright sunlight, I drive along the narrow roads with other people driving too fast. People drive too fast on these narrow roads. It's not safe. Especially with me driving this little go-cart in disguise.

Deadly but beautiful.

The forever snow-capped mountains in the distance glow in the bright sunlight and here in a slightly lower elevation, I drive beneath colorful trees. Maple trees with crisp red leaves. Aspen trees with golden leaves. All interspersed with the green of blue spruce trees.

Passing by some of the fancy houses on the edge of town, woodsmoke creates a haze from the fireplaces.

Would Jack and I have built a house out here if we'd stayed together? Or would we have stayed closer to his family's ranch? I always figured we'd take over his family's ranch one day. Not that I'd been in any hurry for that to happen. It just seemed like one of those inevitable things in life.

Back then everything had seemed so easy. Back then Jack and I'd had time to kick around and do pretty much whatever we wanted to do. We'd had a good life.

Then Purdue happened. And everything fell apart.

I never should have come back here.

Olivia had been wrong. Coming here hadn't helped.

I hadn't left with divorce papers because there weren't any.

I loose cell phone service for a few miles, then as I reach Interstate 70 heading into Denver, I'm back in range.

My phone starts ringing.

A glance tells me it's Theo. Another glance tells me I have messages from both Olivia and Madison.

Had my phone not been working in Alpine Falls? Apparently not. Either that or everyone just decided to wait until now try to reach me.

I pull off at a rest area and call Theo back first.

"Hey," he says. "I've been looking for you. Where are you?"

"I had some business to take care of."

He doesn't say anything as I get out of the car and quietly close the door. The air is cold, somehow colder than it had been in Alpine Falls. Or maybe it's just me. Maybe it just feels colder because I feel like I'm going in the wrong direction.

I actually feel a little adrift right now. It's a feeling I'm not unfamiliar with. I'd just hoped that getting married to Theo would abolish that feeling once and for all.

"Olivia told me you had to go out of town."

I stop walking. Stare at the phone.

"I did." And if Olivia wasn't keeping Bandit, she and I might have words.

"You went to see your parents, didn't you?" he asks, sounding accusing.

Theo knows I'm not on speaking terms with my parents, but I hadn't told him why. Just that we didn't see eye to eye and I'd had to get away from them to make my own way.

"She wasn't supposed to tell you I went to Denver," I say.

"Hannah. Don't you think *you* should have told me? I would have gone with you."

"I haven't even seen them," I say, telling him the truth.

"Why not?"

"I'm still working up to it." It's not a complete lie.

"Okay," he says. "I know this must be stressful for you. Take all the time you need. But Hannah?"

"Yes?"

"Let me know if they're going to be coming to the wedding. You know I don't like surprises."

"Of course," I say. "But I don't think that's going to happen."

"Good. We'd have to make adjustments to accommodate them."

I can't help but compare his reaction to a possible reconciliation with my parents to Jack's. My parents had wronged Jack and yet he'd seemed genuinely sorry that I wasn't talking to them.

"I have to go," I say.

"Okay. Call me when you get home."

I disconnect the line and walk to the restroom.

Theo doesn't want my parents to come to our wedding because we'd have to make accommodations. And yet we haven't even agreed on where we're going to live after we're married. Less than one week away.

If he knew I'm planning on keeping Bandit, he'd probably blow a gasket.

And to think that I'm going to marry this man.

Was going to marry this man.

It occurs to me as I head back out to my car that I have to postpone the wedding. I can't get a marriage license without divorce papers.

With the wind blowing through my hair as I stand next to my car, I call Olivia.

"Hey," I say. "How's Bandit?"

"Hey to you, too. Bandit is fine and I'm fine, too. Thanks for asking."

I don't answer.

"What's wrong?" she asks, her voice serious now.

"I can't get married."

"You didn't get the divorce papers."

"Nope. They apparently don't exist."

"Thank goodness. Theo has been hounding me about where you are and what you're doing. You know I support you in anything you do, but Hannah. Maybe you should take another look at Theo."

"Don't worry," I say. "I'm pretty sure that he's going to vanish once I call off the wedding."

"You're calling it off?"

"I don't think you're supposed to sound that happy."

"I can't help it. I'd pick Bandit over Theo any day."

Biting my lip, I smile. My thoughts exactly. "I guess I'll come home."

"You don't sound super excited about it."

"I have to call Madison and see if she can arrange for me to use her points for a flight."

"I don't even know what all that entails."

"Neither do I." I look at the go-cart in disguise Madison arranged for me to drive. "Somehow I'm not too optimistic."

"Everything is going to work out," Olivia says. It always does. Just come home."

Home.

Why is it the word home evokes a memory of Alpine Falls?

It's because I just left there.

That's all. Nothing more.

Madison's call goes straight to voicemail.

I leave a message and continue my journey to Denver.

Chapter Twenty-Two

Jack

My mother is not happy with me. She'd been counting on me to be the tour guide for a ride into the mountains for a small group of tourists.

Right now, the thought of getting onto a horse and riding into the backcountry is the last thing I can imagine doing.

"Mom," I say. "Ask one of the neighbors to come and sit with Dad. What I'm doing right now is important. Long term important."

"Alright. I'll try to get someone." She still doesn't sound happy about it.

"If not, just cancel the ride."

"I can't do that," Mom says. "It's our business. People paid good money."

"Tell them there was a bear sighting."

"Jack. Maybe I need to rethink leaving the ranch to you."

"Maybe. Refund their money and give them a discount on their next ride."

"I worry about you."

"No need to worry. Just take care of it. Either way. And I'll see you soon."

"You're taking a flight, aren't you?"

I look across the desk at McKenna squinting at a document on her computer.

"I might be," I say. "It's a little scary that you know that."

"I know my son," she says on a sigh. "Just be safe."

"Always."

As I disconnect the line, McKenna removes her reading glasses and looks up at me. "Do you happen to have her social?"

I rattle it off.

"Okay," she says. "Most people getting divorced can't do that."

"We aren't most people," I say.

McKenna puts her elbows on the desk and leans toward me. "Are you sure? Are you certain there's no way to salvage this? I'm getting the sense that you really don't want this."

"I don't want it," I admit. "But it's the only way. It's the right thing to do."

McKenna is from the city. Houston, I think. There are lots of rumors surrounding how she ended up here, married to my friend Caleb Lawson. Caleb doesn't talk about it. But he doesn't have to tell me that they're happy.

I always liked McKenna. I have a good sense that if Hannah and I were together, McKenna and Hannah would be good friends.

"Okay," she says, then sends the file to the printer. She slides a printed copy of divorce papers across the desk. "Read over it. See if you want to change anything."

"I'm sure it's fine," I say, but I get comfortable in the chair and start reading from the beginning.

It's the right thing to do.

Knowing that it's the right thing to do doesn't keep it from making me feel sick to my stomach.

And it doesn't help knowing that these are divorce papers that I will actually sign, unlike the ones I tossed into the fire.

As I turn to the second page of the three page document, I see that McKenna walked off. I guess she wanted to give me some privacy and some space to take my time.

She's a good attorney, but even more importantly, she's a good person.

Caleb is a lucky man to have ended up married, really married, to the girl he loves.

But I'm doing the right thing.
I'm setting Hannah free.

Chapter Twenty-Three

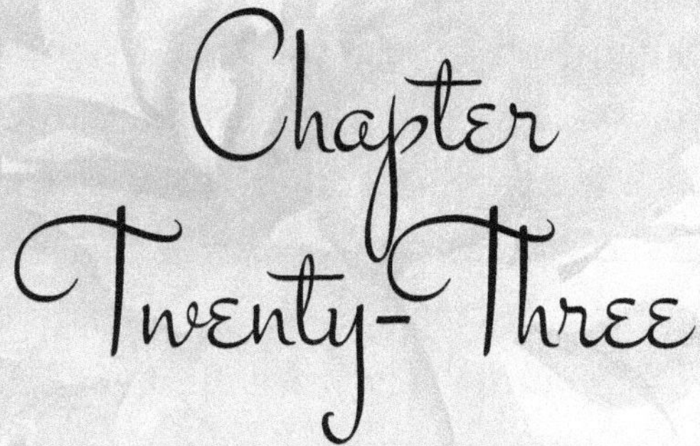

Hannah

A Yankee Dime

Although I'm more than happy to be rid of the go-cart, I'm not enjoying standing in line at the airport. Getting a flight last minute, even with points, maybe especially with points, is a hassle to say the least.

After an hour, I'm beginning to think that I should have stayed in Alpine Falls until I had the whole flight thing worked out. That had been my plan and I should have stuck to it.

But I'd been so upset, I'd just rushed away from Alpine Falls as quickly as possible.

After splurging on a designer coffee, I sit at one of the little tables to wait. The young lady behind the desk tells me it could take some time. She'll call me back up when she has something. If she has something.

The concourse is crowded. A lot of people traveling from Denver to Houston. The usual. Business people. Families. A teenager traveling alone, headphones on his head. Oblivious to the world around him.

As I sit there holding my coffee, all those people blend into the background.

I'd been upset when I'd left Alpine Falls, but I hadn't been upset *at* Jack. Not exactly. I'd been more upset at the situation.

Ten years. Wasted. Ten years I could have spent with Jack.

But he let me believe we were divorced.

And now there's Theo.

Theo had checked my boxes. He'd been handsome. Successful. Let me do my own thing.

That last bit doesn't quite add up with who I really am.

When I'd been with Jack, we'd been together all the time. I didn't even know the concept of a boundary. We didn't need boundaries. We were a couple in every possible way. Hardly ever apart.

But pushing thirty-years-old had freaked me out a bit. Maybe more than a bit. When my doctor had asked if I wanted to make an appointment with the sperm donor clinic, something inside me had churned. That was the best way I could describe it.

All I heard was her telling me I was waiting too long to start a family. My aunt hadn't had children and she told me how much she regretted it. She told me she felt like she'd missed out on a big part of life by not having children.

For some reason those words stuck with me. Because she wasn't married and didn't have children, everything went to my parents when she passed away. I remember looking on in horror as they went through her things. Tossing. Donating. If something was important to my aunt, no one knew it.

It had been heartbreaking. I had a snow globe I'd gotten from her belongings, but I have no idea if she cherished it or not. I cherish it because it had belonged to her and I like to imagine that someone special gave it to her or maybe she went on a trip that she enjoyed and bought it or...

"Would you like some company?"

I look up, blinking, thinking I'm imagining things.

But Jack is standing there at my table.

"Jack. How did you get back here?"

"Being a pilot has its perks. I have clearance."

"But... Why? What are you doing here?"

"I thought you might want a ride to Houston."

I look into his beautiful blue eyes. Eyes so familiar.

I can't even say how happy I am to see him. Seeing him just makes my world brighter.

"I'm not sure I want to go to Houston," I say, surprising myself.

"Where would you like to go?" he asks, sitting down across from me in the other aluminum chair.

"I don't know." I look down at my untouched coffee. Alpine Falls is the answer, but I don't tell him that. I can't tell him that because there's nothing there for me.

I shake my head. "Everything is in Houston. I have to go there."

"Right," he says and a shadow crosses his face.

"I'm having trouble getting a flight," I say.

"I just happen to have an airplane." A little smile plays about his lips.

I spent the last of my credit card balance on this coffee. "Might be a little out of my league."

"Not when you know the pilot."

I take a sip of my coffee, finally, to give myself time to think of something witty to say.

"What's the fee?" I ask.

"A Yankee dime."

"A what?" I ask on a bubble of laughter.

"A Yankee dime. Surely you remember what that is."

"Of course I remember what it is. That's your fee? For flying me to Houston?"

"Yes. Innocent. Affordable."

I glance toward the airline counter where I have feeling I'm so not going to be getting a flight anytime today. "Okay," I say.

"Really? Okay?"

"Yes. I'm not getting out of here any other way."

"There's something I have to give you first," he says,

reaching into his jacket pocket and pulling out a packet of folded papers.

He sets them in front of me, a black pen on top of them.

"What's that?"

"It's what you came looking for."

The peach pit of dread is back in my stomach. Things had been going so well and now he goes and puts papers in front of me.

It has to be divorce papers. That's all it could possibly be.

Keeping my gaze on his, I slowly unfold the papers.

When I look down, I think I'm going to be sick.

It's exactly what I thought it was going to be.

Divorce papers.

Chapter Twenty-Four

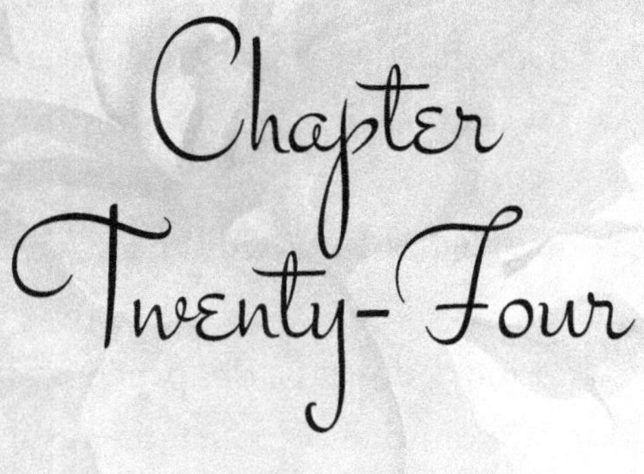

Jack

"You tracked me down to give me divorce papers?" Hannah asks, her voice barely above a whisper, her gaze locked on mine.

Her hands are in her lap now, the papers lying there as though she can't stand to touch them.

"Yes." I feel like I should say more, but the lump in my throat is keeping me from saying much of anything at all. I swallow, needing the silence to go away. "Caleb's wife is an attorney."

She looks away then, her eyes welling with tears.

I should know her well enough to know if they're tears of joy or tears of unhappiness. But I don't. I don't know.

So I just sit there quietly, waiting to see what she does.

"Is this what you want?" she asks, turning back to me finally.

"This was never what I wanted," I say, my heart in my throat.

She nods and looks down at the papers as though deep in thought. But, still, she doesn't touch them.

She valiantly fights the tears that threaten to spill from her eyes. When a tear slips down her cheek, despite those efforts, she doesn't wipe it away. She doesn't even seem to notice it.

I reach across the little table and lightly wipe it away with a finger.

She bites her lip and blinks, forcing what passes as a little smile onto her lips.

"How much for a round trip?" she asks.

"A round trip? To Houston and back? Here?"

"To Houston. And back to Alpine Falls. It would require at least one overnight's stay."

I don't know what she's saying. I know what I hope she's saying, but I don't know for sure. I don't want to make assumptions. I know better than to make assumptions.

"Overnight stays are customary," I say, keeping a straight face. This sounds suspiciously similar to a conversation she and I'd had already.

"What about pets? Are pets allowed on the plane?"

"You can bring anything you want on the plane."

She slides the papers back in my direction, touching them with only one finger. "I don't think I'll be needing these," she says.

My heart swells and I'm nearly consumed with happiness.

"So let me see if I understand the terms. You want me to fly you to Houston. Pick up a cat. And fly you back to Alpine Falls."

"That about sums it up," she says, holding onto the coffee cup with both hands.

"I see." I run a hand along my chin in a show of thoughtfulness. "That might be a little different."

"Oh?" I see disappointment cross her features and she looks away again. "It's okay. I know it's a lot."

I can't stand to see that disappointment on her face, especially knowing I'm the one who put it there.

"A down payment," I say. "I'm going to need a down payment for that."

"What kind of down payment?" With her brow creased, she slides her coffee in my direction. "I have this coffee. I've barely touched it."

As though coffee was worth anything nearly as much as a Yankee dime. Poor misguided young lady.

"No. The coffee won't do unfortunately."

"I don't have a lot to offer." There's a seriousness in her tone now. And a sadness. It's almost more than I can bear to hear.

"A kiss," I say. "A kiss for down payment."

Her eyes widen and I lean forward.

"A kiss, my sweet, and I'll take you anywhere."

She leans forward, meeting me halfway, and I press my lips against hers.

The moment is as magical as that first kiss all those years ago.

The same fluttering sensation in my stomach. The same feeling that everything is right with the world and things will never be the same again. In a good way. In a future that is lovely and bright way.

That had been in a noisy, crowded football stadium.

This was in a noisy, crowded airport.

Then someone calls Hannah's name over the speaker.

"Hannah Thompson."

Leaning back, I look at her with raised eyebrows.

"Is that you?" I ask. "Hannah Thompson?"

"I sort of never changed my name on my passport." She shrugs sheepishly.

"Things are just falling into place, aren't they? Mrs. Thompson."

"Yes. Mr. Thompson. They are."

I snatch up the divorce papers and stuff them back in my pocket.

We won't be needing these. Not ever again.

Epilogue

Hannah
Three Weeks Later

Living Our Someday

The Thompson's ranch house is one of those rambling comfortable two-story mountain houses that can easily accommodate more than one generation at the time. It's an old house. With log cabin walls, but much too modern to be considered a log cabin by any means.

Although the house is nearly a century old, everything has been updated including the kitchen with the latest appliances available on the market.

The house has lots of windows, letting in natural sunlight, especially at the back of the house, floor to ceiling windows with breathtaking views of the forever snow-capped mountains surrounding the high elevation valley. There are either wood burning fireplaces or gas burning fire-places in practically every room and even in the middle of summer, they keep them burning. Like the gas flames burning silently in the breakfast room.

I sit at the kitchen table with Jack and his parents. It's early in the morning. The sun is barely over the horizon. But it feels right to be up this early. Getting up in time to see the sunrise is one of those things too beautiful to miss. Sleeping in is not worth missing nature's splash of color across the sky.

A rooster crows outside and a dog barks. Typical sounds that come with living on a horse ranch.

Bandit sits on my lap, rubbing his face on my chin. He's adapted quite well to being here in the house and he never sets foot outside. He spends his days sleeping in the warm sunlight or exploring the big house. Mostly sleeping.

Mr. Thompson sits across from me, a newspaper spread out in front him, his crutches leaning against the table next to him. Mrs. Thompson shuffles a stack of papers. "We have a group of ten today," she says. "A larger group than I normally like to take into the back country."

"We'll handle it," Jack says, flipping eggs in a skillet. "Hannah is good with them."

"She's a natural," Mr. Thompson smiles.

"She always was," Mrs. Thompson says.

I look over at Jack. He winks at me.

My place.

I've found my place.

I'd known it was my place all along and even though I strayed from it for a while, I've found my way back.

"Have you set a date yet?" Mrs. Thompson asks.

"Christmas," Jack says. "Christmas Eve. Right?" He looks at me for confirmation.

"That's right," I say. "The most magical day of the year."

Bandit jumps down from my lap and hops into the window ledge to chitter at a bird fluttering in the marble bird bath outside.

"I didn't know he did that," I say.

"The country air agrees with him," Mr. Thompson says. "It's good to have you back."

"It's good to be back," I say.

"I don't mind grandcats," Mrs. Thompson says, reaching over and scratching Bandit's ears. "Not one bit, but we wouldn't mind some two legged grandchildren."

Jack rolls his eyes, but I just smile. Jack and I have had this conversation. We're both on board with children.

"We have to get married first," I say, feeling a little heat on my face.

"Bah," Mr. Thompson says with a wave of his hand. "The two of you have been married plenty long enough that no one's going to be doing any math."

Jack sets a plate of eggs on the table and pulls me to my feet. "See? What did I tell you? Everyone knows we're married."

I give him a dubious look, but he just smiles and kisses

me. "It's okay. We'll have our small, intimate wedding. Get our photo in the newspaper."

"I don't care about the newspaper," I say, but it's only partially true. I do actually want everyone to know that I'm Mrs. Jack Thompson. Officially and technically.

"We have our plans," Jack says, keeping me wrapped in his arms.

"Speaking of plans," Mr. Thompson says with a glance at his wife. "We don't know what you two are thinking long-term. Probably still have things to work out. But I saw that Noah Worthington has a little Cessna for sale."

With his arms wrapped loosely around me, Jack looks from me to his father.

"You don't happen to know him, do you?" Mr. Thompson asks with a straight face.

"Only if it's the same Noah Worthington I work for," Jack says.

"Right," Mr. Thompson says, feigning innocence. "Well. Anyway. Your mother and I were thinking about buying it so you can keep living here at the ranch. And fly when you want to."

I see the emotion on Jack's face. Emotion he tries to hide, but it's there.

He and I have talked about this. Long conversations late into the night. We just hadn't figured out how we were going to come up with the money.

I'm still doing a few pet adoptions from here, but it doesn't pay much more than coffee money.

"Jack," I say, then smile over at Mr. and Mrs. Thompson. "It's perfect."

"It's what we had hoped to do some day," Jack says, kissing me again.

"Someday," I say, looking into his sky blue eyes.

He pulls me close against him and I rest my cheek against his chest. "We're living our someday," he says against my ear.

"Yes, we are."

My someday with Jack is here. This very moment.

Maybe it took us some years to find our way back around to our someday, but we're living it now.

We're living our very own happily-ever-after.

THE END

KATHRYN KALEIGH

SOMETIMES FOREVER JUST NEEDS A LITTLE HOLIDAY MAGIC

Yours for Christmas (Maybe)

THE ALPINE FALLS (MAYBE YOURS) SERIES

Yours for Christmas (Maybe)

*She came for her best friend's wedding...
not to fall for the groom's brother.*

Chapter One

Olivia Harris

"I NEED TO CONFIRM MY RESERVATION." I put the phone on speaker and drop it onto the bed next to my over-stuffed suitcase.

Of course the automated system goes to music. Elevator music. At least it has a Christmas beat to it. So there's that.

Why did Hannah, one of my two best friends, have to get married in winter? In the mountains, no less. She could've had a wedding on a warm beach somewhere like most December brides.

Doesn't she know that packing for a cold weather trip requires ten times as many clothes?

I pull out a chunky, oversized cable sweater that's taking

up a fourth of my whole suitcase and toss it aside. I'll just take it with me. I'll need something warm when I get off the airplane in Denver anyway.

At least now I have room for my maid-of-honor dress. And shoes. I almost forgot my heels.

I dash to the closet and grab the box of sparkly high heels I've only worn once. But they are a perfect match for my new burgundy evening gown with its sparkly waistband.

My dog, a little Yorkshire terrier with an adorable caramel colored head and a white body, trots into the room carrying her leash in her mouth.

She drops it at my feet and barks once.

"Hey Cupcake. Time to go outside?"

Instead of answering, she sits down and looks at me with big puppy dog eyes.

Shoving my phone, still playing nondescript music, into my back pocket, I snap her leash onto her collar and together we head to the back door of my little cottage.

Since I own the house outright after inheriting it from my grandmother, I can have as many dogs living with me as I want to.

Right now I only have Cupcake. I've taken her around to two different families for possible adoption, but they both declined. Something about her fur color not lining up.

It was their loss and since I personally think Cupcake is cute as a bug's ear, I'm keeping her for myself.

The temperature outside is warm. Currently in the seventies. Not like December at all. Cold weather is one point in favor of a mountain wedding. Christmas weather is supposed to be cold.

Cupcake runs down the steps and straight out to her favorite tree where she promptly does her business. Standing at the top of the stairs, I let the leash roll out and somehow she knows exactly when to stop before it runs out and stops. It was a one-trial learning for her to figure out just how far out she could run without her leash running out on her. She has impressive spatial skills in that way.

Not one to dilly dally, Cupcake comes bounding back up the stairs.

I pick her up and carry her the rest of the way inside. Just an excuse to bury my face in her soft fur.

When the doorbell rings, she goes on alert and wiggles until I let her down.

Not expecting anyone, I scowl at the door.

A peek outside tells me its Stan, my current boyfriend. I pick Cupcake up again so she won't run outside and open the door.

"I know," he says, holding up a hand. "I know you're leaving in the morning and don't have time for me tonight, but..." He holds up a paper sack. "I know that you forget to eat."

With a sigh, I open the door. I did forget to eat. Sort of. I got busy packing and didn't bother with it.

He smiles and kisses me on the cheek as he comes inside. "Hello Cupcake," he says to the dog in my arms.

"You're right," I say, taking the bag from him and sliding

two ham sandwiches and two bags of chips out onto the table. "I didn't eat."

"Interesting music," he says.

"What? Oh." I pull my phone out of my back pocket and disconnect the call. "I was trying to confirm my reservation. I'll check online later."

"I brought Cupcake a treat." He pulls a dog treat out of his pocket and Cupcake stands up for it, then runs off to chew on it in private.

"I've decided to keep her," I say, sitting down in one of the wooden chairs at my well-worn square kitchen table that seats four.

"I know," he says.

"How do you know?"

He sits down next to me, unwraps one of the sandwiches and slides it in front of me.

"I know because you like her." He opens a bag of chips. "Besides. You need a dog."

"A pet makes a house a home," I say with a sigh. It's the tagline on our pet adoption agency website.

My two friends, Hanna (the one who ran off to Colorado and is getting married) and Madison and I have our own pet adoption agency. When we started Madison and I were handling the dogs while Hanna was handling cat adoptions.

But now that Hanna is in Colorado, we all do what we can. Quite truthfully, Hanna isn't doing much pet adoption work at all. She lives in a tiny little mountain town and helps her husband/fiancé's family with their horse ranch. Yes. Her relationship is complicated. Long story. She was married, but thought she was divorced for ten years. So they're getting married again.

"Are you sure I can't go with you?" Stan asks.

"You've got finals to grade and two grad student dissertations to chair," I say. "And your sister is coming in from Portugal for Christmas."

"I know. I was hoping you'd be here to spend some time with her."

I smile. "Maybe later." It's about as noncommittal as I can get.

I like Stan. He's a good guy. Thoughtful. Dependable. Always thinking about me.

Is there a spark? Define spark.

He knows, should know, because I've told him, that I don't want to get married. It's not him. It's me. I like being single.

"It's okay," he says. "You need to be with your friend. Maybe my sister will be still be in country when you get back."

"Maybe," I say with a forced smile before I bite into the sandwich.

"Are you sure you don't want me to keep Cupcake for you?"

"That would be the sane thing to do. But no. Cupcake is coming with me."

"When you adopt, you go all in, don't you?"

"You know I do. That's why I try to get the dogs — and cats — out of here as soon as I can. I get attached."

He grins. I try not to roll my eyes. I know exactly what he's thinking. He's thinking that I must surely be getting attached to him by now. We've been seeing each other since spring.

It's impossible not to like Stan. It's also almost impossible to keep him from getting his hopes up that we're ever going to be something we're not.

<h1 style="text-align: center;">Chapter Two</h1>

Olivia

Shortly after landing at the Denver airport, I discover that the car rental agencies were not prepared for the number of people heading into the mountains for the holidays.

It makes no sense to me. Hannah warned me that Alpine Falls and Whiskey Springs and a couple of the other little towns like Silver Pines, are Christmas destinations.

Every year.

If I was managing a car rental agency, I would make sure to have enough cars on hand for this time of year. Most especially enough cars to cover the reservations.

But they don't. I send Hannah a text.

> I'm in Denver. But there are no cars.

HANNAH

> Somehow not surprised.

> Options?

HANNAH

> I'll come get you.

I've already studied the map in preparation for my drive. It's a good three hour drive up to Alpine Falls. Then she'd have to drive here, then back into the mountains. At least six hours for her. Plus I have to wait here for her.

> No. Let me think.

I do a quick online search.

> I'll get a car to the train station and ride the train up there.

Thought bubbles.
Then nothing.
I shift the pet carrier on my shoulder. Cupcake is getting heavy.
I sit down on a bench and look for an Uber.

HANNAH

> We have a better solution. Jack's brother is in Denver. He can swing by the airport and pick you up.

> Jack's brother?

HANNAH
Trenton

So Trenton Thompson. I vaguely remember Hannah mentioning that Jack had a couple of brothers. I know absolutely nothing about them.

But. I like the idea of hitching a ride far better than I like the idea of sitting here for three plus hours waiting for Hannah to get here or worse, riding a train.

I had enough trouble with airplane staff leaving me alone about Cupcake. The thought of going through that again to try to get Cupcake on a train is daunting at best.

Speaking of Cupcake, she needs to go outside for a potty break.

Okay. I'll go outside and wait.

HANNAH
Can't you wait inside the airport?

I can. But I have to take Cupcake for a bathroom break.

HANNAH
Oh. Okay. Let me get in touch with Trenton.

I stare at the people hurrying past. Something about being in an airport makes people feel like they have to rush from one place to the next. It's part of the energy that comes with being here.

So this guy, Trenton, doesn't know he's giving me a ride.

Isn't that just great.

After I take my dog outside for a walk, I'll read up on the train. It might end up being my best option after all.

I hoist Cupcake's carrier back over my shoulder and, dragging my overstuffed suitcase along behind me, head for the nearest door to the outside world. If I ran an airport, I'd put in a park where people could walk their dogs. But, of course, that isn't going to happen.

Chapter Three

Trenton Thompson

My meeting went well. I'm not sure why the meeting had to be in Denver. I think the owners of the little company were trying to impress people with their fancy meeting space and city attorneys sitting at the table.

If I get the job, great. If I don't, that's okay, too.

Either way, my building design is solid and they'd be crazy to walk away from it. If they walk away, I'll use the ideas in my next projects. Sure. I'll only be able to use bits and pieces for the next client. Each client has their own unique needs.

As an architect, I pride myself on listening to what a

client wants, hearing what they need, and putting it all together into something they can be proud of.

I'm back in my car before I turn my phone back on. I learned the hard way that the phone has to actually be turned off during presentations. Otherwise, even a phone on silent is a distraction.

When my father fell from a horse and had to be rushed to the hospital, I'd had my phone on silent. Keeping my focus on the presentation while watching those texts come through had been brutal. If I could rewind time, I'd probably stop my presentation and go to my family. At the time, however, I'd been determined to land the contract on the table in front of me. I'd done it, too. No one had ever suspected what I'd been going through. Fortunately it all turned out well with my father. But things could have gone badly in so many different ways.

I have a string of messages from my brother, Jack.

Jack is getting married in a couple of weeks. Married to the girl he's been secretly married to for ten years. Long story. He didn't sign the divorce papers. She thought he had.

They're doing the right thing renewing their vows in a small ceremony.

Small, but Hannah's two friends are going to be there. One of them, Olivia, is apparently already on her way here.

And she's stuck at the airport with no rental car. Typical. There are never enough rental cars.

I send my brother a message.

> Why don't you just fly down and pick her up?

My brother is a pilot with his own small jet. He literally could just fly down and fly Olivia back up to Alpine Falls.

JACK

Because I'm out on a trail ride
with eight guests.

Right. Of course. My brother Jack is running the ranch while our father is off his feet. I have a feeling that Jack and his wife are going to continue to run the ranch from here on out. Our parents are getting up in age and running a horse ranch is brutally hard work.

Makes sense.

JACK

Just swing by the airport and pick
her up.

I'm on the other side of town.

JACK

She's waiting. Her name is Olivia.

Olivia. Yes. I know. I read your
other ten messages.

JACK

Thanks Bro.

Sometimes having a family is a pain in the ass. This is exactly why I live in Boulder. It's just close enough to my family that I can visit, but I don't have to be involved in their day-to-day lives.

Living too close and things like this happens.

And apparently things like this happen anyway.

Not really having a choice about picking up Olivia from the airport, I buckle up and back out of the parking spot. I can't very well leave a young lady stranded at the airport.

Being a gentleman has been pounded into me since I was a boy. My mother raised her three boys with an iron fist and made sure we understood how to treat women.

Traffic is brutal, as always. I turn on the radio and make the best of it. Christmas music on every channel. I try not to be a scrooge, but by Thanksgiving, I'm pretty much sick of all the Christmas festivities.

As the airport comes into sight, I realize I don't know what Olivia looks like. How am I supposed to find this woman when I don't know what she looks like?

I send my brother a message, but his phone is obviously out of range.

I'm on my own on this one.

After making it to the airport, I watch as a large commercial airplane takes off practically right over the road. With my brother being a pilot, I've spent my share of time at airports, but unlike Jack, I don't have that draw to airplanes. Feeling the allure of the sky is something I can appreciate, but never share with Jack.

Instead of parking in the parking lot, I pull up to the main doors.

A woman comes out the doors, walking a little dog. The dog, a Yorkshire terrier, if I know my dogs, is rather odd looking. Cute, but odd. The woman is... actually quite stunning. She has a sassy short bob of blonde hair that just barely brushes her shoulders. She's wearing a chunky sweater over jeans and sneakers on her feet. Casual but with an urban vibe about her.

She's holding the dog's leash with one hand and pulling her suitcase with the other, a pet carrier secured to the top of the suitcase. She carries a computer bag on one shoulder and an oversized handbag on the other, balancing it all with surprising grace.

But, seriously, who brings a dog to an airport?

Since I can't leave my car, I get out and lean against the hood. Maybe someone had the good sense to send Olivia a description of me or even what kind of car I drive. Either would be helpful.

I send my brother another text.

> Would help if I had her number.

After a few minutes, the woman walks back this way, picks up her dog and sits on a bench with it in her lap. I cross my arms and keep my eyes open for someone who looks like she might be waiting for a ride.

Maybe I should just park the car and go inside to look for Olivia.

I glare at my phone.

Try sending Hannah a message, but her phone is out of range also.

Why did no one think to send me Olivia's number?

I scroll back through my previous messages, but I definitely don't have her number.

A few people come out the door, but none of them look like a woman heading to Alpine Falls. I try to imagine what a friend of Hannah's might look like.

Hannah is thin and casual-looking, but then Hannah is different because she's actually from Alpine Falls. Her friend won't be from Alpine Falls. Her friend will be from Houston.

My gaze strays back to the young lady sitting with the dog. She's also typing on her own phone and not looking too happy.

I need a sign. That's what people do in the movies.

Annoyed with myself that I didn't already think of that, I climb back in my car and write *Olivia* in big letters on a blank piece of paper.

Taking my sign, I go back to my station near the hood of the car. Now I'm feeling pretty much like a dumbass standing here holding a sign.

Jack and Hannah owe me big time.

Chapter Four

Olivia

I WALK outside the front doors of the airport. The air out here smells like exhaust. And not only that, the air is dry. I can tell as soon as I step outside that the air is different. Hannah told me to bring moisturizer and now I understand why.

There are cars lined up, waiting for people. Dropping people off. Typical airport.

Not seeing any grass anywhere where Cupcake can take her potty break, I find a private space with a little patch of rocks and after making sure Cupcake's harness is secure, lift her out of the carrier to do her business.

Since she was cramped up in the carrier for so long, I keep her leash short and walk around with her some, letting her get some exercise. It's not like we're going anywhere right now.

My stomach growls and I realize it's mid-afternoon and I haven't eaten anything all day. Thanks to Stan, I ate last night, so I can make it to Alpine Falls. Maybe. If I ever get there.

I sit down on a bench, happy to take from break from the weight of my computer bag and purse from my shoulders.

A man pulls up in a new sedan, gets out of his car, and leans against the hood.

He most definitely does not look like someone from Alpine Falls. Not that Jack did either when I'd seen him in Houston a few months ago.

The guy leaning on the car looks like a guy out one of those men's magazines. Perfect hair and perfect business suit. Definitely not from Alpine Falls.

Gathering Cupcake up into my lap, I send Hannah a message.

How am I supposed to find Trenton?

No response. It doesn't even look like it's been delivered.

Great. The train is sounding better and better.

The magazine guy gets back into his car. I study the train

schedules. The last train leaves in... I glance at the time... thirty minutes.

Well. So much for that. My next option is to get a hotel room and try again tomorrow.

If there still aren't any rental cars, which I am almost certain if there were no cars today when I actually had a reservation, there's no way I'll get a car tomorrow when I don't have one, I can at least get on the train. Or maybe I'm going to have to let Hannah come and pick me up after all.

Now I'm thinking crazy thoughts like maybe I should have let Stan come along. Not that Stan could have produced a rental car, but this whole ordeal would seem less daunting with someone else along.

And if I'm quite honest with myself, that's probably the main reason I keep Stan around. To have someone to do things with. Maybe it's not the best reason, but it seems like as good a reason as any all things considered in this world we live in.

Stan is dependable and safe. That's not easy to find in someone these days, at least not in my experience.

The handsome magazine guy gets out of his car and, leaning on his hood again, holds up a piece of paper. A sign?

I squint in his direction. It looks like he's holding up a sign. It's too far away, of course, for me to read it.

A sign would have been a good idea. People do that in the movies all the time. It's how strangers find each other at the airport.

It suddenly occurs to me that I need a sign. I need a sign

that reads *Trenton.* That way when he drives up, he'll know I'm waiting for him.

Of course, I have no paper. An iPad, but no paper. Maybe I can make a sign on my iPad.

Or... I get up, set Cupcake on her feet, and after gathering up all my things, securing my handbag and computer bag over my shoulder, grabbing the handle of my suitcase with my other hand, and walk over to the man. If a man has a sheet of paper, he'll have more than one. It's some kind of law.

"Hi," I say, smiling at him.

"Hi." He looks a little startled that I'm talking to him.

"I'm sorry to bother you, but I was wondering if maybe I could borrow a sheet of paper."

"Okay," he says, but doesn't move.

"I'm supposed to be meeting someone, but I don't know him and I need to make a sign."

"Sure." Now he seems a little annoyed. Oh well. "Hold this." He thrusts his own sign into my hands and opens up his car door.

I glance down at the sign.

Olivia.

Chapter Five

Trenton

I'm leaning into the back seat of my car, digging in my briefcase for a sheet of paper when the woman with the dog says "Never mind."

I back out of the car, straighten and look at her. "So now you don't need any paper?"

"I won't be needing to make a sign after all," she says, biting my bottom lip.

"Okay," I say, closing the car door. "Fine by me."

She holds up my sign. "Olivia," she says.

"That's who I'm waiting for."

"I'm Olivia," she says as though I'm the stupidest person she ever met.

I glance down at her dog, then back up to look more closely at her. She has forest green eyes framed with thick dark lashes.

My gaze snags on her plump, kissable lips curved into a little amused smile.

"You're Olivia? Hannah's friend?"

"Yes. Are you Jack's brother?"

I take a deep breath. Let it out slowly. "Yes."

"What's your name?" she asks, suddenly suspicious.

"Trenton." She looks at me with one eyebrow lifted. "Thompson."

She seems satisfied with that. "I think you're my ride."

"You're headed to Alpine Falls?" I try to keep the disbelief out of my voice.

"Yes."

"Okay. Let's go."

I pop the trunk and after she drags her suitcase around, I grab it up and toss it in. It weighs a ton.

"This is Cupcake," she says.

"You brought a dog on an airplane?" I ask.

"Yes," she says somewhat defensively.

"I didn't know that was allowed."

"It's allowed. But. I don't think people like it very much."

"I wouldn't think so."

"You don't like dogs?"

"I like dogs fine. I just didn't know they were allowed on airplanes."

"I guess I lucked out and got a lenient crew."

"Cupcake needs to ride in her carrier," I say, opening the back door and taking her computer bag to stash it in on the seat.

"Why?"

"Safety. And it's the law." I honestly don't know if it's the law or not, but even if it's not, it should be.

"Okay." She secures the dog in the carrier and sets it on the back seat. "Do you want me to ride in the back, too?"

"Why would you do that?"

"I don't know," she says. "You just don't seem very friendly."

I open the passenger door and hold it while she climbs inside. She's absolutely right. I'm not being very friendly. I've been annoyed by the whole ordeal. Not exactly the way to welcome one of my sister-in-law's friends.

"Please accept my apology," I say before I close the passenger door, not waiting for an answer.

This woman reminds me of my mother. She doesn't seem like one to put up with bullshit.

I walk around and get into the driver's seat.

"How was your flight?" I ask as I buckle up and start the motor.

"Fine," she says.

"You must be hungry."

"A little."

"When was the last time you ate?"

"I ate last night."

"That's too long to go without eating," I say.

"You sound like my... friend."

"Hannah?"

"No. A different friend." She looks away.

"We'll stop and get something to eat before we leave the city. Can't have you going hungry."

"I'll be okay."

"I have no doubt about that, but as your welcoming committee, it's my job to make sure you're taken care of."

"Welcoming committee?" she asks with clear skepticism.

"I thought I apologized for not being friendly."

"You did. I'm just not sure I forgive you yet."

With a smile, I get us onto the interstate. This girl might be odd enough to bring a dog with her to an airport, but she's also entertaining.

Chapter Six

Hannah

JACK'S BROTHER is nothing like I expected. Although he's good looking, he doesn't look like Jack. Of course I only saw Jack that one time and only briefly, so I could easily be missing the resemblance.

He's also a bit of a smartass and not very friendly.

And although he claims he likes dogs, I'm not so sure I believe him.

All in all, Trenton comes across as quite disagreeable.

On the interstate now, it looks like we're going to be stuck in traffic.

"Not the best time to be driving in the city," he says.

"Is there ever a good time?"

"In Denver? Not really? It seems like rush hour is all the time."

"It's not quite that bad in Houston."

He changes the channel on the radio. Then changes it again.

"Nothing but Christmas music," he says.

"What's wrong with Christmas music? It's almost Christmas."

He changes the channel again. More Christmas music. "It's been almost Christmas for a month now. Don't people get tired of hearing the same old songs over and over?"

"I don't know. I play my favorite songs over and over again. I don't get tired of them."

"I guess you have a point."

We pass by a pickup truck with a freshly-cut Christmas tree secured in the truck bed.

I turn back to Trenton. "Are you one of those people who doesn't like Christmas?"

"I didn't say I didn't like Christmas. I just get tired of the hype. We barely get into November and everything is all about Christmas. Normal business practically shuts down for weeks. Then after that one day gets here, it's all over. All that hype for that one day."

"So why don't you tell me how you really feel?"

He glances over at me with a perplexed expression, then smiles.

"I guess you're one of those people who loves the holidays."

"What's not to love? There's an energy in the air that isn't there any other time."

"I guess so," he says. "It just makes it hard to conduct any business."

I tuck my hair behind my ears and turn my gaze back to the traffic. We're heading west, toward the snow-capped mountains. Having never been to the mountains, I'm finding the prospect of finally getting to be in the high elevation a little exciting.

"What kind of work do you do?" I ask.

"I'm an architect."

"Oh." I nod and keep my thoughts to myself. It seems to me like any kind of architectural work could easily wait until after Christmas.

"You don't think my work is important," he says.

I look at him with a vexed expression. "I did not say that. I'm sure what you do is very important."

"There are people who want to move forward with their building plans during the holidays but can't because everything slows down."

"Doesn't building slow down in the winter anyway? What with the rain and, up here, the snow?"

"Sure. But mostly just for the external part of the buildings. Work on the interiors continues."

"You do interior work?"

"I'd say that's the bulk of what I do."

"Oh. Well. I'm sorry your work slows down in December."

"What about yours? What do you do?"

"Pet adoptions. We usually see an upswing. But not so much this year."

"People want pets for Christmas." I can't tell if he's being sarcastic or not. "What's different this year?"

"I don't know. I think it's our focus. With Hannah moving up here and getting married, it's splintered our company."

He changes lanes and we're able to speed up for a bit.

"You do know that Hannah is already married, right?"

"Oh no," I say, shaking my head.

"Oh no what?"

"Don't tell me you not only don't like Christmas, but you don't believe in romance either?"

"I didn't say that. There's a little diner about a mile up ahead."

"Okay. I guess since it's not hot outside, Cupcake can stay in the car, but I need to feed her, too."

"Sure." He exits and finds a parking space near the door. "Wait here for a minute," he says. "I need to check on something."

"Sure." Wondering what he could possibly have to check on, I watch him go inside the little diner. Maybe he's checking to see if they have any tables.

I check my phone for messages. Still nothing from Hannah.

Not wanting to keep sending unanswered messages, I don't tell her I found Trenton and that I'm on my way. She'll find out soon enough.

Trenton comes back to the car. "I spoke to the manager," he says. "You can bring Cupcake inside."

"Oh. Okay." I did not expect that. It's the first really kind thing he's done since I met him.

Maybe he isn't so bad as I initially thought after all.

Chapter Seven

Trenton

THE HOSTESS USHERS us to a booth in the back of the
diner.

It's just a little diner in two old train cars put together,
very retro and very architecturally creative. Someone took
one of the long walls off each of the two cars and then
welded them together. Worn maroon colored leather seats at
the dozen or so booths. Metal stools with matching seat
covers at the bar.

Christmas music plays in the background, but it's old
music from early last century. It fits the diner and doesn't
bother me.

The cook is hard at work at the grill. Everything here is

fried. I don't think they bake anything, except maybe the apple pies that are impossible to resist. I usually get a whole pie to go when I'm headed to Alpine Falls and just a slice if I'm heading home to Boulder. This is a whole apple pie day.

The diner is one of my regular stops on trip from Denver into the mountains. I was first drawn to it because of its creative use of a couple of old train cars, but then I discovered its excellent food and eventually became friends with the staff. Some would call me a regular even though sometimes I go weeks without stopping in.

We borrow a couple of bowls, one for water and one for food, and set Cupcake up a place on the floor beneath our table to eat. While Cupcake devours her food, Olivia checks out the Christmas tree that just so happens to be next to our booth.

"Look at how cute this tree is," she says. "All the decorations are little dogs and even a few cats. So sweet."

Alice, the waitress, comes to our table to take our order.

"Can I get you something to drink?" she asks.

"Just water," Olivia says. "I love your tree."

"Thanks," Alice says, smiling. "It was my idea."

"And it was a wonderful idea," Olivia says.

"I'll be right back with your water and a coke for you Trenton."

Olivia sits down at the booth and looks at me.

"Come here often?" she asks.

I smile at her way of asking how I know the staff. "Whenever I'm down this way."

"Well. Cupcake likes it here."

"If Cupcake likes it, that's saying something."

She tilts her head as she looks at me. She can't tell if I'm being sincere or smartassed and quite frankly I'm not sure which way I'm leaning at the moment.

I'm still getting over being annoyed at having been strong-armed into giving this woman and her dog a ride to Alpine Falls.

The problem with my annoyance is that I'm struggling to hold onto it. Olivia is actually a delight to be around and Cupcake is weirdly cute in her own way.

Alice quickly brings Olivia's water and my coke to the table.

"Need some time to look at the menu?" she asks, holding a little pad and pencil at the ready.

"Yes, please," Olivia says. "What's good?"

"Everything," Alice says, then looks at me. "Don't let her leave without apple pie."

"Wouldn't think of it," I say. "In fact, I'm heading to Alpine Falls, so save me a couple back."

"Consider it done," Alice says. "I'll be back in five to take your order."

"What do you like?" I ask, sliding a menu over to Olivia.

She opens it up and studies it. I fully expect her to order a salad, maybe the chicken salad. Something light. Dressing on the side.

After a quick perusal of the menu, she sets it aside.

"Find anything to your liking?" I ask.

"I think I'll have the ham sandwich with fries."

"Good choice," I say, trying to hide my surprise that she would order something so robust. "I'll have the same."

Cupcake finishes her meal and Olivia puts her on the seat next to her. The dog curls up and goes to sleep. The dog being so well behaved surprises me, too.

"I want to get a photo of the Christmas tree," she says. "For our website. Do you think they would mind?"

"I don't know why they would."

She pulls out her phone and proceeds to photograph the Christmas tree with pet decorations.

Alice takes our order. "I'll have it right out."

Sitting back down, she zooms in on one of the photos and holds it up for me to see. "Look. Some of the lights are even shaped like dogs. Where do you think they found something like that?"

"I wouldn't know. We can ask."

I don't dislike Christmas. Not exactly anyway. It's more like I tolerate it.

I've never had one of those magical Christmasses like they show in the movies where everything comes together. Sure. I enjoy the time spent with my family. The food. The football games. Even the presents are sometimes fun, but as for magic, not so much.

This year, the focus is going to be on Hannah and Jack, as it should be since they're getting married (again) on Christmas Eve. Apparently Christmas Eve is Hannah's favorite day of the year.

Personally, if I were in Jack's shoes, I'm not sure I'd want to combine occasions. One good thing is he won't be forgetting his anniversary. Hard to forget an anniversary that's also Christmas Eve.

Just after we order our food, both our phones chime with messages.

"Message from Hannah," she says.

"I got one from Jack. He sent me your phone number."

"And Hannah sent me yours. Took them long enough, didn't it?"

"Yes. It did. I'm think we keep them in suspense a little while."

"You mean not tell them that we found each other."

"It seems like a small price to pay for leaving us hanging like that."

"I don't think it was intentional," she says, setting her phone aside. "But okay. Maybe next time they'll think things through a little better."

"My thoughts exactly."

Alice drops our ham sandwiches off and a bottle of Ketchup. "Can I get you anything else?"

We both say no.

"Good." Alice says. "I'll get those pies wrapped up for you. Sure you don't want a piece for now?

"Maybe later," I say with a glance at Olivia who's already eating her French fries. "We'll let you know about that."

"Enjoy," Alice says, leaving us to it.

"How's your sandwich?" I ask.

"Good. I haven't had a ham sandwich this good since I used to live at home with my parents. My mother made the best ham sandwiches ever."

"Will you see your family for Christmas?" I ask.

"No. They died when I was fifteen."

"Olivia. I am so sorry." And I'm such a dumbass for making assumptions when the truth is I know nothing about her. Sometimes it's hard for me to remember that not everyone had a happy childhood like mine. Even if my family does annoy me sometimes. It's easy to forget just how lucky I am.

"It's okay," she says, picking up her sandwich. "It was a long time ago and I learned at an early age to take care of myself."

We eat in silence for a few minutes.

"You're quite impressive," I say.

"How's that?" she asks with amusement.

"You've been on your own for what, five years."

"Ten."

"Okay. So you've been on your own for ten years and you're not afraid to take risks."

"What makes you think that?"

"You have your own company, for one. Mostly it's just an impression I'm getting from you."

"It's true. I don't have a lot of fear. Losing my parents as a teenager taught me that we don't have a lot of control over our ultimate fate. So I just put my all into everything I do. I figure I have everything to gain and not a lot to lose."

"Boyfriend?"

"Nothing serious. I don't do serious." She stops herself and looks down, focusing on her food. I get the impression she said more than she intended.

It fits. Losing her parents at such a young age, she would have trouble with relationships. But I'm no psychologist and it's not my business.

"Do you want a piece of pie now or do you want to wait until we get to Alpine Falls to eat with the family?"

"Definitely wait," she says. "I couldn't eat another bite right now if I had to."

"I know what you mean. This place has great food."

"Thank you for sharing it with me," she says, her eyes bright and not looking a little bit sad.

I wonder two things in this moment. I wonder if maybe bringing up her parents made her sad and her bravery is a front for something more vulnerable beneath.

And second, I wonder how she could have known that I don't share this place with a lot of people. It's sort of my own little private sanctuary for when I travel into Denver.

Chapter Eight

Olivia

I DON'T USUALLY TELL people about my parents. Madison and Hannah know, of course. But I don't go around telling random strangers.

Technically, I guess, Trenton isn't a random stranger. He's the brother of my friend's fiancé (husband).

Still. I don't know why I told him. It was more information than he needed to know over a late lunch in a quaint little diner made out of a train car.

So I do what I know how to do well. I change the direction of the conversation.

"As an architect, you must be especially able to appreciate the design of this diner. It's made out of old train cars? Or just made to look like it?"

"Yes. It really is. They took two train cars and welded them together. It's really quite fascinating."

"Is this the kind of thing you do or do you do more modern designs?"

"I can go either way. I listen to what the client wants. Try to get an image of what they must be picturing. And then I draw it up."

"Is it hard? Trying to figure out what someone else is seeing in their head?"

"They usually have pictures. In fact, I ask them to bring photos from magazines and websites of things they like."

"What's your favorite project you ever designed?"

"That's a hard question to answer."

Alice stops and picks up our empty plates. "Pie now or just to go?" she asks.

"Just to go," I say. "Thank you Alice."

"Come back and see us again," Alice says to me.

"I will." I smile, but I also can't imagine a scenario where I would be back here.

"I guess if I had to pick a favorite," Trenton says handing Alice a credit card. "It would be a small cottage I built for an older lady on a little plot of land just outside of Boulder."

"What did you like about it?"

"Like you, she liked animals. I think she had about ten cats and a couple of dogs. She wanted a courtyard in the middle so her pets could go outside. I built the house around that. A firepit and a fountain in the middle. Gas fireplaces in every room, even one in the bathroom. Very cozy."

"I think you just described my dream house."

He laughs, softening his features and sending little tingles of awareness down my spine.

When he laughs, his handsomeness becomes more approachable.

"I have photos. Not with me. But I can show you photos."

"I'd like to see them."

"Okay. I'll bring them by next time I'm in Alpine Falls."

"You don't live in Alpine Falls? At the ranch?"

"God no. I have my own place in Boulder."

"Of course," I say, wondering why I feel disappointed. I suppose I was looking forward to seeing him at the ranch while I'm there. Hannah will be busy with Jack and even though I just met him, Trenton is someone I'm comfortable being around.

"I'll be spending most of the next couple of weeks at the ranch though," he says. "It'll take me a couple of days to finish up some work at my place, pack, and drive back up there."

I bring up a mental image of the map I'd studied when I'd thought I was going to be making this drive myself.

"Giving me a ride is way out of your way, isn't it?"

"A little," he says with a little smile. "But it's okay. I'm enjoying the company."

"I hope you know how much I appreciate it. I had a

rental car reservation, but when I got there, they didn't have a car."

"Think nothing of it," he says. "You ready to get back on the road? I'd like to be there before dark."

Chapter Nine

Trenton

When I told Olivia I was enjoying her company, I'd been speaking from the heart. The words just sort of spilled out and honestly it was the kind of bland statement I would say to acquaintances. The problem is that as I said the words to Olivia, I realized how much I actually meant them.

With Cupcake back in her carrier and safely in the back seat, we get back on the interstate and head toward the mountains.

I put on my sunglasses to combat some of the bright sunlight we're driving toward.

Olivia doesn't seem concerned, but she seems to see everything.

"Is this your first time to Colorado?"

"Yes. My first time out west. To the mountains."

"You've never been to the mountains?"

"Never. With Houston being in the south, my friends always just sort of gravitated to the beach."

"I've never been to the beach."

"You're kidding!"

"No. I prefer the higher elevations."

"Huh. We're like total opposites."

"Maybe," I say. "We'll see how you feel about that after you've been in the mountains for a few days."

"Hannah loves it."

"Well. She's from Alpine Falls. So I'm not sure that really counts."

"True. But it counts. I think she went to the beach with us one time. She didn't care for it." Olivia pulls out her phone. "Speaking of Hannah. She's texting me again. I should probably let her know I'm still alive."

"Probably."

She sends me a smile before she answers the text.

"Okay. I told her we managed to find each other and we're on the way."

"You're a good friend."

She shrugs. "Hannah always seemed like she needed a friend, you know. Madison and I knew each other from where we grew up in Katy, but we sort of just adopted Hannah."

"Katy? Isn't that a suburb?"

"Yes. West of Houston."

"Hm. That fits." I adjust my shades and lower the visor to help combat the bright sun.

"What makes you say that?"

"You sort of have a city girl vibe, but it's different from most of the city girls I've known."

"You've known a lot of city girls?" she asks.

"No one from Houston," I say, keeping my answer purposely vague.

"Well. My grandmother had a house in Houston. I inherited it from her. So I guess I sort of grew up in Katy then lived in Houston from age fifteen."

Another piece of the puzzle falls into place.

If she inherited a house from her grandmother, that explains how she can venture out on her own. Most people seek security, but if she had an inheritance sizable enough that she got a house out of it plus whatever she would have gotten from her parents, she wouldn't have to. She would have the freedom to do whatever she wanted.

"They said your other friend Madison will be coming up, too."

"She will. She's actually more like you. It's hard to get her away from work. I think you'll like her."

"Trying to set me up?"

"No. Not unless you want me to. If you want me to, I can."

"I'm good."

And no. I do not want Olivia to set me up with her friend Madison. Not when I'm enjoying Olivia's company like I am. That just wouldn't make any sense.

I keep those thoughts to myself though. The next couple of weeks are going to be interesting to say the least. And for the first time I'm not dreading spending the two weeks leading up to Christmas at the ranch. In fact, I'm rather looking forward to them.

Chapter Ten

Olivia

I SPEND the next few minutes sitting in silence, mentally kicking myself.

Why would I offer to set Trenton up with Madison? First of all, that hadn't been where I was heading when I said they were alike. I was simply stating a fact.

I like Madison and Trenton is a lot like her so I like him, too. That had been more along my line of thinking.

But he'd jumped the other way. That told me he's not interested in dating me. Good to know. And probably for the best considering that I do technically have Stan in my life.

He deftly changes the subject, pointing out landmarks as we go.

We go through the Eisenhower Tunnel and I am officially impressed.

We take the next exit after we come out of the tunnel.

"Just for full disclosure, we could have taken the exit before the tunnel, but I thought you might like the experience of driving through it."

"I did. Thank you. Wow. It's just. Impressive."

"One point for the mountains," he says.

"You're funny. You think you're going to convert me from a beach person to a mountain person."

"You say that like you don't think it's possible."

"Anything is possible," I say. "But you're looking a life-long beach-goer. You have your work cut out for you."

"I'm not worried. The crisp mountain air will do the work for me."

"I don't doubt that. I'm not really a fan of hot weather."

"Oh. The beaches are going down."

"Are you always this sure of yourself?"

We're on a two-lane road now. A winding two-lane road with lots of trees. Some bare with no leaves. Others look like Christmas trees in the wild.

"Only when I can see that the odds are stacked in my favor."

"A betting man." I nod. "Okay. I have to keep an eye on you."

"Busted. Just whatever you do, please do not tell my mother."

"You would seriously keep something like a propensity for gambling from your mother?"

"Once you meet my mother, you'll understand."

I feel a flutter of butterflies in my stomach.

I came up here to Alpine Falls to help my friend get ready for her wedding. Not that she needs help getting ready for her small, intimate wedding, but I took the excuse to spend time with her. And if I'm honest with myself it's as much an excuse to spend Christmas with Hannah and her fiancé (husband) as it is to avoid spending Christmas with Stan and his family. Spending Christmas with Stan would only encourage him to think our relationship is heading toward marriage.

It doesn't help that I finally told him I don't want to get married.

The problem is he doesn't believe me. He seems to think he can sway me over to his side of wanting to get married. Not that he comes right out and says it. I can just tell.

At any rate, even though I came up here to spend time with Hannah, I've met a guy.

And now through circumstances outside of my control, I'm on my way to meet this guy's family.

It's all quite surreal.

And I need to keep my thoughts together.

Trenton has already made it clear to me that he's not interested in me that way.

Maybe he doesn't even like girls. He's certainly good looking. Not exactly a rugged kind of guy and he spends most of his life away from his family.

"What about your girlfriend?" I ask. "Will she be coming up to the ranch for Christmas?"

"Did Hannah tell you I have a girlfriend?" he asks.

"Hannah didn't tell me anything about you or your other brother. I was just making conversation."

"No. I don't have a girlfriend."

"Boyfriend?"

He looks at me sideways, but I can't see his eyes behind his dark sun glasses.

"I don't have a girlfriend because the last two women I dated didn't understand why I spend so much time working."

"I see. I understand that. A lot of people struggle with that." Madison for one, but I'm not bringing her up again.

"Like Madison?" he asks.

So much for that. I send him a sideways look. "Yes. Like Madison."

"What about you? You don't put yourself in that category?"

"I work plenty when I need to. But I don't have to always be doing something productive."

"I envy that quality," he says.

"Do you now? Maybe you just need to hang around someone you enjoy spending time with."

"You sound like you're speaking from experience now?" he says, turning off the highway.

We're definitely in the mountains now and the sun has dropped behind the mountains, leaving us in twilight. The sky is streaked with beautiful shades of pink.

"Wow. This sunset."

"Better than the beach?"

"Maybe."

Maybe it doesn't have so much to do with the beach versus the mountains as it has to do with the company.

"We're here," he says turning down a long dirt driveway.

Hannah hadn't been kidding when she'd said the ranch was deep in the mountains, off by itself.

Chapter Eleven

Trenton

THE DRIVE UP from Denver had gone quickly with Olivia to talk to. The travel time had passed by more quickly than I could ever remember.

"The house is huge," Olivia says, looking out of the car window at the two-story house, all the windows aglow with Christmas lights around the roof and all the windows. A Christmas tree twinkles with clear lights in the front window. "You grew up here?"

"Yes."

"This house must have inspired you to become an architect."

"Maybe. I never really considered that." I glance out at the house where I'd grown up. Maybe it was subconscious inspiration, but somewhere along the line, I started taking it for granted.

As I drive around the circle drive and park in front of the door, Hannah and Jack come outside to meet us.

Hannah runs up to the car and opens the door. Olivia gets out and the girls hug.

I open the back door and set Cupcake's carrier on the ground. Knowing she's wearing her leash, I open up the carrier and lift her out. The dog licks my hands as I set her on the ground. She runs over to Olivia, putting her front feet on her legs.

"This is Cupcake," Olivia says.

Hannah picks up the dog and gets her face licked for it.

"You'd think she's known you forever," Olivia says.

"I think she likes me," Hannah says.

"What's not to like?" Jack asks. "Hey Bro," he says to me. "Thanks for going out of your way to do this."

"It was surprisingly not a hardship." I walk around to the trunk and drag out Olivia's suitcase.

"Coming from you," Jack says. "That's saying a lot."

"Olivia is... pleasant."

Jack laughs. "I guess I should go introduce myself."

"Olivia," Hannah says, obviously overhearing that last comment. "This is Jack."

"Yes," Olivia says, giving Jack a quick hug. "I remember."

"Welcome to the Thompson Ranch."

"Thank you." Olivia looks around. "It's beautiful here."

"I told you," Hannah says. "You're going to love the mountains.

"I think I already do." Maybe I'm imagining things, but she sends me a quick glance. "Trenton is an excellent welcoming committee."

Jack looks at me. "Are we talking about the same guy?"

"Nobody asked you, Jack," I say, handing Cupcake's leash to Olivia.

"I need to take Cupcake for a walk. Hannah. Can you come with?"

"Sure. We'll be right back." Hannah gives Jack a quick kiss and the two girls walk off with an excited Cupcake leading the way.

"Do I detect an attraction here?" Jack asks me when the girls are out of earshot.

"Just being hospitable to your wife's friend," I say.

Jack runs a hand over his chin and nods. "Thank you. I appreciate it."

"Don't mention it," I say, pulling Olivia's computer bag and after a moment's hesitation, her purse, from the car, I put them over my shoulder and drag her suitcase to the front door.

Jack watches me with obvious amusement.

"Get the door, would you?" I ask.

"Sure. It's the first time I've ever known you to fall for a blonde."

I send my brother a scathing look as I set Olivia's things down in the foyer.

"Just doing what you asked me to do."

"And you're doing a fine job of it," Jack says, clapping me on the shoulder. "A fine job."

Chapter Twelve

Olivia

With Cupcake leading the way, sniffing every tree, every fallen branch, we walk along a little path that winds through the trees.

"You'd think she's been here before," I say.

"Probably smells Lucas's dog. They walk out here sometimes," Hannah says.

The dirt path is dry and firm, rocky in places. The silver bark of aspen trees contrasts with the green spruce trees that smell like Christmas. The air is light and almost painfully clean.

"So," Hannah asks. "What do you think?"

"It's beautiful here. Definitely not humid. I brought moisturizer."

"I meant about Trenton," Hannah says.

"Oh. He and Jack don't really look alike, do they?"

"Not really. Lucas and Jack look more alike. But if you watch Trenton, you'll see the resemblances."

"Different personalities."

"Jack is better with people," Hannah says.

"I don't know," I say, looking back toward the house, but the guys have gone inside. "He warms up nicely."

"You like him," Hannah says, pleased.

"No. I don't like him. I don't not like him, but he's not interested in me."

"Please tell me how exactly you know that."

I shake my head and tug gently on Cupcake's leash when she tries to circle a maple tree. "He and I are complete opposites."

"So? That doesn't mean anything."

"I think he and Madison will get along better," I say.

"Definitely not," Hannah says. "They will clash like two like magnetic poles."

"Maybe," I say, then I change the subject. "So how about you? Do you miss Houston?"

"Sometimes, sure. But Alpine Falls is home. And Jack is home."

"You look good," I decide. "Happy. And relaxed."

"I don't know about relaxed. The ranch is a LOT of work."

"What about his parents? How is it living with them?"

"Oddly enough, I don't mind. They let us do our thing and the house is big enough that we don't run over each other." She looks back toward the house, too. "It's actually kind of nice being part of a family."

"Yeah. You and I haven't done too well in that department, have we?"

"No," she says. "But for entirely different reasons. I keep thinking I should reconcile with my parents."

"If that's something you want to do, then yes. But Hannah? Do it now. While you can."

"Maybe after the wedding."

"Hannah." I take her hand. "Doesn't it make more sense to go see them before the wedding? Maybe they'd like to be here for it."

Hannah bites her bottom lip. "Maybe that's what I'm afraid of."

"Just because Theo was an ass about your family doesn't mean Jack would be. I think Jack would be supportive if your family wanted to come."

"I know he would. And you're right. He's nothing like Theo."

When Theo, Hannah's ex-fiancé, thought Hannah might be in Denver to reconcile with her family, he'd been an ass about having to accommodate them for their wedding. The joke was on him, though, because Hannah ended up reconciling with Jack and breaking up with Theo.

"Do whatever you think is right. We're all right here behind you."

"I know," Hannah says. "I'm so glad you're here."

"Me too."

"And I think you and Trenton would make a cute couple."

"Don't get ahead of yourself there," I say. "I know how you married people are. Wanting everyone around you to be married, too."

"I plead the fifth. Let's go inside," she says. "Get you settled in."

Chapter Thirteen

Trenton

MY PARENTS ARE good with people. Taking guests on horse rides every day has definitely given them lots of practice with getting along with new people.

As such, I shouldn't be surprised that they take to Olivia.

"What can I do to help?" Olivia asks as she comes back downstairs after getting settled into one of the guest rooms.

"Not a thing, Dear," Mother says. "Jack is just about to slice one of those apples pies."

"It smells delicious," Olivia says.

"You know," she says. "Trenton doesn't tell us where he gets these pies, but they're always delightful."

Olivia glances over at me. "He's a man of many secrets."

"He wants us to think that anyway," Father says.

Jack pulls the pie out of the oven and proceeds to cut it into six even slices.

"Where's Lucas?" I ask. "Out with the horses?"

"I think he went into town," Jack says.

"Girlfriend?" I ask. Our brother is usually out with the horses so it's quite unusual for him to not be around somewhere.

"Who knows," Mother says. "Lucas does whatever Lucas wants to do."

Mother puts a slice of pie in front of Father and sits down next to him.

"Have a seat, Olivia," Mother says. "Make yourself at home."

I take two plates of pie and set them down on the other side of the table.

After Hannah and Jack sit down, Olivia sits next to me. I hand her a fork.

"Thank you," she says.

"You're welcome." My gaze snags on her forest green eyes and I smile.

When she smiles back, the ground beneath me seems to shift.

It's funny because no one else seems to notice. They keep talking like nothing has changed.

But for me, having Olivia here feels like everything has changed.

I don't feel like just the third wheel around Jack and

Hannah. Or the son who's never here because he doesn't really fit in.

I realize that Hannah is saying something to me, but I missed it.

"I'm sorry, Hannah," I say, tearing my gaze away from Olivia. "I was distracted."

Hannah just smiles and repeats herself. "It's okay. I was saying that maybe you should wait until the morning to drive into Boulder."

"Yes," Mother says. "You know how dangerous these mountain roads can be at night. And you have a perfectly good room here to sleep in."

"I might do that," I say. "I've already been driving a lot today."

"Thank you for rescuing Olivia," Hannah says.

"I had a rental car reservation," Olivia says. "And now I know to get to Denver early enough to take the train."

"You don't have to take the train," Hannah says. "Next time we'll make sure Jack is there with his airplane."

"I wouldn't want to put anyone out. It was bad enough for Trenton to go to all that trouble to pick me up and drive me here."

"It wasn't any trouble," I say, taking a bite of pie and making a concerted effort not to look at her. Not when everyone is watching us. Plotting us getting together.

"So you'll stay?" Hannah asks. "Jack and I were thinking we could fire up the firepit out back."

The thought of getting to spend more time with Olivia is dangerously delicious. I should say no. I should use any excuse I can find to drive back to my place tonight. I'm going to be back here in a couple of days anyway. I always spend a couple of weeks at Christmastime here with my family. So I'll have plenty of time to spend getting know Olivia.

That's what I should do. Just go home tonight.

Distance myself from Olivia and her undeniable allure.

"Yes," I say. "I'll stay."

Chapter Fourteen

Olivia

After we have pie, Hannah and I sit on the sofa in the living room while the guys go outside to get a fire going in the firepit. His parents went upstairs to bed.

Cupcake, having discovered the fireplace, sits in front of it, fascinated by the flames.

Bandit, Hannah's Snowshoe cat, walks over and stands in my lap, rubbing his chin on my face.

"I missed you, too," I say. I kept Bandit while Hannah was up here seeking her divorce papers, but instead learning that she was still married to Jack and subsequently reconnecting with him.

It was all dreamily romantic. I scratch Bandit behind the ears and he purrs happily in response.

"What made you decide to keep Cupcake?" Hannah asks.

"I took her around to a couple of people thinking about adopting, but they didn't appreciate Cupcake's unique coloring. I think she's adorable. So. She's mine now."

"Good for you. You've been needing a dog of your own."

"Seems we both needed pets."

"Pets make a house a home," she quotes from our website.

"It really is true," I say. "The guys are coming back inside. I should bring Cupcake outside with us."

"I think Cupcake is happy where she is."

"I guess so."

Both guys are not only wearing heavy coats, they're each holding a coat in their hands.

Hannah goes right over and slides into the coat Jack holds up for her.

"We're assuming you don't have a coat," Trenton says to me.

"I have a jacket," I say.

"Well. It's cold outside. I think you might be glad you have this."

"Whose it is?" I ask, looking skeptically at the coat.

"I don't know," Trenton says. "Guests are always leaving things behind."

"I'll go up and get my jacket," I say.

"Stop it," Hannah says. "That's one of their mother's coats. She keeps extra coats around. I've never even seen her wear that one. I think it's even new."

Grinning, Trenton holds up the coat. "It's fine," he says. "Trust me."

I slide one arm into the coat, then the other.

I can't keep from getting the feeling that it would not only be easy to trust Trenton, but it would also be somewhat dangerous in one of those I could really start to like him kind of ways. Reminder to self: I have a boyfriend.

Walking alongside Trenton, we follow Hannah and Jack outside.

I know immediately that he's right about the coat. I'm glad I'm wearing the heavy coat and not my jacket.

The air has a definite bite to it.

We sit on the chairs gathered around the firepit. Hannah sits next to Jack and Trenton sits next to me.

This pairing off comes a little too naturally. I'm getting the feeling that Hannah is pleased that Trenton and I are getting along so well.

I'm also getting the feeling that I could easily fall into being comfortable with it.

"When do you think it's going to snow?" Hannah asks.

"Any day now," Jack answers. Their chairs are tucked up against each other and Hannah has her legs draped over Jack's lap.

Trenton stabs at the fire with an iron poker. "The first snowfall is always the best. After that, people start to get tired of it."

"Speak for yourself," Hannah says. "Olivia is going to love the snow."

"Have you ever seen snow?" Trenton ask, looking over at me.

"Of course I've seen snow."

"Flurries," Hannah corrects. "She's seen flurries."

"Oh. She's in for quite the treat," Jack says.

"Sometimes they get snowed in here," Trenton tells me."

"For how long?"

"Days. Weeks. Eventually someone comes around with a snowplow."

"How do they survive?" I ask, a bit aghast.

"They have an extra freezer," Hannah says. "There's never a shortage of food."

"Oh. I see." Just the mention of a possible snow or ice has the population of Houston scurrying to the grocery store to stock up on... well... everything.

"They keep a nice supply of anything you could possibly need," Trenton says. "No need to worry."

"I'm not worried," I say with a forced smile. Besides, I'm certain I'll be safely back in Houston before they get snowed in here.

"Olivia doesn't worry about much," Hannah says.

I hide a yawn behind my hand. It's been a long day, starting with an Uber to the airport early this morning.

"You know," Trenton says. "Somebody is sleepy and tomorrow is another day. Why don't I walk you to your room?"

"Okay," I say, yawning again. "I'm really sorry. It just hit me all of a sudden."

"It's okay," Trenton says. "It can take a few days to adjust to the elevation."

"Maybe that's what it is," I say. "I need to take Cupcake outside."

"I'll take her," Trenton says.

"And I need to feed her," I add.

"We've got her," Hannah says. "Go. Sleep."

"Okay," I say on another yawn.

Trenton stands up and holds out a hand.

Without even thinking, I put a hand in his and let him help me to my feet. He wraps his fingers around mine in a firm grip.

"Goodnight," I say to no one in particular.

"Goodnight," Hannah and Jack say as Trenton and I head for the back door.

By the time we get our coats off and hang them on by the back door, I'm waking up a little.

"I guess I'm a lightweight," I say.

"It's okay," Trenton says. "Getting used to the elevation takes a minute."

"I didn't notice it at first."

"Affects different people differently," he says.

"Good to know. I can take Cupcake out for her walk." The dog is still sitting in front of the fireplace, watching the flames.

"I'll take her. I don't have a dog, but I'm friendly with them."

"I got the impression you didn't like dogs."

"I like them fine," he says as we start up the stairs to the second floor.

"Just not in your car."

"It's a long story," he says. "I'll tell you about it another time."

"Another time. I'll hold you to it."

We stop at my door.

"I won't see you for a couple of days," he says. "I've got to do some things at my place in Boulder before I can be gone for the two weeks I'll be staying here. But I'll be back."

"Okay," I say with a little shrug. "Be safe." My nonchalant words don't reflect the disappointment I'm feeling on the inside.

He doesn't move. in fact, with one arm on the wall next to the door, he studies me. "I'm glad you're here."

"Me too."

Our gazes hold and I realize I don't want him to leave, not even for two days.

But then with a little smile, he turns around walks away.

I open the door to my bedroom and step inside.

Chapter Fifteen

Trenton

I walk back downstairs, clip Cupcake's leash to her collar and, after having to practically drag her away from the fireplace, take her out front to do her business. I don't go out back where Jack and Hannah are still sitting around the firepit because I need a few minutes to think and clear my head.

Olivia, as Jack so bluntly pointed out, isn't really my type. Not that I have a type exactly. I just usually don't go for blondes.

Olivia isn't really like any other blonde I've ever known. She's more serious and responsible.

Cupcake tugs on her leash and I follow her around the

cars. She sniffs every tire before heading toward the trees to do her business.

"You're a good match for Olivia," I tell her while I wait. Cupcake ignores me.

I glance up toward the second floor where Olivia is. Her light is already out. I know exactly where her room is. Even though I don't live here anymore, I know everything about this house. Olivia made a very astute observation when she'd said this house inspired me to become an architect. It had.

Or rather my grandfather had inspired me. He and I had spent countless hours hiking along the trails and riding horses in the backcountry. He'd told me how he'd designed this house. He hadn't built it himself, but he and Grandma had designed it together. They'd sketched out a rough draft and they'd given that to an architect who had put it all together for them.

I hadn't thought about that in forever. It's one of those bittersweet memories that I keep tucked away just for myself.

I take Cupcake back inside and fill her bowl with dry kibbles that belong to my brother's black lab. She gobbles it up like a starving dog.

We hadn't talked about where Cupcake was going to sleep. I can't very well leave her down here in a strange house by herself and I don't want to disturb Olivia who is probably already asleep.

"I guess you're sleeping in my room," I tell Cupcake.

With a bowl for water in one hand and a bottle of water for me in the other, I pick up the little dog and head upstairs.

My bedroom, the same room I grew up in, is right across from Olivia's room. I take the extra pillow off the bed and lay it on the floor for her. She climbs right onto it and after turning around three times, lays down and appears to go right to sleep.

I smile to myself. Again. The little dog has some uncanny resemblances to Olivia.

I fill the bowl with water and set it next to her pillow so she can find it when she wakes up in the night.

After taking a few minutes in the bathroom to get myself ready for bed, I come back out, wearing my sleep pants and a t-shirt. I keep some basic clothes here, so I never have to worry about that when I stay over unplanned.

A spurt of alarm shoots through me when I see that Cupcake isn't on her pillow. I know I closed the bedroom door so she couldn't have gotten out.

Then I see her curled up on the foot of my bed, sound asleep.

Delighted, I laugh out loud to myself.

Chapter Sixteen

Olivia

I SLEPT like a log through the night. Maybe I was exhausted. Maybe it's the clean, light mountain air. Whatever it was, I wake refreshed.

The feeling, however, only lasts for about half a moment before I'm overwhelmed by panic.

Cupcake.

I'm the worst mother in the history of dog mothers.

I slept like a baby and I don't even know where my dog is.

I climb out of bed, sliding my feet into my slippers. After quickly running a brush through my hair, I decide I don't look too terribly frightening.

Before I head out though, I walk to the window to see if Trenton's car is still out there. It isn't. He had been serious about leaving out early today. Feeling much better about venturing downstairs in my pajamas to look for my dog, I open the door and pad down the hallway to the stairs.

I hear Hannah's voice drifting from below. She seems so incredibly happy here. I confess I'd had my doubts about her being content here after relocating back here from Houston, but she's in the right place. I guess small town roots are very strong.

I shudder at the thought of moving back to Katy, Texas. Not a small town. Just a suburb. I have no reason to ever go back there. I'm a Houston girl now.

Hannah is sitting with Jack at the kitchen table. Several papers are spread out in front of them and she's holding a highlighter. I wonder if it has something to do with the wedding or the guided horse tours.

"Hey," I say. "Where's Cupcake?"

"I'll give you one guess," Hannah says.

I turn around and walk toward the living room. Cupcake is sitting in front of the fireplace, watching the flames.

"Cupcake," I say, walking over and picking her up. She licks my face. "You like the fireplace? Your fur is so warm."

"You're going to have to move now," Hannah says, coming up behind me. "Get her a house with a fireplace."

"Yeah right." Like that's going to happen. "Thanks for looking out for her."

"I can't take the credit," she says. "Trenton kept her."

"Kept her?"

"He thought she'd be lost in a strange place, so she spent the night in his room."

I hold Cupcake out at arm's length and look into her big chocolate brown eyes. "Cupcake. You little rascal, you."

"Jealous, much?" Hannah asks.

"No. I'm not jealous. I'm just surprised." I set Cupcake back down in front of the fireplace. And then proceed to change the subject. "So. What do we need to do today?"

"Today is a rest day for you. Jack and I have to take a family for a guided horseback ride."

"Sounds like fun."

"The horseback ride or the rest?"

"Both. The horseback ride for you and the rest for me. But I'm here if you need anything."

"We might go into town later to pick up some supplies and a few Christmas gifts. You can come with us."

"Okay. What am I supposed to do while you're out horseback riding?"

"You'll have the house to yourself. Mrs. Thompson will be leaving soon to take Mr. Thompson to a doctor's appointment in Boulder so they'll be gone most of the day."

"Is he okay? He seems like he's recovered."

"Just routine. Make yourself at home."

"I feel like I should be doing something." It's funny. I told Trenton that I didn't have to be doing something productive all the time and here I am having trouble at the thought of having nothing to do for most of the day.

I think it has something to do with being a guest in a stranger's house.

"You'll figure something out," she says. "I'm heading out to the stables to get the horses ready. Call my cell phone if you need anything."

I shoot her a look.

"If I have service, I'll answer."

"Have fun." I wave her off. "I'm going up to shower and dress."

"Good idea," she says over her shoulder.

"Alright Cupcake," I say. "You're coming upstairs to keep me company. We'll come back down and sit in front of the fire later." Taking my dog, I head back up to my room.

Chapter Seventeen

Trenton

I GOT UP EARLY, like everyone in the Thompson household, take Cupcake out for a walk and feed her.

I even have breakfast with the family before I head out. When I find myself stalling a bit, glancing toward the stairs for Olivia, I know it's time to get on the road.

Now that I'm at my house, I find that I don't have as much to do as I thought I would. Usually I find things to do in order to avoid going to my family's house in Alpine Falls. Some last minute work or some phone calls. Whatever seems urgent at the moment.

And yet I always end up going there. It's a tradition for me to spend a couple of weeks with them around Christmas and since most business offices are closed, it doesn't hurt me to take a break.

This year, however, I realize that whatever work I need to do, I can do from Alpine Falls just as easily as I can do it from my own home. So I stash everything in my briefcase, fill a suitcase with clothes, and throw it all in the car. It takes me a little bit longer than I would've liked to clean out the refrigerator and haul everything out to the garbage can. Most definitely a hard learned lesson. Throw food out before it goes bad, not after. Much more pleasant to deal with.

I stand in my apartment and look around. It's sparsely furnished even though I've lived here for over three years. Most of the time I spend here is either working at my desk or sleeping.

I can't say that it really feels like a home. It honestly feels a bit more like a remote office.

When I think of home, I think of my parents' ranch house in Alpine Falls. They have a home. And my brother, Jack, lives there with his fiancé (wife). Our other brother lives there too, sort of, but he lives in an apartment over the barn.

He's probably about as distant from the family as I am. They do see him more, though, in passing so it feels like he's around more. As far as actually doing things with the family, he doesn't do any more than I do.

Not that it's a competition.

Right now my intent has nothing to do with spending time with my family, at least not exactly. Sort of. What I *am* plotting is spending time with Olivia. So in a round about way, it is about my family.

Seeing nothing else to do in my apartment that can't either wait or be done remotely, I climb in my car and head out.

I briefly contemplate tracking down my parents who are in town for a doctor's appointment, but decide against it. They can handle themselves and it would probably just confuse them if I showed up.

Instead, I navigate traffic, making my way to the highway that will take me back to Alpine Falls.

This is probably the quickest turn around I've ever made.

My parents will be delighted that I'm there when they get back. Jack and Hannah won't care. Lucas won't even notice.

I will be free to devote all my time and attention to Olivia.

I just hope she's receptive to my attention.

If she isn't, then I have my work cut out for myself.

As I drive back along the road weaving through the mountains, I realize that I have no choice but to make this thing with Olivia work.

I've always heard that when a man knows, he knows.

And I know.

I'm going to marry Olivia.

Chapter Eighteen

Olivia

I BLAME THE ELEVATION.

Back in my room, I decide to hold off on the shower and take a much needed morning nap.

By the time I wake up, it's nearly noon and I still haven't showered.

My stomach is grumbly with hunger and I need caffeine.

I can't explain why I didn't have coffee when I was downstairs earlier. Hannah had coffee and would have gladly shown me how to work the coffee maker.

I get up and slide my feet into my slippers and don't even bother to brush my hair.

Cupcake is waiting by the bedroom door and most definitely needs to go outside for a walk.

She needs a potty break and I need coffee and food.

The house is quiet. I can tell before I even open the door and head downstairs, Cupcake leading the way. Houses have a different feel to them when they're empty. Or practically empty.

Bandit is asleep on the sofa and barely even stirs as I hook Cupcake up on her leash and step out the back door with her.

The sun is warm on my head as I walk around the back yard with her, but the wind is chilly.

The forever snow-capped mountains surrounding the area on three sides have a little cluster of wispy white clouds hovering around them.

It's quite picturesque. If I had any artistic talent at all, I'd pick up a paintbrush and paint it. Instead, I open up my phone and take some pictures.

I can hear the rushing water of the river not far from here and decide that I'll take Cupcake for a walk down to the river later. But now, we need to go back inside in search of food. And coffee.

Back inside, I unhook Cupcake's leash from her collar and she runs straight for the fireplace. Fascinating.

I don't know if she likes the warmth or if she's intrigued by the flames. Either way, Cupcake has found something to entertain herself with.

I go into the kitchen and study the fancy coffee maker sitting on the counter. The last thing I want to do is break it.

Walking into the pantry, I find a jar of instant coffee. I consider that success along with the electric tea kettle on the counter.

Within minutes, using hot water, instant coffee, and milk from the refrigerator, I have something that resembles drinkable coffee in a mug.

"You know. If you use the coffee maker, the coffee is much better."

I yelp and nearly spill coffee everywhere. Holding the mug in both hands to keep from spilling it, I look straight into Trenton's eyes.

"You aren't supposed to be here," I say, setting the mug on the kitchen island and resisting, barely, the urge to brush at my hair with my hands.

"I got finished earlier than I expected," he says with a grin. "Can I make you some real coffee? That looks rather undrinkable."

I look down at my feeble attempt using instant coffee and cold milk.

"I wouldn't say no," I say.

He goes to the counter and, taking out two mugs, proceeds to make a latte using the coffee maker.

He slides the first cup over to me, then gets to work on a second cup for himself.

"Have you had lunch?" he asks.

"No." I take a sip of the hot coffee. Wonderful. "Not yet."

"Want to go into town? Get a pizza?"

"I'm not dressed," I say, shifting from one foot to the

other. I'm so not dressed. Or showered. And my hair must look like a bird's nest.

"It's okay. I can wait."

"I need to shower."

"I can unpack while you shower."

"Okay," I say. What else can I say? He's shot down all my feeble arguments. "Thanks for taking care of Cupcake last night."

"Cupcake is no problem at all."

He's looking at me with a sideways expression and I cave, running my hands through my hair, hoping it doesn't look as awful as I imagine it must. "I'm just going to go up," I say, trying not to sound as awkward as I'm feeling. "And start getting ready. I'll be a few minutes."

"Take your time."

I feel him watching me as I walk toward the stairs. He must think there's something wrong with me still wearing my pajamas in the middle of the day.

Chapter Nineteen

Trenton

OLIVIA IS adorable in her pajamas. And her hair, slightly mussed. She runs her hands self-consciously through it. Her features have that soft quality that comes with just waking up.

To say that I am inordinately pleased, considering that I've decided I want to marry her, is an understatement. She'll be delightful to wake up next to every morning for the rest of my life.

Of course. There is a huge chasm between where we're standing right now and getting to that point.

I busy myself with going out to the car, bringing my

things inside, and taking them up to my bedroom. I take my time unpacking and setting up my little workspace.

I usually spend several hours up here working on projects while I'm home for the holidays. It's the logical thing to do. To do my work while everyone else is doing their thing.

But this year, it's not going to happen. This year I have Olivia.

And whatever work needs to be done can quite simply wait.

I've only just met her yesterday and already she's changed my whole outlook on life. In the best possible way.

After I hear her door open, I finish up hanging my clothes in the closet and follow her downstairs.

As I near where she's sitting on the couch, I hear her talking softly and I assume she's talking to Cupcake.

But then, too late to avoid overhearing, I realize she's talking to someone on the phone.

"No," she says into the phone. "You can't. You can't come up here for Christmas. I'm staying at Hannah's in-laws' house."

I stop. Not sure if I should turn around and walk away.

"You can't just invite yourself to someone's house. Even if there aren't any rooms in town."

She sounds vexed.

"No. Stan. Just enjoy your sister. Yes. We'll do something for New Year's. I have to go. We'll talk again later."

With a sigh, she lowers the phone.

I'm feeling pretty much like an idiot right about now.

I know she'd told me she doesn't have a boyfriend.

But she definitely does. A boyfriend that she has New Year's Eve plans with. A boyfriend who wants to come out here and be with her for Christmas.

"There you are," I say, walking the rest of the way to the couch.

She looks different now. No longer wearing her pajamas. Her hair is freshly dried. She looks good. Whether she looks she just woke up or whether she looks like she's ready to go into town, she looks good.

But I have to dial things back. If she has a boyfriend, then I don't have the right to date her.

"Hey." She straightens and gives me a little smile. "Sorry I took so long."

"You didn't. I just finished unpacking."

"We can take Cupcake?" she asks.

"We have to take Cupcake."

"I just didn't know if she could go into the restaurant."

"This is Alpine Falls. Dogs are welcome."

She scratches Bandit on the head. "I guess that means you get to stay here," she tells the cat. Bandit just yawns and turns over. "I think Cupcake would be content to just stay here, too."

"We had a cat that did that one time. He spent hours watching the flames in the fireplace. His name was Bradley."

"Huh. I wonder if it's the heat or the flames."

"I guess we'll never know. I'll get our coats."

"Right. I forgot about coats. I went out earlier and it wasn't bad."

"It's a good idea to take one just in case the temperature suddenly drops. I'll be right back."

I really wish she'd told me about Stan. This changes everything.

Chapter Twenty

Olivia

TRENTON PARKS the car in a lot at one end of town and we walk down Main Street toward the Pizzeria.

I keep Cupcake on a short leash to keep her from running ahead more than a few feet.

Even in the daylight, the town is decorated with brightly colored twinkling lights. Every little shop that we pass has a Christmas tree in the window and a variety of Christmas songs spill out the doors as we pass.

There are a lot of people out. Families mostly with children of all ages from infants to teenagers.

Most people are carrying brightly colored shopping bags. Christmas shopping.

Hannah had mentioned that she wants to come into town later today for Christmas shopping.

It occurs to me that I'm going to have to get gifts for the Thompson family. I've already gotten Hannah's wedding gift from her registry, but now I've got to figure out something for the rest of the family.

I shouldn't have answered the phone when Stan called. I'd gotten downstairs before Trenton and I guess I had a weak moment.

Now I'm regretting it. He and I had agreed that we'd spend Christmas apart. Now he's changed his mind and he wants to come up here for Christmas.

I've hardly even thought about him since I left Houston. I should probably feel bad about that, but I made it clear from the outset that wasn't looking for anything serious.

He just doesn't seem to get it.

He keeps pushing for more.

"Everything okay?" Trenton asks.

"Yes." I smile over at him. "Why do you ask?"

"You seem a little preoccupied. That's all."

"There is something," I say.

"What is it?" he asks, looking a little wary.

"I need to get your parents something for Christmas. Maybe you can help me figure out what they might like."

"Oh well. I'm not going to be much help there. That's something I struggle with every year."

"It's okay," she says. "I'll ask Hannah."

"Hannah is probably the better person to help you with that."

"Maybe she can help you, too."

"Maybe."

A little girl, about three-years-old, her father right behind her, runs up to Cupcake.

"Doggie," she says, wrapping her arms around Cupcake.

"I'm so sorry," the father says, with obvious embarrassment.

"It's okay. She likes children."

The father watches helplessly as Cupcake licks his daughter's face.

"She's been eating ice cream," he says as though that explains the licking. He doesn't know that Cupcake would lick her face anyway.

"Cupcake loves ice cream," I say.

"Cupcake!" the little girl squeals.

"Come on Abigail," the father says, scooping up his daughter. "We have to let this nice couple be on their way."

"Cupcake. Doggie." Abigail starts to cry.

"You don't happen to know where I can adopt a dog like Cupcake, do you?"

"Not at this particular moment. But in my work, I sometimes come across pets who need homes. If you want to give me your name and number, I can send out some queries."

"Would you? That would be great." Abigail wiggles out of his arms and drops back down to frolic with Cupcake. Her giggling is much better than her crying.

"Sure. It's no problem."

"My name's Caleb. My sister and I run Lawson Outfitter's Supply Store just down the street. You can find me there."

"Okay. My name is Olivia and this is Trenton."

"Trenton Thompson?" he asks, turning his attention to Trenton.

"Yes."

"I've heard about you. The architect."

"That's me."

"Your parents talk about you all the time. I'm surprised we haven't met before."

"Guess you were a few years ahead of me," Trenton says, holding out a hand.

Caleb wipes his hand on his jeans before shaking hands. "I might a little sticky."

"That's okay. Cute girl."

"She's a handful. And we've got another one on the way."

"Congratulations."

"Let me see what I can find to distract this one with. Come on Abigail. Cupcake has to go home now and get something to eat."

"Ice cream."

"Yes. We just had ice cream. Let's go see if we can find your mommy."

"Mommy!"

"Yes." He looks at us. "I'll see you around. Nice to meet you both."

After they walk away, I bend down and pick Cupcake up. "Good girl. You know. He just barely missed his chance."

"What do you mean?"

"I just recently decided to keep Cupcake. I showed her around to a couple of families, but they didn't like something about her coloring."

"Their loss," Trenton says.

"Definitely." I run my hands through her fur. "She's a good dog."

"And apparently good with children. Did you know that?"

"I do now."

"Is that something you want?" he asks as we start walking again. "Children, I mean."

I'd had this conversation or one like it with Stan. I'd specifically told Stan that I do not want children. I'd also told him I don't want to get married. And yet he persists in his endeavors to push me in that direction.

But here, walking along Main Street in Alpine Falls, I feel something shifting inside me. Not a seismic shift, but something like a tiny crack. Enough though that it has me questioning everything I thought I knew about myself.

"I'm not sure," I say. "It hasn't really come up."

"I guess you still have time to figure that out," Trenton says.

"No hurry, right? Looks like we're here." I stop and look at the little Pizzeria. A big sign over the door just identifies it as "Alpine Falls Pizzeria." "Are you sure it's okay if Cupcake goes inside?"

"Everyone in Alpine Falls loves dogs."

I'm beginning to get that impression. A little town where dogs are welcome in restaurants is my kind of town.

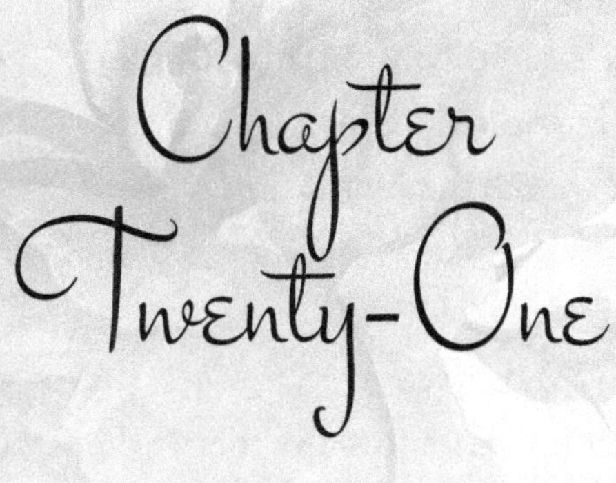

Chapter Twenty-One

Trenton

AFTER LUNCH, we make a detour on the way to the car, to walk around the little town park. Just as I predicted, we need our coats.

"Do you think it's going to snow?" Olivia asks.

"I think it might."

"I hope so." She looks up toward the tall, jagged mountain peaks.

"Do you want me to tell you a secret?"

"Sure."

"See those clouds hovering around the mountain peaks?"

"It's hard to see the mountains for them."

"Right. Those clouds are a sign that it's snowing up there in what we call the high country."

"Right now?"

"Those are snow clouds."

She nods. "Makes sense."

"There'll be fresh snow up there when they clear. But here's the real secret. It usually means that it's going to snow down here tonight."

"Really? How cool is that."

We walk through a grove of blue spruce trees mixed with the white barked aspen trees that shed their leaves months ago.

I suppose I'm easily encouraged.

Olivia said having children hadn't come up. If she's in a serious relationship with that Stan fellow, it would have come up one way or another.

It's such a little thing, but it gives me encouragement anyway.

I don't know enough about her to make assumptions about her relationship with Stan. They could just be friends.

Friends do things together on New Year's Eve.

We reach the river and stop to sit on a wooden bench. The river's rushing water tumbles over itself.

"Cold?" I ask.

"A little. But I like it. It makes me feel alive."

"It does, doesn't it?"

The cold air looks good on her. Her face is flushed prettily and her eyes are bright.

It occurs to me as we sit there on the bench, Cupcake sitting in Olivia's lap, that Stan, whoever he is isn't here, but I am.

Olivia is here and I heard her tell Stan not to come here.

It's not much, but I'll take it.

"Do you really think you can find a dog for Caleb?" I ask.

"I don't know. Cupcake was a rescue dog, so I don't know where she came from. But maybe. I work with some larger agencies in Houston who might could help." She wraps her coat around Cupcake. "The problem, though, is getting it here."

"Jack has an airplane," I say.

She turns and looks at me. "Yes. He does."

"A dog would be a great Christmas gift for Abigail."

"Oh. Do you think he was serious? Adopting a pet is a big commitment."

"He seemed serious to me."

"We'd have to figure the cost of the flight into the adoption fee."

"Has anyone ever told you that you worry too much?"

"Me? Worry? I don't know why you would say something like that."

I just grin at her.

Olivia is an amazing woman. She has me thinking about traveling to Houston, on a private jet nonetheless, to pick up a dog for a man's daughter, people I don't even know.

Getting into the Christmas spirit is a new experience for me.

I think I'm going to like it.

I know I like her.

And that changes everything.

Maybe she has a boyfriend named Stan. Maybe she doesn't.

Either way, I am determined to enjoy her delightful company.

Olivia

Sitting in the little park, Cupcake barking and dashing after a chipmunk she couldn't possibly catch even if I didn't have her on a short leash, I feel a new kind of contentment settle me.

Trenton sits next to me, looking relaxed, like he has nothing else he'd rather be doing.

"Am I keeping you from work?" I ask.

"No."

"Yesterday you seemed annoyed that the holidays take

you away from your work."

"I'm making allowances."

"Allowances? What does that mean?"

"It means I'm allowing myself to take some time that doesn't involve working."

"Okay."

Cupcake runs back, giving up on her current quest to tree a chipmunk and jumps into Trenton's lap.

"I think Cupcake approves of that approach."

"Okay," he says, turning his head to keep her out of his face. "No dog kisses."

"See. I knew you don't like dogs."

"I love dogs. Loving a dog and kissing a dog are two completely different things."

I laugh. "Okay. I can't argue with that logic."

"A man has to have his limits."

"I think you're OCD."

"What makes you say that, Dr. Olivia?"

"I took psychology in college. And..." I wave a hand. "You have this thing. You don't like dog hair in your car and you don't like dogs licking you."

"Maybe you should've been a psychologist. Wait. What was your major?"

"I majored in business like everyone recommended, but I really liked the psychology classes best. I actually got a minor in it."

"Is that so? You do know that you can go back and get your degree in psychology?"

"I don't know. Maybe. I don't think I want to go back to

college. I want to grow my business."

"The pet adoption business."

"That's actually Madison's business. I'm just helping her out."

"What's your business?"

"I can't tell you. You'll laugh at me."

"Why? Is it funny? You want to be a clown?"

I shudder. "Clowns terrify me."

"Now you have to tell me what it is you really want to do."

I glance over at him, then turn back to face the lovely mountain view.

Water from the river splashes in our direction, but it evaporates before it lands on us.

"I won't laugh," he says, pulling a serious face. "But if you don't tell me, I'm going to imagine all sorts of crazy things. Like maybe you want to be an airplane mechanic."

"No. Not that," I say with a little smile. "I want to be an interior designer."

He tilts his head to the side. "What's wrong with that?"

"I have no training in it. It's a whole new field and I just told you I don't want to go back to school." I take a breath. "And you're an architect. It's sort of your field."

"It's very much my field. And I can tell you it's hard to find an interior designer who's decent to work with. I think you'd be good at it."

"I'd be competing with people who've studied it and I just don't want to go through that. That's why the pet adoption thing is working for me right now. It's low stress."

"You, Olivia, are selling yourself short. Some of the best interior designers don't have degrees. They have passion and experience. You have passion and experience just comes with time."

"People always say that. But how does someone get experience without experience?"

"They have to know someone," he says definitively.

"I don't know anyone," I say. "It's just not realistic."

"You do know someone," he says.

"Who?" I turn and look into his grayish blue eyes.

And then it hits me. I do know someone.

I know him.

Chapter Twenty-Three

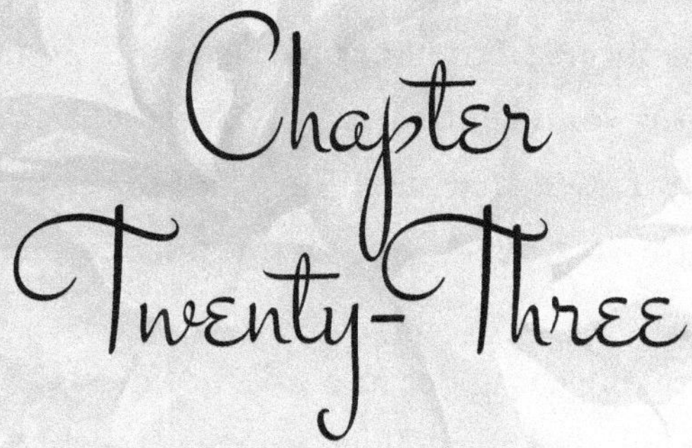

Trenton

JACK

Where are you?

I'm in town. Alpine Falls. Why?

JACK

We can't find Olivia. And she
doesn't answer her messages.

"I THINK someone's looking for you," I tell Olivia.

"Who?"

"Jack and Hannah."

"Hannah wanted me to come into town with her later." She pulls her phone from her purse and pulls a guilty expression. "I had my volume off."

"It's okay. I guess they were just worried about you."

"I'm not used to that," she says, typing a quick response on her phone.

I don't say anything because I don't know what to say. I find it incredibly sad that Olivia isn't used to having people worry about her. It was just one of those off-hand, throw away comments, something she probably didn't even intend to say, much less for me to hear.

But I did hear it.

And hearing it makes me want to change it.

Even though I know she's already texting with Hannah, I send Jack a quick message.

> She's with me.

I want them to know that she's being taken care of and that if I have my way, I'll be taking care of her from here on out.

Olivia has no family. From what I've gathered, listening to her, she has a couple of friends, Hannah and Madison, and maybe a fellow named Stan, but that's it.

Olivia is a good friend. She's here in a strange place, giving up her time to help her friend, Hannah, get ready for a wedding. A wedding in name only since Hannah's divorce never went through and she's still married to my brother.

"I told her I'm with you," she says. "I hope that's okay."

"Why wouldn't it be?"

"I don't know. You aren't really supposed to be back until tomorrow."

"It's okay. I just told Jack that you're with me."

"Oh. Okay. We're good then."

Cupcake scrambles down and sits at Olivia's feet, looking up at her with big brown eyes.

"I think Cupcake is ready to return to her place in front of the fireplace," I say.

"You might be right. She does have an affinity for it."

"Do you have a fireplace in your house?"

"No. No fireplace. Unfortunately."

"You might have to move."

"That's what Hannah says."

"You need a house with a fireplace. For Cupcake."

"I can't just move because my dog likes to sit in front of the fireplace." So she says and yet I hear doubt in her voice.

"Maybe you'll have to hire an architect to help you figure out how to install one.

"Maybe." She looks at me sideways, pulling her coat more tightly around her. "Can that be done?"

"I don't see why not. You're cold. Cupcake is shivering. We need to go." I stand up, deciding that part of my job in making sure that Olivia is cared for is making sure she stays warm.

"Maybe Cupcake needs a coat," she says.

"They sell those at Caleb's Outfitter's Store."

"Dog coats? I was joking."

"Dogs need coats, too."

"Okay. Well then. I'll have to go there and get her one."

"I'll take you by there. Do you want to go now or later?"

"Later is okay. I kind of promised Hannah I'd hang out with her. She wants to come shopping."

"You're a good friend."

"I try."

She may try, but I think it comes naturally to her.

But either way, it's a quality I admire.

She's going to fit in just fine with my family.

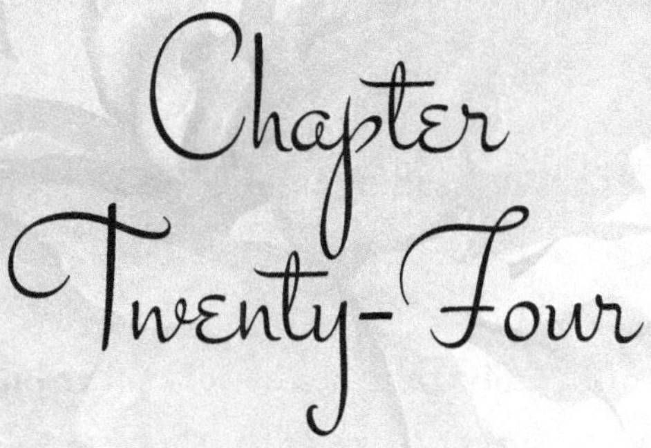Chapter Twenty-Four

Olivia

Two hours later, I'm back in Alpine Falls, this time with Hannah. We're standing in a quaint little bookstore with wooden floors and books stacked everywhere. The building looks like it belongs in an historic district, but no one seems to notice that it's anything other than just any other store with people rushing in and out.

It has a certain charm though. A cat curled up on the counter next to the register. A fireplace in the back with three chairs in front of it.

"What are we looking for?" I ask Hannah.

"I want to get Jack's mother something light and fun to read."

"A novel."

"Yes. She's always reading nonfiction and it just seems so dull."

"Maybe she likes it."

"I know. But." She puts her hands on her hips and looks up at the row of books on one of the shelves.

"How about a cozy mystery?" I suggest. "People really get into them."

"Maybe. Like what?"

"Here's one with a cat and a dog on the cover. Can't go wrong with that."

"Seems fitting." Hannah takes the book and flips it over to read the back cover. "It's not the first in the series."

"Let me see." I read the series title then study the books on the shelves. "Here it is. First in the series."

"I should get the whole series," Hannah decides.

"Okay." I shouldn't feel annoyed. After all, I'd come up here to Alpine Falls to spend time with Hannah.

But now that I'm here, I can't stop thinking about Trenton. I can't keep myself from wanting to get Hannah to hurry up so we can meet Trenton and Jack at the Hungry Biscuit.

In and of itself, meeting the guys at a restaurant called the Hungry Biscuit has nothing to do with me wanting to hurry her up.

It has everything to do with me wanting to see Trenton again.

I'm pretty much a hopeless case at this point and I know it.

I'm just not ready to admit that to Hannah.

I help Hannah find all the books in the series, there are nine of them, and we head up to the checkout counter.

"I need to find a dog," I say. As strange as the comment sounds to most people, Hannah knows exactly what I mean.

"Here or Houston?" she asks as the young lady behind the counter rings up her books.

"Here, oddly enough. Trenton and I ran into a guy named Caleb."

"The Outfitter Store Caleb?"

"Yes. His little girl fell in love with Cupcake."

"Aw. That's too bad. He almost had his chance."

Hannah knows what it's like to decide to keep one of the pets we have up for adoption. She did that with Bandit. Just didn't put forth the effort to find him a home and she ended up adopting him herself.

"I know. But not now."

"Thank you," she tells the girl behind the counter as she takes her bag of books.

"Merry Christmas," the young lady says with a bright smile.

"Merry Christmas to you, too, Jennie." She turns her attention back to me. "You might have some luck in finding him a dog like Cupcake in Houston, but I don't know about Alpine Falls."

"I know. Trenton seems to think that Jack could help out with the transport if we can find one. I don't know if Caleb is serious enough to pay those kinds of fees."

We step outside into the chilly air.

"Trenton knows that Jack wouldn't charge him for the flight."

"Really? So that's what he meant."

"About what?" Hannah asks, amused.

"Trenton told me I worry too much."

"He's not wrong."

"Well. I didn't know. I was thinking we had to figure in the cost of the flight."

"The restaurant's right up here," Hannah says.

I walk alongside her, thankful that we're finally finished with her shopping for the evening.

"Why wouldn't he charge him?" I ask.

"First of all, it's good for business. Caleb sends tourists our way and we, of course, send people to his store. But something like that would go a long way in securing loyalty between our generations. And, besides, it's the right thing to do."

"But what about the cost of the flight?"

"You obviously don't know much about pilots."

"Obviously."

"Pilots use any excuse they can find to fly. Jack would like nothing better than getting the chance to fly the four of us down to Houston to pick up a dog."

"That's just interesting."

"You'll see. They're probably already talking about it."

"Surely not. I have to make some calls. See if anyone even has a dog."

"You will though. You'll find something."

"We're going to waive all the fees, aren't we?"

"Yep. You're getting the idea."

"How do people in Alpine Falls make any money?"

"They just do. It comes back twofold. But to be honest, most of our money comes from tourists."

Our money. Hannah has moved back to Alpine Falls in body, mind, and spirit. My friend, I realize, is never moving back to Houston.

Not that I thought she would, now that she's reunited with her high school sweetheart (and husband), but seeing her here, hearing the way she talks, it's just all so clear.

Stepping inside the Hungry Biscuit restaurant, we're greeted by a brightly colored life-sized cardboard biscuit wearing a big grin.

It's obviously a family restaurant. Packed at the moment. The scent of fried foods filling the air. I'd been told they're famous for their hamburgers and French fries. According to a handwritten note on a chalkboard sign just inside the door, they've recently added fish sandwiches to the menu.

"There they are," Hannah says, drawing my attention away from the cheerful motif.

Trenton and Jack are sitting across from each other at one of the booths at the back of the restaurant.

They both stand up as we walk in their direction. Hannah walks right up to Jack, kisses him, and slides into the booth next to him.

Trenton slides over to make room for me on his side of the booth.

"Hi," he says, his eyes smiling at me.

"Hi." I sit down next to him, suddenly feeling a little nervous.

Hannah shows Jack the books she bought, pulling them out of the shopping bag and lining them up on the table.

"Did you have fun shopping?" Trenton leans close and asks me.

"It was nice to spend time with Hannah," I say. "And the old bookstore is quite impressive."

But what I don't tell him is that I would have enjoyed my shopping trip one hundred percent better if he had been with us.

It must be the clean mountain air.

Chapter Twenty-Five

Trenton

A COUPLE OF HOURS LATER, we're back at home.

While Hannah feeds Bandit, Jack gets a fire going in the fireplace.

Olivia clips Cupcake's leash on her and she and I head outside to take her for her evening walk.

The stars are bright, scattered overhead like a million twinkling lights.

"We don't have stars like this is Houston," Olivia says. "At least not that we can see."

"Oh. That's too bad. So I'm guessing you don't know any of the constellations?"

"No. Don't hold it against me."

"I never would." I stop and look up. "The star pattern most people recognize is the Big Dipper. It's not a constellation though." I point over the trees. "It's part of the Great Bear constellation."

"I see the Big Dipper," she says. "Where's the bear?"

"You have to use your imagination. Follow the Big Dipper down for his back legs. Then over all the way to his head and down again for his front feet."

She stares in the general direction I'm pointing, but shakes her head. "I don't see it."

"Can I show you?" I ask. At her nod, I move to stand behind her. "Hold Cupcake with your left hand. Now." I take her hand and using my hand to guide hers, I point to the Big Dipper, then across. "Imagine that's a big bear walking across the sky."

"I think I sort of see it," she says.

Her hair smells like lavender and it takes all my willpower not to pull her close and wrap my arms around her.

I guide her hand down toward the bear's front legs, then his back legs.

"It's easier to see after you've seen it sketched out."

"I'll look it up," she says, looking up and turning a bit to look at me.

As she turns, her cheek brushes against mine.

"Olivia," I say, just needing to say her name.

Her lips are parted and it's the perfect moment for a first kiss.

But Cupcake races back and, making a circle around us, wraps us together in her leash, breaking the spell of the moment.

"Cupcake!" Olivia says. "She's an imp."

It takes both of us to get ourselves unwound from the dog's leash.

Olivia picks up her dog. "Cupcake, you're a very bad little dog." Cupcake just licks her face.

"She's giving you dog germs," I say.

"I know. Isn't it sweet?" She looks over at me mischievously.

"Very endearing," I say.

She'd been right when she'd pointed out my obsessive-compulsive tendencies.

Those tendencies serve me well as an architect.

But the dog germs, not so much.

"I don't think it's going to snow tonight," she says as we walk back toward the house. "The clouds are all gone."

"Yes they are. But as for the snow, we'll see. Maybe not tonight. But it won't be long. It'll snow by Christmas for sure."

"I really hope you're right. I don't want to go home without seeing snowfall."

"I don't want you to."

I don't want her to go back to Houston at all. I want this to be her home.

But that is something we're a long way from.

Chapter Twenty-Six

Olivia

THE NEXT MORNING before the sun is barely up, Cupcake hops onto the bed and barks once, obvious ready to go outside.

"Why?" I ask, rolling over, away from her. "It's too cold to get up."

She barks again.

"Okay. Fine."

I get up, but this morning, instead of going downstairs

in my pajamas, I put on jeans and a sweater, wash my face and brush my hair.

Cupcake waits patiently while I slide my feet into my boots and tighten the laces.

I give her a big hug, making her wiggle all over in delight, then we head down stairs.

Hannah, Jack, and Trenton are already up, having coffee.

"I thought I was up early," I say as I walk past the breakfast table where they're sitting.

"It is early," Hannah says. "But we're going out to cut down a Christmas tree."

"In the dark?" I ask as I put on my coat.

"We have biscuits in the oven," Jack says as though that explains everything. "Do you want coffee when you get back?"

"Sure."

By the time I get to the door, Trenton is there.

"Good morning," he says.

"Hi. My dog insisted I get up."

"Dogs will do that."

After grabbing his coat, he holds the door open for me.

There's no snow on the ground, but the air is so cold, it almost hurts to breath it in.

"It didn't snow," I say, stepping out onto the frosty ground.

"Not yet. Did you sleep well?"

"I sleep really good here for some reason."

Cupcake runs ahead and I release the slack on her leash to let her run.

"It's quiet for one," Trenton says. "And there's something about the clean air."

I take a deep breath. "I think I could get used to it."

"Be careful," he says. "There are a lot of people who come here to visit and never leave."

"I have a life in Houston." I have my house. And I have Madison and our pet adoption business. "Which reminds me. I need to make those calls today about Caleb's dog."

"I thought you were the one who doesn't like to work all the time."

"Making a little girl happy at Christmas isn't work."

"You're right. But you're also right that we should probably talk to Caleb while we're at the Outfitter's and make sure he really wants to adopt a dog. Make sure his wife is good with it."

"I think we should have gotten Cupcake's coat yesterday. She's cold."

When she comes racing back, Trenton picks her up before she can wind us up in her leash again.

"Be careful," I say, echoing his words. "A lot of people get attached to those little guys."

"Nothing wrong with that," he says. "In fact, I might have a coat she can wear. It'll be too big, but we can make it fit until we get into town."

"There might be hope for you yet," I say.

He puts an arm around my shoulders, causing my heart rate to trip up. "There's always hope, my dear."

I look over at him sideways, but he doesn't seem to notice that he just called me "dear." Knowing it's not good to read too much into such things, I don't say anything as we go inside where the house is filled with the scent of not only coffee and biscuits, but also bacon and eggs.

A good hearty breakfast for another day in the mountains.

I sigh to myself as I'm reminded that with every day I'm that much closer to having to leave here and go back to Houston.

Chapter Twenty-Seven

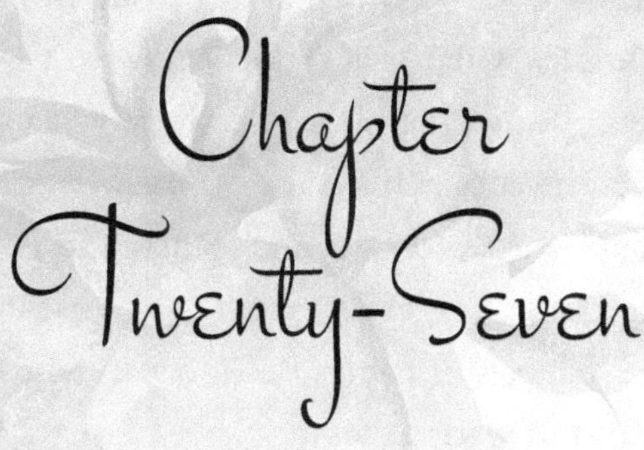

Trenton

My brother Jack has become quite the chef. He's a man of many talents, to say the least.

He can fly an airplane. He can ride a horse like a cowboy while leading a group of people who've never even seen a horse before on guided tours.

And since stepping up to help our aging parents run the ranch, he's become quite good in the kitchen.

After our father's accident, Mother put all her energy

into caring for him and gave the kitchen over to Jack. Everyone knows it wasn't much of a hardship for her.

No one argues when Jack claims he doesn't want anyone in his kitchen and he doesn't argue when we step up to do the dishes after he cooks. It's one of those arrangements that just sort of happened and everyone seems to be good with it.

After breakfast, I excuse myself and go into the attic where there are boxes of things no one wanted to keep lying around, but didn't want to toss.

It doesn't take me long to find what I'm looking for.

When I was a boy, I had a cocker spaniel named Spot. Spot was bigger than Cupcake, but not by a whole lot.

Her old coat is worse for wear, but it's a good warm coat that served Spot well. I take it downstairs and, since Olivia is in the shower, I manage to get Cupcake into it.

"It's too big," Jack says. "It's going to fall off of her."

"It's just for today. Until we can get to the Outfitters. I think I can use a belt to keep it from falling off."

"Olivia is going to have your hide."

"Nah. Olivia's going to be happy that her dog's warm."

"I hope you're right."

After I take the coat off Cupcake, she goes back to her spot in front of the fireplace.

"Has anyone heard from Lucas lately?"

"He's in Denver."

"Denver? Doing what?"

"I don't know. I think maybe he has a girlfriend."

"So I guess you're taking up the slack around here," I say.

"Don't I always?" Jack asks, pulling on a pair of work gloves. "Speaking of. I wouldn't turn down some help feeding the horses."

"You just want me to muck out the stalls."

"Wouldn't turn it down."

"Alright. Let's go."

Jack looks at me a moment. "I never would have guessed that Olivia would be such a good influence on you."

"I don't want to hear a word about it."

Jack holds up his hands. "Not from me. Do you even own a pair of work gloves?"

"I have absolutely no doubt that you're more than happy to provide a pair."

"You're really good at evading questions."

"And you're really good at trying to get into other people's business."

"Let's call it the cook's prerogative."

"Hannah makes you cocky," I say.

"Hannah makes me happy," Jack says. "I highly recommend marriage."

"You always did. I do remember that you got married at eighteen."

He just grins as we step outside and walk along the trail to the barn.

"Any tours today?"

"One. This afternoon. That's why we're getting the tree this morning. Hey. You should bring Olivia on the tour."

"I don't know how Olivia feels about riding a horse."

"If she's going to be staying around, she needs to get used to it."

"She say something about staying around?" I ask, trying to ignore the hope that springs inside me.

"You would be the first one to know that," he says.

"I doubt that. She and Hannah are pretty tight."

"True. But I think you would have more to do with that decision that Hannah."

I decide not to respond to that.

I don't respond because the truth is he might be right.

And even more, I hope he's right.

Chapter Twenty-Eight

Olivia

"WHERE ARE JACK AND TRENTON?" I ask finding Hannah downstairs, her head in her computer.

"Out mucking stalls."

"Mucking stalls?"

Hannah glances up at me. "Replacing the hay in the horse stalls with fresh hay."

"Oh. That sounds like hard work."

"It's very hard work. Hey. Have you heard from Madison?"

"Not lately. I'm sure she's doing whatever she does."

"I'm sure. I wonder what day she's planning on flying up."

"I don't know," I say, sitting down and looking outside at a cardinal sitting on a tree limb. "She'll be here though. In time for the wedding."

"Are you okay?" Hannah asks, closing the lid on her computer.

"Sure. Why do you ask?" I keep my gaze on the cardinal. Must be a male, I decide, with such bright red feathers.

"You look sad. Is there something you want to talk about? Is it Dan?"

"Stan," I say automatically, even though I know she knows his name is Stan. It's one of those running jokes between good friends.

"Has Stan done something?"

"No. It's not Stan," I say. "He called earlier. Wants to come up here for Christmas."

Hannah looks a little startled.

"Don't worry," I say, pulling my gaze away from the bird and looking at Hannah. "I told him no."

"If you really want him to come, we can made accommodations," she says, but I hear the worry in her voice.

"I don't," I say, squaring my shoulders. "You know how I feel about marriage, right?"

"Right."

"He's pressuring me to think about it. And if he comes up here for Christmas... for the wedding... he's just thinks he's making progress in winning me over."

"You don't want to marry Stan," Hannah says.

"No."

"Olivia," Hannah says, leaning forward and looking into my eyes. "I understand you don't want to marry Stan. But... maybe it's not marriage you're set against so much as it is Stan."

"Maybe," I say with a forced smile. "But I've always said I don't want to get married."

"I know. But it's okay to change your mind. Not saying you will, but if you ever wanted to."

"I don't think I will," I say, looking back to the window for the cardinal, but he's gone.

I sigh.

I have my reasons for not wanting to get married. And none of them have anything to do with Stan.

But sometimes I wonder. I wonder if I might change my mind if I was with someone else.

"When the guys get in from the mucking the stalls," Hannah says, obviously changing the subject to something more cheerful. "We're going out to cut down a Christmas tree."

"That sounds like fun," I say.

Sad, Hannah decides. Olivia is most definitely feeling sad about something.

Chapter Twenty-Nine

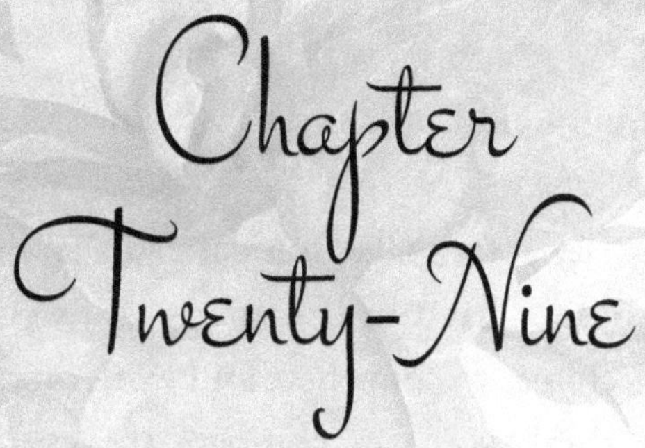

Trenton

"I FEEL LIKE I NEED A SHOWER," I say as we walk up the steps leading onto the back porch of the house.

"We could both use one, but might as well get that tree first." Jack glances at his watch. "I've got to get back and start lunch."

"You're a busy man, Jack," I say.

"I have a lot of people counting on me for a lot of different things."

"How do you do it? Day in and day out?"

"I don't have a choice," Jack says, pulling off his boots before going inside. I do the same. "If I don't do it, who will?"

"You should hold Lucas's feet to the fire. Get him to do more."

"Not my style to make someone do something they don't want to do. That'd be like asking you to give up your career as an architect to come here and work on the ranch."

"I don't think you can compare the two of us. I'm making a living."

"I'm just making a point."

I couldn't do it if I wanted to. I have people counting on me, too. They might not be family, but they're counting on me.

We step inside the warm house to find the girls working on the schedule.

"Where are Mom and Dad?" I ask.

"Staying in their room. Dad's wiped out after yesterday," Hannah says.

"Right."

"Jack took them up some breakfast earlier."

It always amazes me how our mother puts our father above everyone else. She is the epitome of a loving wife.

"Ready to head out?" Jack asks.

"Wait. I have something for Cupcake," I say, veering off toward the living room where I'd left the dog coat.

Cupcake is asleep in front of the fireplace.

"Cupcake," I say. Cupcake stands up and wags her tail. "Come here." She bounds toward me and this time it takes a lot less time to get her into the coat. I tighten it around her with one of my belts.

Walking with uncertainty and not a little bit of difficulty, she follows me into the kitchen.

"Cupcake is officially ready to go tree hunting," I say.

Jack shakes his head and looks away. Hannah looks horrified.

Olivia looks at her dog, then bursts out laughing.

"When you said dog coat, I pictured something else entirely," she says.

"This is just temporary. Until we can get her a coat that fits properly."

"Poor baby," Olivia says, scooping up her dog.

"Told you," Jack says.

"She likes it."

Olivia looks at me over her dog. "Cupcake is ready to go out and find a Christmas tree."

I give my brother a smug look.

"But after lunch, she wants to go into town get herself a proper coat."

"That's what we're going to do then," I say.

She puts Cupcake in my arms and heads to the back door where her own coat is hanging.

Minutes later, the four of us, along with Cupcake, are on our way outside to find the perfect Christmas tree.

Chapter Thirty

Olivia

"STAND BACK," Jack says before he lifts the axe and slams it into the blue spruce we all agreed was the perfect Christmas tree.

"We won't get in trouble for cutting down a tree?" I ask.

"Get in trouble with who?" I ask. Somehow I ended up holding Cupcake again.

"Whoever owns the land."

"No. I don't think so. We have permission."

Hannah leans over and explains. "The Thompsons own this land."

"Oh. This much?"

"The whole mountain. I think it's like maybe a million acres."

"It's not a million," Trenton says.

"Thousands?"

"Closer to that," Trenton says.

"Anyway," Hannah says. "You can walk all day and still be on their land."

"Well, that makes cutting down a tree less complicated," I say.

But for me, things are more complicated. When I first met Trenton, he didn't seem like the kind of person who came from a wealthy family.

Now that I stop and think about it, though, Jack owns an airplane and the family owns a herd of horses.

It's odd, though, because they don't have people working for them. Shouldn't the owners of a large ranch like this have staff to muck out stalls and such?

"Why don't you have a staff of employees?" I ask Trenton before I remember that it's not my business.

"Not in the budget," he says, without elaborating.

But it makes sense. The Thompsons are like me. They inherited their land just like I inherited my house. It helps, sure. But it doesn't mean they're wealthy.

Maybe having a lot of land just gives the illusion of wealth.

"Timber," Jack calls out as the tree crashes to the ground.

"All hands on deck," Trenton says, thrusting Cupcake back into my arms.

"What do I need to do?" I ask.

"Walk alongside me. Keep me company."

The two guys wrap the tree up in some kind of rope to keep it from getting damaged on the way back to the house.

I don't know how far away we are, but it probably isn't as far as it seems. I think maybe we walked around in circles for a bit as we looked at trees. There was never any doubt that we would get a blue spruce tree simply because there are about a thousand blue spruce trees on what I now know is their property.

I feel a bit like an idiot worrying about them having permission to cut down a tree.

On their own property.

But no one seems concerned and everyone seems to have forgotten that I even asked.

Walking along beside Trenton as he and Jack carry the tree over their shoulders, I get the impression that they've done this many times before.

I never had much in the way of family traditions. My grandmother did the best she could, but she was older when she took me in and had her hands full just providing for me.

She and I baked cookies on Christmas Eve and we put up her little artificial tree the day after Thanksgiving.

But this. This is different.

If I ever have children, I want to have at least two. Maybe half a dozen.

If I ever have children, I want to have a big family.

If...

Walking along the trail in the clean mountain air. Cupcake running ahead. I feel my priorities shifting.

Children.

This is the first time in my life that I even gave having children any kind of thought whatsoever.

I don't say anything. I keep these thoughts to myself.

After all, there's a very good possibility that they will pass once I'm out of this thin mountain air.

It's probably just the elevation.

Chapter Thirty-One

Trenton

CALEB and his wife are out when Olivia and I get to the Outfitters, so I end up sending him a text about the dog adoption.

In the meantime, Olivia tries a couple of coats on Cupcake and decides on a bright red one.

"This one does fit her better," I admit. "And it looks a lot more modern."

"Style is very important," Olivia says.

She obviously lives by this adage. After our hike into the woods, she changed into tall knee-high boots, jeans tucked inside, that would most definitely not be good for wearing out hiking in the woods.

She's wearing a red wool cap on her head that makes her look a bit like a Christmas elf, a very fetching one, and a matching red buttoned cardigan.

I give her points for getting into the Christmas spirit, especially now that she has chosen a red coat for Cupcake.

Just as we're checking out, I get a message from Caleb.

CALEB

We definitely want a dog if you can find one. Just don't tell Rachel.

Rachel is Caleb's sister and the one currently taking Olivia's credit card payment.

I look up from my phone and smile at her, trying not to look guilty.

I'm not sure what Rachel has to do with Caleb getting a dog for his daughter, but knowing Rachel, she has an opinion. Rachel has an opinion about everything.

"Do you want her to wear it or do you want it in a shopping bag?" Rachel asks about the dog coat.

"She can just wear it," Olivia says. "I think she likes it."

"What's not to like? Enjoy. And Merry Christmas."

"Merry Christmas," we both say back to her.

"Oh. Trenton?"

"Yes?" I'm surprised Rachel remembers me from school. She and I never really talked.

"Will you give Jack something for me?"

"Sure."

She slides an envelope across the counter.

"What's this?" I ask.

"Just a little refund. He overpaid for some supplies."

"Okay. Sure. Thank you."

Olivia and I step outside.

"I don't think that would ever happen in Houston," she says.

"I'm surprised it happened here. Most people would just pocket the overage and hope you didn't notice."

"I guess Hannah was right."

"What did Hannah say?" I fold the envelope and tuck it in my back pocket.

Cupcake is prancing now up the sidewalk, in her new coat. None of that awkwardness she'd initially experienced when I'd put Spot's coat on her. So much like Olivia.

"Hannah said that in the small town, good deeds come back two-fold. Or something like that."

"Caleb wants the dog," I say.

"For real?"

"He doesn't want Rachel, his sister to know. Rachel's the one who just checked us out, by the way."

"Wonder what that's about."

"Who knows. But if you can find a dog, they want it."

"I'll make some calls," she says, pulling out her phone.

"You don't have to do it right now."

"It's almost Christmas, Trenton. If I don't catch them before they close down their offices, we won't get a dog."

"Okay." I don't ask how they can close down offices when they have pets to take care of.

That is above my pay grade.

Chapter Thirty-Two

Olivia

As THE SUN starts to drop over the mountains, splashing a hundred different shades of pink across the sky, Hannah and I are hanging decorations on the Christmas tree.

Jack and Trenton should be back soon from taking a little family out on a horse ride.

"Are you still planning to have the wedding here?" I ask, looking around the living room and wondering what kind of decorating we're going to need to do next.

"Yes. Nothing big. Just family. And you and Madison,

but you're family." She hangs a solid red ball on one of the tree limbs, then moves it and hangs it a couple of inches over.

Just a sign of the nerves on her. She puts a hand on one hip. "I had an idea."

"What's that?" I ask, choosing another ball, also red, from the box and adding a hook to it.

"I think maybe we should get another tree. Have this one decorated all in red and have another one all in blue."

"Two trees?"

"Sure. Why not?" she asks.

"Are you turning into one of those crazy brides?"

"Two trees does not a crazy bride make," she says.

"No comment." I glance down at my phone resting on the coffee table. "The adoption agency is calling me back."

"Now?"

"I know. I have to take it." I grab up my phone and wander toward the kitchen, leaving Hannah with the tree decorations.

Ten minutes later, I disconnect the line and walk back to stand next to Hannah.

"They have a dog," I say.

"Oh? Wow. I didn't expect that."

"Neither did I. But. There's a catch."

"Always," she says, picking up another red ball to hang on the tree.

"We have to pick it up tomorrow."

"Why?" She looks at me, still holding the decoration.

"I don't know. It's Christmastime."

"But that doesn't make any sense. Somebody has to take care of the dog even if it is Christmas."

"Not this dog," I say, the words feeling bitter on my tongue. "They've decided to euthanize him."

Hannah sets the decoration down. "No. Not going to happen. You told them that, right?"

"I did tell her. She told me that someone has to pick the dog up tomorrow or else."

"Just get Madison to go pick him up. She can go right now."

"Good idea." I dial Madison's number. "Madison isn't picking up her phone."

"Why not?" Hannah pulls her phone out of her pocket and dials Madison's number. "Straight to voicemail."

"We have to get to Houston. We have to rescue that dog."

"Agreed."

"Do I need to look at plane tickets?"

"Not yet. Let me talk to Jack."

"Okay."

I'd been led to believe that Jack would fly us down to get the dog. That it wouldn't be a problem.

"I have to see if the plane's available," Hannah answering my unspoken question.

"I thought it was Jack's airplane."

"It is, but he sublets it sometimes."

"Oh. I'll check with the airlines. Just in case." I drop onto the sofa and start my search.

"I'm worried about Madison," Hannah says, sending Madison a message.

"I am too." I'm worried about a lot of things, including Madison, but mostly, right now, I'm worried about how to rescue the little dog.

That's what our company is all about. Not just placing pets with their forever owners, but keeping animals from unspeakable fates.

Even if Caleb didn't want the dog for his daughter, I'd still do everything I could to rescue him. I'd do it even if it wasn't my job to save him. The thought of not saving the little dog from an unspeakable fate makes me literally sick to my stomach.

Chapter Thirty-Three

Trenton

IT'S BEEN some time since I've gone horseback riding. By the time Jack and I are back at the stables and brushing down the horses, I know I'm going to be sore all over. It was worth it though, getting out, seeing some of the beautiful backcountry again.

I'd planned on taking Olivia, but she'd been doing her thing with trying to find a dog for Caleb.

Next time. Next time I go riding, I'm taking Olivia. It doesn't matter that she's never been on a horse. I have experience with that and I know how to teach her what she needs to know. We have horses specifically for inexperienced riders, so it's definitely not a problem.

Glancing out the open barn door, I'm surprised to see Hannah and Olivia walking this way. Cupcake is leading the way. The dog has an uncanny sense of guessing which way to go, even in places unfamiliar to her.

Both of the girls, Hannah and Olivia, are beautiful, but I only have eyes for Olivia.

"The girls are coming this way," I say.

Jack looks up and grins. I've never known anyone so in love as Jack is with Hannah. That he was secretly married to her for ten years without her knowing it, and never went on a single date during that time speaks volumes.

Hannah walks up to Jack, Olivia standing next to her. "We have to fly to Houston," she says.

"Okay," Jack says. "We knew that was coming."

"Tomorrow."

Jack glances at me. "Didn't expect that. Why tomorrow?"

While she tells him, I put away the horse brush and walk over to stand next to Olivia.

"Didn't know your job was this stressful," I tell her.

"It can be."

"I need to make a call," Jack says. "Make sure the airplane is available."

"Why wouldn't it be?" I ask. "It's your plane."

"I sublet it sometimes."

"Why?"

"Running a ranch is expensive," he says, pulling off his gloves and shoving them in his coat pockets. "It helps to offset expenses."

"I didn't know things were that bad," I say.

"We're handling it," Jack says, washing his hands and drying them before pulling out his phone.

With Jack and Hannah going on ahead, I lock up the barn and, walking alongside Olivia, follow behind them.

"You're not saying anything," I say.

"If Jack can't get the airplane, I have to take a commercial flight down to Houston tomorrow."

"What about Madison? Can't she pick up the dog?"

"We can't get in touch with her."

"Is she okay?"

"I don't know."

"We'll figure something out," I say.

Olivia just nods and looks straight ahead.

So now I know. When things get dire, Olivia gets quiet.

There's another possibility. Her friend, Stan.

I start to ask her about it, but decide against it. The subject of Stan isn't one I want to bring up if I can avoid it.

Chapter Thirty-Four

Olivia

WHILE JACK and Hannah make dinner, I sit at the kitchen table, using my computer to search the web for flights to Houston.

Trenton sits next to me, watching.

"I'm not seeing anything," I say, sitting back in the chair. "Even if we drove, we wouldn't make it to Houston in time."

"Can't you just call whoever has the dog and tell them you'll be there? Tell them to keep the dog safe?"

Olivia exchanges a glance with Hannah.

"The guy who has this particular dog isn't exactly trustworthy."

"Seriously? That's unfortunate."

"Yeah. He's not a nice person."

Hannah whispers something to Jack.

"Maybe," Jack says.

"If Jack gets the airplane," Hannah says. "We're all going."

"Either way, we'll figure something out," Trenton says.

"When did you become so optimistic?" I ask him.

"Someone has to be," he says.

And he's right about that. No one is saying much right now. I've never seen this group so quiet.

We're all just waiting on Jack's phone to ring.

Everything hinges on his airplane being available tomorrow.

I glance outside. And the weather. As Hannah pointed out, the weather has to be good for a flight out of here to be approved.

A little dog's life hangs in the balance.

If I was a writer, I'd make that my tagline for the day.

Needing something to do, I go back and try a different airline website. There has to be something.

"Will you drive me to the airport tomorrow?" I ask Trenton. "If Jack doesn't hear anything?"

"Of course. And I'll go with you. So book two seats." He pulls out his credit card and lays it on the table next to my computer.

"You don't have to do that," I say. But the truth is, I want him to go with me.

"I understand if you don't want me to go," he says. "I'm still buying your ticket."

"It's not that," I say. "I just don't want it to be an inconvenience."

"I wouldn't offer if it was an inconvenience," Trenton says.

Looking up from my computer, I meet his gaze. His grayish blue eyes lock onto mine.

"I have something I need to do," I say.

"Right now?" he asks.

"I don't know." I look away. I hadn't even realized I was saying the words out loud.

I'd been thinking how much I wanted to kiss Trenton. And that thought had led to other thoughts. Like how I need to break up with Stan once and for all.

Hannah had been right. I'm not sure just how right she is about everything, but she was right about Stan not being right for me. She hadn't come right out and said it, but the implication had been there.

I need to break up with Stan. It's never been more clear to me than it is right now, sitting here next to Trenton.

I can't be with Stan anymore. Not when Trenton makes me feel like he makes me feel.

Trenton makes me feel like a different person. He makes me feel like the kind of person who wants to move to a small town in the mountains, preferably on a horse ranch, even though I know absolutely nothing about horses.

The kind of person who wants to get married and have children.

Trenton makes me feel like a different version of myself. Maybe even a better version.

Chapter Thirty-Five

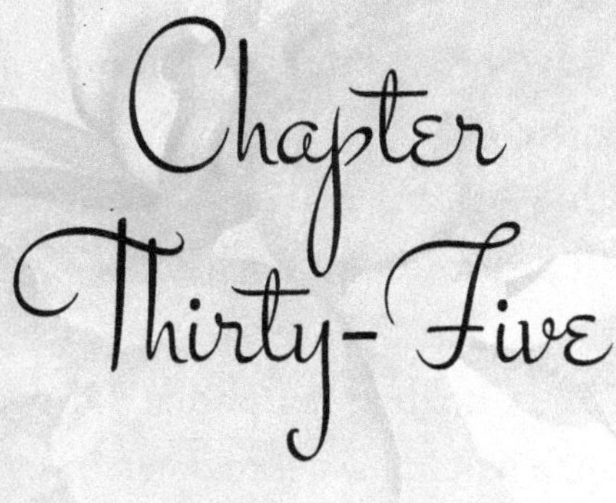

Trenton

JACK'S CALL comes in after we've all gone to bed in our respective rooms.

I know because he sends me a text.

JACK

Got the plane for tomorrow.

Elated, I stare at the message.

I have to tell Olivia.

Wearing a sleep t-shirt, I put my jeans back on and head across the hall to knock on her door.

She must have been standing at the door because she opens it immediately.

She's wearing her pajamas and her face looks freshly washed, her hair damp around the hairline.

"Jack got the airplane," I say.

"I know." She's holding her phone. Of course, I realize, belatedly, Hannah would have texted her, too.

"What time do we leave in the morning?" I ask.

"I don't know. That depends on Jack, I guess."

"I guess. We need to have time to fly to Houston. Then get wherever it is we need to go."

"The earlier the better," she says.

"I think so." I find myself distracted by her green eyes.

Neither one of us moves.

"Olivia," I say.

"I have something I need to do," she says again.

"You mentioned that." I take a step forward, closing the distance between us. "Is it something I can help you with?"

She looks perplexed for a moment, then a little amused. "I think you already have."

I gently cup her face with one hand, then, when her eyes drift closed, I lift my other hand to cup her face with both.

There is nothing I want more right now than to kiss her and only an idiot would let this moment pass without doing so.

I lower my lips toward hers until our breaths mingle.

There's no going back from this. Once I kiss her, there's no going back.

That thought crosses my mind and I know I don't want to go back.

There's only going forward.

My lips touch hers ever so slightly.

Then as she leans forward, pressing her lips more firmly against mine, I sigh and murmur. "I've been wanting to do this since the moment I first saw you." I deepen the kiss.

She wraps her arms around my waist and leans into the kiss.

She doesn't have to say anything for me to know that she feels the same way. Her kiss tells me everything I need to know.

"Olivia," I say, my lips moving against hers. "Will you be my girl?"

"I think I already am," she says.

And that is all I need to hear.

Forward. Everything is moving forward.

Maybe it's the magic of Christmas that's brought us together. Right here. Right now.

Whatever it is, I'm more than grateful.

Chapter Thirty-Six

Olivia

"ARE YOU NERVOUS?" Trenton asks the next day as we're buckled into what they tell me is a little Cessna jet.

The airfield, not big enough to be an airport by any stretch of the imagination since it's literally just a runway is near the Alpine Falls Lodge. There are no other airplane is sight. Just a couple of air socks on either side of the runway.

"No. Should I be?" I look over at Trenton, searching his expression for clues. "Jack's a good pilot, right?"

He smiles. "Of course he is. And no. You shouldn't be nervous. It's just you said this your first time on a private jet."

"It is." Hannah and Jack are sitting in the cockpit, headphones over their ears. Trenton and I are buckled into the two seats behind them. "But it should be like any other flight, right?"

"Right," he says. "It's a little bit different though."

"How so?"

"The plane is lighter, so it feels different. Especially coming out of the mountains. Sometimes there's turbulence."

"Oh." I double-check my seatbelt. "Well. I wasn't nervous."

"In reality, turbulence is nothing to worry about as long as you're buckled in."

"Good to know," I say. "Thanks for the encouragement."

He reaches over and takes my hand. "Maybe I just needed an excuse to hold your hand."

"You don't need any excuse for that," I say.

"Prepare for takeoff," Jack announces through the speakers.

"A kiss for luck?" Trenton asks.

"Looking for another excuse?" I ask.

"Always."

"Again," I say. "Not really needed."

He leans over and plants a kiss on my lips as the airplane picks up speed as the plane races down the little runway.

Trenton's lips are still on mine the moment the wheels leave the ground.

Between that first moment of weightlessness and Trenton's lips against mine, that moment is like nothing I've ever experienced.

It's overwhelmingly intoxicating.

Trenton pulls back enough that his grayish blue eyes meet mine.

We're in the air now. Jack is turning the airplane in a slow arc so that we're eventually heading east.

We are officially on our way.

The thing I notice most about the small private jet is that it's louder. Hannah and Jack can talk to each other through their headphones, but Trenton and I have to lean close to be able to hear each other. Not a hardship.

After he kissed me last night, I felt like my whole world shifted.

Like maybe that kiss breathed life into that alternate version of myself that I'd been imagining.

And now we're on our way to Houston to rescue a dog. A dog that will make a little girl's Christmas one to remember. Things couldn't be better.

Jack and Hannah will be officially remarried in just days.

My thoughts circle around and land on that thought. The wedding. I came to Alpine Falls for the wedding.

Once the wedding is over, I'll have to return to Houston to my home. To my life.

This trip, as wonderful as it is, will soon become nothing more than a memory.

And Trenton will be remembered as the man I fell in love with over the holidays.

He squeezes my hand to get my attention and kisses the palm of my hand.

This is going to be one of those memories that I remember with fondness mixed with heartbreak.

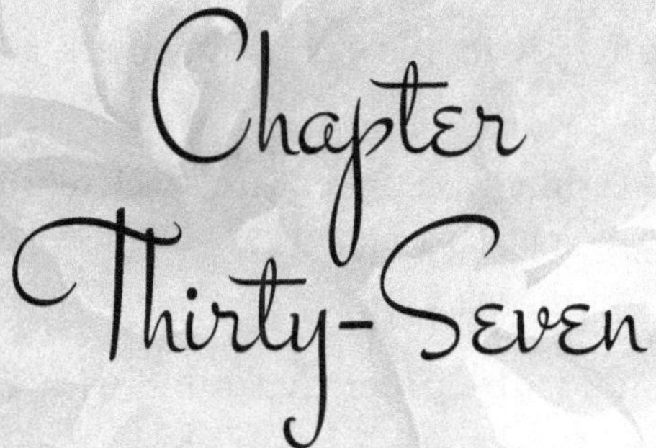

Chapter Thirty-Seven

Trenton

THE GIRLS HAD BEEN RIGHT. The man we got the dog from was not a pleasant man. An asshole if you ask me.

He made it a point to make sure we understood that we barely made it in time to save the dog's life.

There are several things I would have liked to have said in response, but I keep them to myself. This is Olivia's world and I have no business butting into it.

Besides, we got the dog.

Jack is driving with Hannah sitting in the passenger seat, the dog in her lap. "He's so cute," Hannah says.

Olivia and I sit in the back, our knees and shoulders touching.

"It's a good thing you prefer cats," Jack tells Hannah.

"I like dogs," Hannah says.

"What's his name?" I ask.

Olivia unfolds the paper that came with him. "Milo," she says. "But Abigail gets to name him. I don't think I'll even tell her about the name Milo."

"He looks a lot like Cupcake," Hannah says. "Except that his fur is all the same color."

"I can't believe that man was going to just put him down."

"I have a few thoughts about that," I say. "But I'll keep them to myself."

"We're probably all thinking them," Olivia says, putting away Milo's papers.

"Should we go by Madison's place and check on her?" Hannah asks. "While we're in Houston?"

"I don't think so," Olivia says. "Sometimes she just doesn't want to be bothered."

"I've never known her to disappear like this," Hannah says. "Have you?"

"Actually. Yes. She's okay. She's just doing her thing."

"She sounds a lot like Lucas," I say. "We should set them up."

"I don't think you want to put Lucas on anyone," Jack says.

"Lucas isn't bad," I say.

"I'm curious to meet your brother," Olivia says. "He sounds so mysterious."

"I'll have to keep an eye on you," I say. "Women flock to him."

"Really?" Hannah says, looking back at me.

"No," I say, making everyone laugh.

"We can't leave Milo alone in the car," Jack says. "Anyone besides me want to hit a drive-through for some food?"

We all agree that we do want to get some food.

"When do we take Milo over to Caleb's house?" Olivia asks.

"We can't keep him too long," Hannah says. "We'll get attached to him."

"Let me ask Caleb," I say, sending him a text.

"My bets are on Christmas Eve," Jack says. "He'll want Santa to bring the dog."

"We can take him over on Christmas Eve after Abigail goes to bed," Olivia says.

"You'll have to do it," Hannah says. "Remember that's my wedding night." She and Jack exchange a glance.

"I think Olivia and I are capable of taking care of getting Milo to his new home."

"I wonder what she'll name him," Hannah says, the little dog licking her face.

"Hannah," Olivia says. "I think you need to hand Milo over."

"I'm okay."

"She gets attached," Olivia explains.

"We all do," I say, sending Olivia a little grin and putting my arm around her.

We still have a long way to go, she and I, but I think we're making progress. Much better progress than I had expected.

Now all I have to do is to convince her to stay in Alpine Falls.

Chapter Thirty-Eight

Olivia

W E   M A K E it back to Alpine Falls the same day we left.

Flying by way of private jet is the only way to travel. Even knowing it's a mode of transportation outside of my financial reach, it gives me a new goal to work toward.

I find myself thinking more and more about interior design.

Trenton believes he can help me get set up and I'm inclined to believe him.

The biggest problem with going in that direction is that

Trenton can only help me in the Alpine Falls/Boulder area. Maybe Denver, but mostly Boulder.

There are so many implications wrapped up in that.

One. My home is in Houston. I have a home there. The house my grandmother left me.

Two. I don't have a place to live in Alpine Falls or Boulder.

On the plus side, I don't have much of a social life anymore in Houston. One of my two friends now lives in Alpine Falls.

Since Hannah left, I rarely see Madison. Go figure that the newest friend in our little circle would be the glue holding us together.

And of course, there's Stan.

Moving away from Houston could actually be the excuse I've been looking for to break up with Stan.

That and I seem to have a new boyfriend.

Trenton and I can't seem to keep our hands off each other.

He's holding my hand as Jack impressively lands the airplane on the little runway that looks like a postage stamp from the air.

Tomorrow. Tomorrow I'll call Stan and tell him on the phone that I can't see him anymore. It's not as good as telling him in person, but it's better than just sending a text.

Sending a text is so tempting and would be so much easier. But it doesn't seem right. Stan is a good man and he cares about me.

Just doesn't seem right.

Doesn't seem right be kissing Trenton while I'm dating Stan either.

So I'll call him.

Back at the Thompson's ranch house, Cupcake seems to think she hasn't seen me in about a year.

Mr. and Mrs. Thompson took good care of her and Bandit, too, while we were gone.

Cupcake and Milo hit it off like old friends.

"You can visit," I tell them. "But don't get attached."

"You know," Hannah says, running her hands through Bandit's fur. "I don't think puppies are out of the question."

"Oh no. I don't think Cupcake needs to go there."

"Why not?" Trenton asks. "Aren't you in the pet adoption business?"

"I'd probably end up wanting to keep them all," I say. "Anyway, I'm thinking about expanding into another direction."

"What's that?" Hannah asks.

I glance over at Trenton, kneeling front of the fireplace, getting a fire going. "Interior design."

"Interior design," Hannah says. "Where is this coming from?"

I just shrug. There are some things I can't explain. Even to my friend. Maybe especially to my friend. The friend who's getting married (is married to) the brother of the man who instigated this whole thing.

Trenton stands up and wipes his hands on his jeans. "I've asked her to come and help me out with some projects."

I look at him with a raised eyebrow. That's not exactly how I remember the conversation going.

Trenton sits down next to me. "That was my plan anyway," he says.

"I think we missed something," Hannah tells Jack.

Jack just grins and stretches his legs out. "I know you're not surprised by this, my love."

"I guess not," Hannah says. "I just thought we'd be more in the loop."

"Should we let them in the loop?" Trenton asks me.

"I'm not sure I'm in the loop," I say.

"We still have some details to work out," Trenton says.

"I'd say so," Hannah says.

"Let them figure it out," Jack tells her.

"Okay," Hannah says. Then on the next breath. "You could sell your house in Houston."

"And if I sell my house, where exactly am I supposed to live?" I ask, feeling a nervous excitement running through me.

"You could..." Hannah bites her lip. I'm not sure, but I think Jack just elbowed her.

"You could live here," Trenton says, finishing the thought Hannah started.

"I can't just move in here," I say. "Your parents can't just adopt a stray... person."

Trenton takes my hand and clasps his fingers with mine. He seems so relaxed while my blood is racing through my veins. I can almost see my life course changing direction right in front of my eyes.

"No, but I can."

"What?" I say, barely able to speak past the lump in my throat.

"I have an opening to adopt a stray."

Hannah, obviously unable to resist, jumps back into the conversation. "Adopting a... person is a serious commitment."

We all just stare at her. "What?" she asks.

"I'm not a pet."

"There might be some similarities," Jack says, backing up his fiancé (wife).

Biting my bottom lip, I look over at Trenton, and a smile tugs at my lips. I couldn't stop from smiling if I wanted to.

"There's something wrong with you people," I say.

"What people?" Trenton asks. "I don't see anyone else here."

Jack clears his throat and says something to Hannah.

"We have to go feed Bandit," Hannah says and they stand up.

"Didn't you just—?"

Trenton takes my hands. "Let them go. I need to talk to you."

After Hannah and Jack are in the kitchen, talking to each other, I meet Trenton's gaze and look into his grayish blue eyes.

"What do you want to talk to me about?" I ask. "A job?"

"The job is just an excuse," he says.

"An excuse for what?" Butterflies are racing in my stomach.

"I don't want you to go back to Houston to live."

"But that's my home. I have a house there." Even as I say the words out loud, I don't feel the conviction behind them that I would've felt before, even just a few days ago.

In truth, the thought of going back there to live leaves me feeling empty.

"If you're not ready to sell your grandmother's house, you could lease it out."

"I could do that." That's something I hadn't thought of. "But I'd have to get a place here."

"You could live here," he says.

"But... wouldn't you have to ask your parents about that?"

"Do you think I haven't already talked to them?"

"What? You talked to your parents about me?"

"We're a close family," he says with a shrug. "It would only be temporary. Until you and I can figure out what we want to do."

"You have some possibilities in mind?" I ask, the words coming out a little breathless.

"Well. I am an architect. And you need to cut your teeth doing some design work."

"What are you trying to say?"

"We have about a million acres of land here," he says with a grin. "We should be able to find a nice spot to build a house."

"Build a house? Us?"

He tucks a strand of hair behind my ear and kisses my forehead.

"Haven't you figured it out?" he asks. " I want to keep you."

"I'm not a pet," I say, feeling a little weak because I like where he's going with this.

"No. You're not a pet. But you're a person I'd like a lifetime commitment with. If you're interested."

"I might be interested," I say.

"Sounds like a strong maybe. I'm guessing you have that thing you have to do before you can say for sure."

"I do have that thing," I say, even though that thing is a definite given at this point.

He nods slowly. Hannah and Jack's laughter drifts from the kitchen. "Let's get those two married off. Officially. Then you and I can see what a future together looks like."

"Okay. But I have to tell you something."

"You can tell me anything."

"It's looking pretty good from here.

With a grin, he leans forward and kisses me.

"A definite maybe then," he says.

"Yes. A definite maybe."

Cupcake jumps up in my lap and licks Trenton on the mouth.

He closes his eyes, but lets her lick his face without recoiling.

I put the back of my hand over my mouth as I laugh. "I think Cupcake approves," I say.

"And now you know that I'll do anything for you," he says.

"Aw. Your OCD is cured," I say.

"Come here," he says, kissing me again.

Wagging her tail, Cupcake licks both our faces until we're laughing so hard it hurts.

I've found my place. My forever home.

Right here in Alpine Falls.

The End.

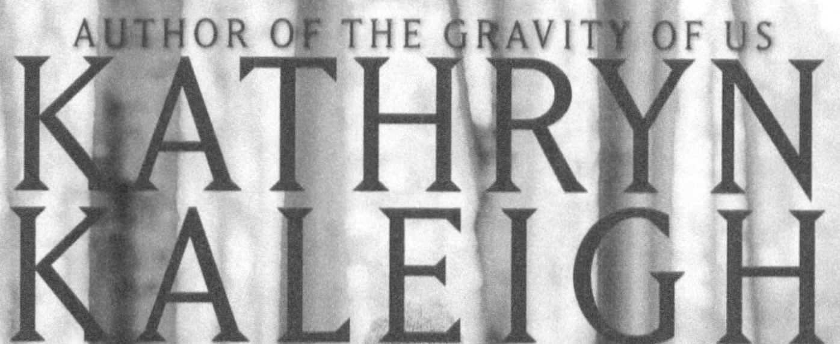

AUTHOR OF THE GRAVITY OF US
KATHRYN KALEIGH

SOMETIMES FOREVER JUST TAKES AN UNEXPECTED TURN
Forever Yours (Maybe)
THE ALPINE FALLS (MAYBE YOURS) SERIES

Forever Yours (Maybe)

One wrong turn. No way out.
And the last place she expected to fall in love.

Chapter One

Madison Lane

IT SEEMED like a good idea at the time.

That's my life. Or so it seems at this juncture in my twenty-seven years.

It seemed like a good idea to take a road trip, by myself, instead of flying to my friend's wedding. When I'd studied the map, the drive hadn't looked all that bad. Just get on Interstate 10 and head west from Houston, then north on Interstate 25 to Denver and east on Interstate 70 to Alpine Falls.

Simple enough.

It was simple enough until I got out of the car in El Paso and my cell phone fell out face down onto the concrete parking lot, smashing the screen, making it impossible for me even unlock it.

Unfortunately, of course, I lost all my phone numbers. It was quite a shock to realize that I don't have a single phone number other than my own memorized.

I don't even have my friend Hannah's address. All I know is it is somewhere in Alpine Falls, Colorado. So that's what I put in my GPS and hope for the best.

After that the trip is uneventful until I leave Denver and head into the mountains.

It's two days before Christmas Eve, Hannah's wedding date, and the weather is appropriately cloudy and gloomy for December. The forecast is calling for snow.

I don't have a lot of experience with mountain life, but I'm determined to make it to Alpine Falls before it starts snowing.

I take the designated exit off of Interstate 70 and head north along a curvy two-lane highway. It's picturesque. I have to give it that. Mountaintops covered with caps of snow. Wispy clouds hovering below the tops of those jagged mountains.

The road follows alongside a rushing mountain stream with shallow, sparkling clear water tumbling over a rocky riverbed. And there are trees everywhere. Blue spruce trees on either side of the highway mixed with white-barked aspen trees and maple trees, both of which lost their leaves months ago.

I drive past a little cabin with smoke wafting out of the chimney sending a wave of nostalgia washing over me. I imagine a family gathered around the cozy fireplace, watching a movie or reading or just talking. The scent of fresh baked cookies fills the air. Or maybe an apple pie.

It's Christmastime and that's what families do. But not my family. My parents decided that since my brother left home, they would take advantage of the long anticipated freedom and take a cruise somewhere warm.

My brother is in Atlanta spending Christmas with his girlfriend.

And that's basically how I ended up here. Driving along a lonely country road in the mountains. Blindly following my GPS to a little town called Alpine Falls.

I could have (probably should have) stopped somewhere to get my phone replaced, but I didn't want to waste the half a day I knew it would take.

Being late for my friend's wedding is not an option. It's already taking longer to get there than I planned. Being my first road trip and all, I might have underestimated the time it takes to drive halfway across the country.

"Turn right on Birch Road in five hundred feet." The female voice of my GPS says with no uncertainty.

"Seriously?" I confess to keeping up a conversation with my GPS since losing my cell phone. Not that it ever responds.

Since I'm at the mercy of my GPS and it's gotten me this far, I slow down and leave the highway to turn right onto Birch Road. Birch Road, a blacktopped country road, winds its way further up into the mountains. Definitely increasing in elevation.

My GPS then suggests I stop for food. Not a bad idea. Except that I don't see any signs of a town up ahead. In fact, I cross an area with a steep drop off on one side.

Beautiful, but deadly. That's what I call it.

After about a mile, I round a little curve and that's when I see the road sign. "Luchara. Elevation 8,540."

Not the population. The elevation. It's interesting how these little towns seem prouder of their elevation than they are of how many people live here.

But there's a little diner. The sign out front identifies it as "Luchara Diner." Not a very creative name, but it looks like it only attracts locals. There aren't enough cars on the highway to suggest that it's much of a tourist stop.

Well, why not? My GPS brought me here, so I might as well stop. I have to go to the bathroom anyway.

I turn down the gravel road and park next to the only other vehicle near the restaurant. The town's only street is a gravel road with parking on either side. There are only a few other parked cars scattered here and there along what I guess they would call Main Street.

The restaurant is the only building labeled with a sign. The other buildings are unidentified shops of one kind or another.

The restaurant has outdoor seating in the form of picnic tables, but it's too cold for anyone to be seated outside. The outside seating area looks quite inviting. A wooden deck with a live, very tall and old oak tree right in the middle of it, a circled bench around the perimeter of its trunk.

A little bell jingles over the door as I step inside and a man calls out to me from behind the kitchen.

"Have a seat wherever you like," he calls out in a gruff smoker's voice. The man is wearing a white apron and apparently is both the cook and the host.

Only two of the six tables are filled. A couple of bearded men in flannel shirts are seated at one of those tables. An older couple, obviously tourists from the way they're dressed are seated at the other one. He's wearing slacks and a polo shirt. She's wearing a casual dress and sandals.

I take a seat next to the door and pick up the sheet of paper that serves as a menu. Not a lot of variety. Everything has eggs in one form or another.

The man comes to stand next to me.

"That's the breakfast menu," he says, looking over my shoulder. "You can order from it if you want to, but this here is the lunch menu." He hands me another piece of paper with items that sound a lot more like lunch items. Hamburgers. French fries. A fried chicken plate.

"Can I get a hamburger? Well done?" I ask.

"Sure thing. Anything to drink?"

I hold up a bottle of water I brought in with me. "I'm good."

"Suit yourself. Got bottles of beer if you change your mind."

"I'll keep that in mind."

The cook/server leaves me alone at the table and heads back behind the counter to the kitchen.

The men laugh loudly at something one of them said.

I tap my fingers on the table. Without a cell phone, I have pretty much nothing to do to entertain myself.

I'm certain my friend Hannah and Olivia have tried to reach me by now. Hannah will be concerned that I'm not answering my phone, but Olivia, whom I've known since grade school, will think I'm just in one of my work mode periods.

I do that sometimes. I close myself off in my apartment and don't want to talk to anyone.

I might be introverted. But it's the only way I know to get everything done.

Right now I'm trying to start a business and it's not going like it's supposed to.

I literally have my life planned out on a spreadsheet. I'm twenty-five now and I'm supposed to have gotten my business off the ground by now.

It might be time for a pivot.

Fortunately, I have contingencies built into my spreadsheet.

It's definitely time to rearrange some things.

My hamburger and fries arrive. Finally. One thing I've discovered is that eating at restaurants alone without a cell phone is not fun. There's not only not anyone to talk to, but there's nothing to read or watch.

My first order of business after I make it to Alpine Falls is to get my cell phone replaced. I just have to get there first. To let them know I'm okay and that I'm not going to miss the wedding.

The wedding is a long story, but it's important to Hannah.

She's marrying her high school sweetheart Jack Thompson.

The funny thing about it is she spent the last ten years thinking she and Jack were divorced when in fact, they've been married all this time.

So technically Jack is already her husband, not her fiancé.

But since Hannah dated other guys and was actually engaged to someone else when she learned that she was still married to Jack, they feel like they should have a wedding to reset their marriage.

Personally, I think it's a good idea.

The hamburger isn't bad. I eat half of it and all my fries before going up to the counter to pay. Now that I've eaten, I'm ready to get going. I should be in Alpine Falls by the end of the day if my GPS is correct and I'm ready.

I'm wishing I could just fly home after the wedding, but, of course, I have my car.

Again. It seemed like a good idea at the time.

Chapter Two

Lucas Thompson

I LOCK the door to the cabin and walk the distance to the Luchara Diner. It only takes me fifteen minutes to get there, door to door. My big gangly black lab, Scout, runs along at my heels.

The old log cabin built in the last century is perfectly located for someone who cherishes privacy. A writer maybe. Or a retired couple. Maybe an investor who wants to rent it out in the summers.

So many possibilities.

The air has a definite bite to it and I shrug deeper into my fleece-lined coat. My boots crunch on frosty snow protected from the day's sunlight. The trail winds among a variety of trees, most of them, aspens and maples, with bare winter branches. Others, blue spruce trees mostly, have full branches that smell like Christmas.

I automatically glance at my watch. Two days before Christmas Eve. Two days before my brother's wedding. Tomorrow I need to pack up and make the short drive back to Alpine Falls.

I have little doubt that they've been trying to reach me, but since there's no cell phone service in Luchara, I wouldn't know.

Fortunately, since I have a habit of disappearing for weeks at the time, they don't expect much out of me. I established that habit during my party days. I never would have predicted that bad habit established in my college years would serve me well in the future. This time I have a legitimate reason for being off by myself.

As I near the diner, a police car pulls up and parks between two tourist's cars.

Luchara doesn't get very many visits by the police, certainly not state troopers. Either something happened or the policeman is just passing through. Luchara is a quiet little community. Another thing that makes it attractive.

That and it's just half an hour's drive from Alpine Falls.

The bell rings as I go inside the diner.

Mel is standing behind the counter, hands on his hips. The state police officer drags off his sun glasses and says something I can't hear.

There's a young lady standing at the counter, credit card in hand, waiting to pay.

The only other people in the diner are two loggers working in the area and an older touristy couple. Everyone is quietly watching the interaction between Mel and the policeman.

I walk up and lean an elbow on the counter. It has the desired effect. Both men look at me. Scout sits down behind me, but no one notices him.

"Everything okay?" I ask with my disarming expression that makes it hard for most people to admonish me for interrupting.

"No," Mel says in his gruff smoker's voice. He doesn't smoke anymore, but the gruffness stuck even after he quit. "There was an avalanche on Birch Road."

My gut twists. Birch Road is the only way to get from here back to the highway. I'm honestly surprised I didn't hear the avalanche. Was probably running the power saw when it happened.

"Anybody hurt?" I ask.

"Don't think so," the policeman says. "But the road is going to be blocked indefinitely."

"Wait," the young lady jumps in. I immediately detect a distinct southern drawl. She has the same accent as Olivia, a friend of my brother's fiancé/wife. Not from here. "I have to get to Alpine Falls."

"Not going to happen," the policeman says with nothing more than a halfway glance in her direction. "The road was washed off the side of the mountain."

She's shaking her head, but the policeman is talking to

Mel again. "Make a list of supplies you're going to need. I'll make sure they get helicoptered in."

"How are you getting out?" I ask the policeman.

"I'm not. No one is getting out." He looks at Mel again. "I hope you have a room for these people."

"The loggers have a trailer," Mel says. He nods in the direction of the older couple. "They're staying at the B&B. No other guests."

I look at the woman waiting to pay for her food. She crosses her arms.

She looks like a vexed elfin princess. Delicate features. Long brunette hair pulled back loosely, leaving a few strands framing her face.

Long dark eyelashes and the greenest eyes I've ever seen. Green like a lush verdant forest after a rain.

"I don't know where you're going to sleep," Mel says to the policeman, ignoring her.

"Hoping you have an extra room."

Mel sighs. "We'll figure something out."

"What about her?" The policeman asks, finally acknowledging the young lady's presence.

Everyone is looking at the young lady now.

"I can't stay here," she says, with a stubborn lift of her chin.

"Lady," the policeman says. "Unless you're planning on hiking out of here, which I don't recommend with the snow coming, you're not going anywhere."

"She can stay in my cabin," I say, blurting out the words

before I have time to think about just how impossible that will be.

Chapter Three

Madison

"I GUESS EVERYTHING IS SETTLED THEN," Mel, the cook and apparently the owner of this diner, says.

"I don't think so," I say, sliding my credit card into my coat pocket. Right now I have more important things to worry about than paying for a ten dollar meal.

Mel turns back to the stove and flips a burger while the policeman turns and walks outside, murmuring something into his radio.

With nothing left to do but to address the man who just offered me his cabin in the midst of this unfortunate event, I turn to face him.

He looks like he hasn't shaved in a couple of days, but

beneath that stubble is a handsome man. A breathtakingly handsome man with steel blue eyes pinned on mine.

"I can't stay in your cabin," I say.

"Suit yourself," he says with a little shrug.

"I have to get to Alpine Falls."

"Don't we all?" he says, signaling Mel. Mel throws together a hamburger, scoops up some fries, and slides the plate over to the man. He follows that up with a cold bottle of beer.

The man takes the plate and the beer to the nearest table and sits down to eat.

I'm at a loss. Stranded.

"Aren't there any rooms here?" I ask Mel. "There has to be someplace I can stay."

"Sorry ma'am. We have two rooms in town and they're both taken."

"What about your place?"

"Oh no," Mel says with a glance toward the policeman standing outside. "I've already got one unwanted guest in my one bedroom house. My wife is already going to kill me."

"Well," I say, looking over at the man who offered his cabin. "I don't know that man."

"Name's Lucas. I reckon he doesn't know you either."

Mel makes a good point. I glance over my shoulder at Lucas. He seems to have forgotten about me.

"I need to pay for my food," I say, sounding as weary as I feel.

Mel sends me a look that I interpret as him really not wanting to be bothered with ringing up my burger. Like everyone else, he suddenly has far more important things to think about.

If the avalanche washed out the road and snow is on the way, it could be spring before we have a way out of here.

I need to sit down.

I just drove over that road. Birch Road.

The avalanche could have so easily have happened as I was driving up here.

"Ten dollars even," Mel says.

I don't question him. Maybe there are no taxes here. Not seeing any place to scan my card, I hand it over to him. He places it on a little machine and manually makes an imprint of it. Then hands me a piece of paper to sign. I haven't seen one of these since I was a kid.

I sign it and hand it back.

"Is there some place in town where I can buy a cell phone?"

"A cell phone?" He scoffs. "We don't even have cell phone service here. Why would anyone try to sell a cell phone?"

"Has this ever happened before?" I ask him. "An avalanche?"

"Lady," he says. "As much as I'd like to stop and chat." He obviously does not want to chat with me. "I don't have the time. If you have any sense at all, you'll go over and intro-duce yourself to Lucas. He's your best bet right now and unless you want to take up sleeping in your car, you'll make nice with him."

I walk over to where Lucas is finishing up his burger and fries and drinking his beer.

"Hi," I say. "I'm Madison."

"I'm Lucas," he says, his expression blank, wiping his hands on a napkin.

"You said you have a cabin I can rent until we can get out of here?"

"The offer stands," he says, pushing his plate away.

"I didn't mean to offend you. I was just..." Looking away, I tuck a strand of hair behind an ear. Asking for favors is not one of my strengths. But he did offer. "Well. I was caught off guard."

"We're all a little caught off guard right now."

"Has this ever happened before?" I ask. "Just wondering how long we're going to be stuck here."

"It happens in the mountains. But it hasn't happened here. It could be a year before they have a road open again. Depends on the engineers."

My jaw drops along with my stomach. "A year?" I drop into the seat across from him. "Surely not."

"I'll walk down there tomorrow and take a look."

"Can I go?"

"Do you have hiking boots?"

"No."

"Then it's not a good idea." He pulls a treat out of his pocket and hands it to his dog. The dog sets it down at his feet and looks at me with big brown eyes.

"You have a dog," I say as though I just now noticed. "In a restaurant."

Lucas hesitates a moment as though he can't quite decide if he's supposed to provide an explanation. Finally he simply says. "His name is Scout."

"Scout." I slide out of my chair and kneel in front of the dog, holding out a hand for him to sniff. "Hi Scout. I'm Madison."

The dog licks my hand, then stands up and wags his tail, letting me pet him.

At least I've found one positive thing in the little community of Lachara. A friendly black lab.

As for what I'm going to do about being stranded here is another matter entirely.

No way out of here. My trusty GPS sent me into an impossible situation.

No cell phone and I don't have phone numbers to call my friends.

No place to stay unless I stay in Lucas's cabin.

Chapter Four

Lucas

WHILE SCARFING down my burger and fries, my thoughts are racing.

The avalanche changes everything, especially if it's as bad as the state trooper suggested. It's bad enough that the officer isn't able to get out, so there's that. I'll hike down at some point and take a look for myself, but I'm not optimistic.

The timing is the worst. I'd been planning on leaving here tomorrow. I should have left today, but that's tricky because leaving today, I could have been caught in the avalanche.

I'm so close to getting the outside of the cabin finished. If I don't get it finished before the snow settles in, it'll be spring. So I might as well resign myself to going ahead and moving to the inside renovations. This sets me back a bit, but not a lot and...

"Hi." I look up to find the young lady I'd seen standing at the counter now standing at my table. "I'm Madison," she says with a tentative smile.

"Lucas," I say.

I'm not from the south, but my mother, having grown up in the south, drilled being a gentleman into my head. My brothers and I all got a steady dose of how to treat a lady.

There's no way I could just leave a damsel in distress standing there. On the flip side, I'm not going to force my help onto someone who doesn't want it. I blame our independent mother for that one, too.

In the heat of the moment, as a gentleman, I'd offered for her to stay in my cabin. I'm quite familiar with Luchara and there really isn't anywhere else for her to crash.

Luchara is a small town community with a population of 65. There's not even a sheriff.

It's not a tourist town. Just a little community of people who live thirty minutes from Alpine Falls. There are all of two rentable rooms and they're obviously occupied at the moment.

And now we're all stranded for God knows how long.

My cabin is in no way whatsoever set up to have someone staying there. There's not even a bed. I'm sleeping on the floor in what can only be described as a construction zone.

But I do have heat and running water and electricity. So there is that.

Now that I've made the offer, I can't very well go back on it.

Besides, Scout obviously approves. In fact, he's making a fool of himself over her.

"I hope you don't mind dog germs," I say, thinking about my brother, Trenton, who likes dogs well enough as long as they don't lick his face.

"I'm friendly with them," Madison says, looking up at me with a happy grin on her face. "I don't have anywhere else to go," she says. "So thank you for letting me stay in your cabin."

"You might change your mind when you see it," I say. "I should warn you it's under construction."

"From what I'm told, it's my only option."

"Okay then," I say. "Did you already eat?"

"Yes. I was just about to leave."

"Good. The cabin doesn't have any food or a stove."

"Sounds like my kind of place."

I look at her sideways and wonder if maybe she misunderstood me. I decide to let it go. When she sees the cabin, she may decide that sleeping in her car isn't such a bad option after all.

Luchara does have a little gas pump hidden behind what passes for a General Store so if she decide to do something crazy like that, she'd at least have plenty of fuel.

"We should get you settled in then," I say.

"Okay." She stands up and secures her scarf around her neck. "I'm parked just outside."

"We walked," I say. "It's not far, so just follow us."

"Do you want to ride?" she asks.

"No. We'll walk. Scout has a propensity to shed and lick car windows."

"I don't mind dog hairs," she says.

"It's seriously not far," I say.

She shrugs. "Okay."

The little bell rings overhead as we step outside. It feels like it's dropped twenty degrees since I walked into the diner.

I hold onto Scout's collar and watch as she gets into her car.

We start walking ahead as she backs out.

I can't help but wonder what I've gone and done.

The cabin is so far from ready to have anyone other than me seeing it, much less staying in it.

I'm going to need to cut some firewood to make sure it's warm. And I'm going to need to come back and buy some more blankets and a pillow while she settles in.

The cabin is tucked deep in the trees sitting on the edge of the river. At night, the sounds of the river drift through the windows like a lullaby—one of the things that initially attracted me to the cabin.

Two sets of sawhorses are out front, a stack of lumber near them. Another stack of logs that I'm using to give the outside wall a refresh isn't far away.

While I wait for Madison to park her car, I pick up the

power saw I left outside when I went to lunch and stash it in metal storage crate in the back of my truck.

"This is it," I say as she gets out of her car. "I warned you. It's a work in progress."

"I don't mind. It's in a beautiful location," she says, closing her door. "The river sounds like a water fountain."

"Makes for good sleeping," I say. "Want help with your luggage?"

"Sure," she says. "I have an overnight bag in the back seat."

"Computer?" I ask.

"Didn't bring one," she says. "I don't have a laptop."

"Sometimes it's nice to take a break from technology."

"Sometimes that just happens," she says. "whether you want it to or not."

As I toss her overnight bag over my shoulder, Scout runs excited circles around her.

"He's just a puppy," she says, smiling.

"Yeah. Not sure how old he is. He was a stray."

"Aw. That makes me appreciate him—and you—even more."

Those little words of praise have me puffing out my chest with pride. I like it that I did something that pleases this girl.

I push open the door and let her walk in first.

"I feel like I should apologize for the state of the cabin, but it has heat and running water and electricity."

"No need to apologize," she says, stepping over a two by four lying in the floor.

"I need to pick up these hazards. Wasn't expecting company."

She walks to the bedroom door. Peeks inside.

The she turns around and faces me. "I don't see a bed," she says.

"There's no bed. But I'll light a fire and you can sleep on the floor. It'll be cozy."

"Cozy is good."

"I'm just going to put your bag over here on this counter."

"Thank you so much," she says.

"Don't mention it. I'll let you get settled in. I'm just going out to chop some firewood."

"Okay. Do you live nearby?"

"Not exactly," I say. "I'm stranded here. Like you."

She tilts her head and looks at me. "What do you mean?"

"I'm staying here, too. In the cabin."

Chapter Five

Madison

I STAND at the window and watch Lucas chopping firewood.

The cabin is warm inside. Heated by an electric heater and will be heated by the fireplace shortly.

There's no bed. Just a little stack of blankets, neatly folded in one corner. I give him points for the neatly folded blankets and equate it to a made up bed.

But there's no bed.

No kitchen. No problem. The diner is within walking distance and I don't eat all that much anyway.

There's a bedroom. But the bedroom doesn't have a fireplace. Or a heater.

According to Lucas, he's living here while he renovates the house. Not unusual.

Just a bit inconvenient considering that I'm going to be staying here with him—a perfect stranger.

Since Mel at the diner sort of, halfway, recommended I stay with Lucas, I suppose he's not a bad guy. Someone I can trust. It's not like a have a whole lot of choice.

Besides he has a sweet, loving dog. Only a good man could have a sweet, loving dog.

I turn away from the window and survey the cabin.

It could use some picking up.

I find a box of trash bags on the counter and gather up things that are obviously throw away. Like takeout coffee cups and food wrappers left lying around. I make a stack for things I'm not sure about. Like little chunks of wood. Lucas could have plans for those.

A few minutes later, Lucas comes inside, a load of firewood in his arms.

"You cleaned up," he says. "It looks better."

"I just picked up a few things," I say, inordinately pleased that he noticed and approved.

He stacks the firewood near the fireplace, then proceeds to lay logs in the hearth.

"Can you grab that newspaper over there?" he asks.

"Sure." I kneel next to him and crumple up pieces of newspaper for him to stuff in between the logs.

He pulls out a lighter and before long the fire is giving off a nice bit of heat.

"Do you need anything?" he asks. "I'm going to walk into town and buy some extra blankets."

"I don't think so. But I wouldn't mind going with you."

He takes a deep breath. "I need to bank the fire before we go."

"You just built it."

"It's okay. I can build it again."

"No. I didn't think about the fire. I'll just stay here."

But he's already putting out the fire. "Easy enough to build again when we get back. You might see something in town that you need."

"You're very kind," I say.

After he washes the soot off his hands, we put on our coats on and head back out into the cold.

Maybe staying here in front of the warm fireplace would have been a good idea after all. I don't know what I could possibly need from one of the little stores.

Scout runs ahead, circles through the trees, and comes galloping back up behind us.

"The cold weather agrees with him," I say, shoving my hands in my coat pockets, looking for warmth. My little wool coat is southern weight. Hannah had assured me that they have plenty of coats and I shouldn't worry about bringing anything heavy to wear.

Unfortunately I'd taken her at her word. Unfortunate because it looks like I'm going to miss the wedding.

A haze of wood smoke lingers over the town. All the buildings, it seems, have wood burning fireplaces.

"Is this all of Luchara?" I ask as Main Street comes into view.

"This is it."

"How far is it from Alpine Falls?"

"Twenty minutes or so. It's just a little community of people who wanted to be away from town."

"It sort of gives the term small town a new meaning."

"Yeah. I guess it does. It's super secluded for those who like that sort of thing."

"Do you? Like it? Or are you just working here on the cabin?"

"I don't mind it," he says, not really answering the question. Leaving me with even more questions than I had to begin with.

We walk past the diner, deserted now that it's the middle of the afternoon, and walk along a wooden sidewalk to one of the stores.

As Lucas opens the door and we all three, Scout included, step inside, a little bell overhead jingles, and an older man comes out of the back.

"Hello Lucas," he says. "I guess you came in to stock up on avalanche supplies."

"Hey Roosevelt. Guess you could say that. At least you have a good attitude about the whole thing."

"What else am I going to do? Not like I can change it."

"You working with Mel on putting together a list of supplies?"

"Sure. Mel called over here. I'm about to head over there so we can put our lists together."

"I won't keep you," Lucas say. "We just need some blankets and whatever Madison needs."

"I'll look around," I say.

The little store is tidy and has a variety of things from laundry detergent to bags of snack to postcards on the counter.

Apparently, even though it only has two rooms for rent, there's some touristy traffic.

Since I'm not sure how quickly the little town vendors are going to run out of supplies, I grab a big bag of chips and a tube of toothpaste.

I hesitate at the candle section. The cabin has heat, but we could always lose electricity. I grab a candle and tuck it in the crook of my arm.

Not seeing anything else I need, I rejoin Lucas at the front of the store. He's already got a stack of blankets and a pillow on the counter. A box of canned dog food. And a flashlight.

Seems he and I were thinking alike.

Roosevelt must be in the back again.

"I don't know if you noticed," he says. "but there's no cell phone service in Luchara. Do you need to use the phone? To let anyone know where you are?"

I shove my hands in my coat pockets and make a wry expression. "I hadn't noticed because my cell phone is broken. And yes. There are people I need to call, but their numbers are forever lost in my phone."

"Oh," he says, studying me. I can't help but wonder

what he's thinking. If this were one of those bad movies, he'd be thinking how if he killed me, no one would know.

"You said you're headed to Alpine Falls?"

"That's right."

"Hey Roosevelt." Roosevelt comes back out carrying a bag of dog food. "You got an Alpine Falls phone book?"

I look over at Lucas. I could almost kiss him. He's a genius.

"I had one. Haven't seen it since someone borrowed it. I'll look for it, though."

"Thanks. I'll check back with you."

"You need help carrying all this to your cabin?" Roosevelt asks.

Lucas glances at me. "Nah. I think we've got it." I nod in agreement.

"I'll put it on your tab."

"Thanks, man. And remember to look for that phone book."

"I'll ask Mel if he has one lying around someplace."

Lucas and I load up everything. He throws the bag of dog food over his shoulder. I take my lighter bag of chips and toothpaste and my candle. He takes the rest.

"Thanks for thinking of the phone book," I say. "I'd forgotten that they still make those."

"I've had to use one out here a couple of times. They're older. Probably at least ten years old, but unless someone is new to town, they should be in there."

Hannah and Jack grew up in Alpine Falls, but Hannah's parents don't live there anymore.

Now all I have to do is remember Jack's last name.

Chapter Six

Lucas

It doesn't take me long to get a nice cozy fire going again.

Madison arranges blankets and a pillow in front of it and sits down to read one of my science fiction novels I'd left lying around.

"Let me know if you need me to do anything," she says.

"I will," I say. "I just need to think through some plans for the bedroom."

"You're going to make some changes?" she asks, sitting up, her legs crossed Indian style and setting the book aside. "What kind of changes?"

I pull out a sketchpad and pencil and open it up to one of my previous drawings with precise measurements. I'm not an architect, but my brother is and I might have picked up a few things from him.

With Madison here, I've changed my perspective on some of my previous ideas.

"First of all," I say, studying the drawing. "I'm thinking to add a fireplace to the bedroom."

"That's a great idea." She gets up and walks into the bedroom.

"It should go right here," she says, correctly assuming I followed her to the door. She points to the outside wall between two windows. "It's the logical place. You won't disturb the load-bearing walls and there's still plenty of room for the bed on the other wall. With the windows on either side, add a couple of comfortable chairs and you've got a reading nook."

"Makes perfect sense," I say, wondering why I didn't think about just walking in here and looking around instead of trying to use the drawing to figure it out.

"What else?" she asks, but doesn't give me time to answer. "A free-standing bathtub. You could expand the bathroom and put the tub in front of a window overlooking the river. Do they make glass that's one way?"

"I'll check on that. I'm not sure I have time to add another room though. At least not right now." And since I'm planning on selling the cabin as soon as possible, probably never.

"That's okay. There's enough room in the bathroom for one if you take out one of the sinks and just have one."

"You don't like dual sinks?"

"I think a bathtub wins."

I run a hand over my chin. "It's good to get a female perspective."

"Happy to help."

"Where did you learn so much about design?"

We walk back into the living room and she sits back down on her little makeshift bed.

"It's just a hobby. I hope to make enough money someday that I can build my own house and when I do, I'll know exactly what I want. What about you? Are you an architect or a contractor?"

"Just a handyman," I say.

She nods towards the drawing I have open. "I think maybe you're selling yourself short."

"Maybe," I say. "But it's a just a hobby." I grin at her.

The truth is, since I don't have a degree in architecture, no one has ever taken my design work seriously. I've always been seen as the youngest son who parties and never held a real job. I was the football player who didn't make it to the pros.

But this cabin, if I can make it work, is my chance to save our family's ranch and prove that I can do something besides play sports.

No one had to tell me that the ranch is struggling financially. It's obvious. They laid off all the staff. Sold a few horses. The signs are all there.

After my father's accident, my oldest brother came home to run the ranch and he's doing all he can do. Now that he's getting married, his fiancé (wife) helps out, but it's still not enough. The income just doesn't outweigh the expenses. He has his own small jet and is able to help out by offering flights, but the truth is, they need a windfall.

If I have anything to do with it, I'm the windfall.

Missing my brother's wedding, though, is going to put me back in the doghouse. A doghouse I'm not sure I'll ever be able to climb out of. Even if this avalanche is out of my control.

I sketch in the ideas that Madison gave me. She is so right on target. Sometimes it just takes a fresh perspective.

"I'm going to take Scout out for a walk," I say.

"Okay," she says, not glancing up.

"Come on, Scout. Let's go out." Scout doesn't hesitate to get up and rush to the door.

I put on my coat and open the door. "Hey Madison," I say. "Come see."

Madison gets up and comes to the door.

Her whole face lights up. "It's snowing," she says, stepping outside. No coat.

She stands in the snow and turns her face up to it, her hair soon adorned with snowflakes.

Scout, equally delighted, rushes around trying to catch snowflakes with his mouth.

Crossing my arms, I stand there and watch them. My puppy trying to catch snowflakes and Madison, a southern girl delighted with falling snow.

It's almost worth missing my brother's wedding for.

I'll give her about two minutes before I'm going back inside for her coat.

Chapter Seven

Madison

THE FALLING SNOW, fat fluffy flakes fluttering from the sky, is delightful. I've seen flurries a couple of times. Houston is not without its winter moments. They're just few and far between.

But this snow, falling among the undecorated blue spruce trees is different. As I stand there with the first few flakes falling onto my face, the snow starts falling like silent rain.

Scout, who had been chasing snowflakes, trying to catch them with his mouth, sits down and barks.

I guess he decided if he couldn't catch the snow, he'd bark at it.

Lucas is standing at the cabin doorway watching us both with amusement.

"I'll get your coat," he says.

"It's okay," I say. "I think I'll go inside now."

"Good idea."

But instead of going inside, I stand beneath the alcove next to him while he waits for Scout to decide if it's safe to do his business.

"It's his first winter," I say.

"I think you're right."

"The snow makes it all seem like Christmas."

"It is Christmas."

"But doesn't it make you want to have hot cocoa and sit in front of the fireplace?"

"I guess so."

"You need a Christmas tree," I decide.

He looks over at me sideways.

"If we're going to be stuck here for Christmas, we should have a tree."

"I haven't decided that we're going to be stuck here," he says.

"But the avalanche."

"I'm going to hike down there tomorrow and take a look. See if we can walk out. Both of us need to get to Alpine Falls." He glances down at my sneakers.

"I know," I say. "I need hiking boots."

"Wouldn't hurt. But I don't think anyone in Luchara is going to have any you can buy."

"That's unfortunate," I say. "But these aren't bad."

"They'll be ruined if this snow keeps up."

"It'll be worth it. But... I do have a suitcase full of clothes I need to take with me."

"That might be a problem."

I sag against the door. "How do these things happen?"

"I don't know," he says. "From where I'm sitting, things could be a whole lot worse."

I smile to myself. Same. Things could be a whole lot worse.

Yes. It looks like I'm going to miss my friend's wedding. And yes. I broke my cell phone and now I can't get in touch with her.

And I'm stranded here in the middle of nowhere for who knows how long.

But. On the plus side, I'm stranded in the middle of nowhere with a handsome man who's interesting and has a super cool dog.

Things could most definitely be worse.

Scout finishes up and rushes toward us, ready to go back inside, too.

He goes straight for the blankets I'd arranged on the floor and flops down on them.

"Hey, Mister," I tell the dog. "What makes you think that's your bed?"

Scout just looks at me with big puppy dog eyes.

"He's think you're a sucker," Lucas says.

"I guess I am," I say as I sit down next to the dog. "At least maybe we can share."

Scout actually seems delighted to share the makeshift bed. I settle in and he puts his head on my lap.

"And she stole my dog," Lucas says.

I smile up at Lucas who's sitting on an old wooden chair, sketching on a drafting pad.

I don't say anything, but I wonder, maybe even hope, if maybe he might be just a little bit jealous of his dog.

Chapter Eight

Lucas

As the sun sets over the mountain tops, I go outside to bring in another load of firewood.

It's still snowing and the temperature has definitely dropped a little more.

It's almost time to walk back to the diner to get dinner. I hope Madison isn't one of those girls who needs something different to eat at every meal. I've dated girls like that. The ones who like a variety, always wanting to try something new.

Personally, when I find something I like I can eat it every day. When I was a college student, I ate spaghetti every day for lunch for two years. Two years. I never got tired of it.

Then I moved back to the ranch and my family broke that up.

If Madison needs variety, she's going to be hurting. Mel doesn't have spaghetti, even though he has a decent menu, but since he cooks everything himself, he doesn't branch out much.

I spend a few minutes outside making sure all my tools are put away for the night. Lock up my truck. Not necessary, but a habit. And watch the splash of pinks across the sky as the sun drops behind the mountains. Nature's sand mandala. Every day the world creates a beautiful sunset lasting only moments, letting go of the beauty that returns in a few hours as a brand new day full of promise.

Tomorrow, after I check out the avalanche damage, I'll call my family and give them the news. They've probably heard about the avalanche by now, but they don't know I'm here. They probably think I'm in Denver wasting time.

If they only knew. I'm here. Trying to do my part to save the family ranch.

I refuse to tell them until it actually happens. Until I get the cabin renovated and it sells. This way, in the event that the project falls through somewhere, I don't have to deal with disappointing them. If it works like I hope it does, it'll be a pleasant surprise.

With everything secure for the night, I go back inside where my dog is curled up on the blankets with Madison.

Although she's reading, she looks like she's about half asleep.

I decide to surprise her with some hot cocoa.

I might not have a stove, but I do have an electric tea kettle and some hot cocoa packets.

It doesn't take long to heat the water and stir in the hot chocolate mix.

"I don't have any marshmallows," I say, kneeling next to her and handing her a steaming mug of hot chocolate. "But you might like this."

She straightens up and smiles. "You made hot chocolate."

"I think I heard you mention that you want to drink hot chocolate in front of the fireplace."

She takes a cautious sip. "It's just one of those Christmassy things people do when it snows," she says. "In my imagination."

I stretch out my legs. "And what else do people do in your imagination when it snows at Christmas?"

"They make cookies."

"I can't help you there. Not without a stove."

"It's okay."

"What else?" I sip the hot chocolate and decide it needs to cool before I can drink it.

"A Christmas tree," she says.

"We can do that, but I don't have any decorations."

"Do you have popcorn?"

"I think I can get some. Mel has a microwave."

"We can string it up and use it for decorations. Get some pinecones. We can make origami decorations, too."

"You do origami?" I ask, feeling a little concerned that this just got complicated.

"No. But we can look it up."

"No Internet."

"Oh. Right."

Even though I'm relieved that I'm not going to have to suffer through learning to do origami, I hate seeing that disappointed look on her face and would do just about anything to avoid it. "But," I say. "We can make paper chains."

Her face lights up again. "We did that as kids. We just need construction paper and some glue."

"Are you hungry?" I ask. "We can go by the store on our way to dinner and see what kind of supplies we can find." I glance at my watch. "We have to leave soon, though, if we're going to get there before they close."

"Do we have time to finish our hot chocolate?" she asks.

"Sure. We'll make time."

"So tomorrow we'll go out and cut down a tree," she says. "Christmas Eve is in two days."

"You're not upset that you most probably going to miss being in Alpine Falls for Christmas?"

"I'm not upset about it so much as I hate to disappointment my friends. They were counting on me and I don't like it they're probably worried about me."

"What happened to your cell phone?"

"Dropped it right onto the concrete in an El Paso parking lot. Must have hit just right."

"Must have. I drop my phone all the time."

"I do, too. I should have stopped to replace it, but it always takes hours to do something like that."

"Coulda. Woulda. Shoulda. Life is full of them."

"You're not kidding," she agrees. "This is good, but speaking of shoulds, we should go , shouldn't we? I don't want the store to close on us."

"You're right. I'll just take that mug." I set them aside and hold out a hand. "Can I help you up?"

She puts her hand in mine and I pull her to her feet. Scout gets up, too, and shakes off the nap he'd been indulging in.

"Scout is always ready to go," I say.

"A sign of a good dog."

"The fire looks okay," I say, spreading the ashes around to make sure. The last thing I need is for the cabin to burn down.

We put on our coats and head out into the snow.

I have to admit, even for a jaded local, used to the snow, it's all quite charming.

But it's not the snow.

It's the delightful girl walking along beside me.

Chapter Nine

Madison

SOMEHOW NO ONE in town has a phonebook.

"People take them for artifacts," Mel says. "They sell them online."

"Why would they do that?" I ask.

"Anything for a buck," Mel says. "What can I get you to eat?"

"Let us take a minute to study the menu," Lucas says.

"If you don't have the menu memorized by now," Mel says. "I'm worried about you."

Lucas gives him a scathing look. "I'm not the only one here, am I?"

Mel shrugs and walks back to the kitchen.

"He seems grouchy," I say, leaning forward to whisper to Lucas.

"He is. Always. But he's a good cook."

"I guess that makes up for his grouchiness," I say, but I'm not so sure. "Are you planning on putting in an oven?"

"So now you want to start cooking," Lucas says.

"Just making conversation," I say, looking over the menu that wouldn't take any time at all to memorize.

"I actually have one on order."

"Well, so much for those plans," I say. "We have hurricanes. You have avalanches."

"At least you get some warning for hurricanes," he says.

"Usually. That is true."

Scout is sitting on the floor on one side of us and we have bags of supplies we got from the store on the other side. I never thought I'd be so happy to find a pack of construction paper, scissors, and a glue stick.

I might be stuck out here in the middle of nowhere for Christmas, but that doesn't mean we can't have the little cabin looking at least a little bit festive.

"Do you know what you want?" Lucas asks.

"The tuna sandwich and fries."

"Good choice. I'll have that, too." He holds up a hand and after getting Mel's attention, relays our order.

"Why doesn't he hire some help?" I ask.

"I guess he doesn't think he needs it."

"I guess. It just seems a little weird having one person doing everything."

"You have to remember that there aren't that many

people coming in. In fact, I think I'm his only regular when I'm in town."

"Good point." Especially since there aren't any other customers in the diner at the moment. "Is your family expecting you for Christmas?"

"Of course. I'll call them in the morning after I check out the damage from the avalanche. Tell them I'm not going to make it."

"If they happen to know Hannah and Jack, ask them to let them know I'm not going to make the wedding."

Lucas just looks blankly at me. Seconds pass. "Hannah and Jack Thompson?" he finally asks.

"That's his last name. I couldn't remember. Wait. You know them?"

"You could say that," he says.

"Oh. Wow. Do you think you could get a message to them?"

"Madison," he says. "Jack is my brother."

Chapter Ten

Lucas

MADISON IS LOOKING at me as though I've lost a marble.
I'm probably looking about the same at her.

"So you're Hannah's friend. The one coming up from
Houston for the wedding."

"Yes. And you're one of Jack's brothers."

"Yes."

"That's all I know about you. Hannah hasn't told me
anything else. Just that Jack has two brothers."

"That kind of figures," I say. "They don't see me much."

"Why not?"

"I guess because I spend a lot of time here." I don't tell

her that I live in an apartment over the barn at my family's ranch. That I don't spend a lot of time over at the house.

"That and she's overly preoccupied with Jack."

"I've never known two people to be more preoccupied with each other," I say. "Except maybe my parents. They're pretty much that way, too."

"I guess that's where Jack gets it."

"I suppose so."

"You don't take after your parents?"

"Not in that way. Trenton, that's my other brother, swears I was adopted."

She smiles. "Were you?"

"Hardly. Our mother will box anyone's ears who even hints at that."

"Your mother sounds like a tough woman."

"She is. She and Dad have worked really hard taking care of that ranch. After Dad's accident, though, she just sort of shifted everything over to Jack."

"What about your other brother? Trenton?"

"Trenton? He's an architect and lives in Boulder. He's not interested in the ranch life."

"That's too bad."

"Why do you say that?"

"No reason," she says with a little shrug. "It's just that it's a family business and it seems like everyone would want to pitch in."

"Yeah. It does, doesn't it?"

She's not wrong. Mucking stalls has never been my thing, but I'm doing my part now. In my own way. Or at least I'm trying to. I'm just crossing my fingers that this cabin venture pays off.

The avalanche has definitely put a damper on things.

Madison leans back in her chair. "I feel so much better now."

"How is that?"

"For one thing, you'll be able to let Hannah know where I am. So that's a relief. And the other thing is selfish on my part."

"Now you have to tell me."

"I don't feel so bad about being the only one to miss the wedding."

"Misery loves company."

"It's not that," she says. "It's almost like you're part of the family. And if we're stuck here in the middle of nowhere, at least I—."

"Hey." Mel stops at our table and sets our plates in front of us. "Be careful about your comments."

"Sorry," she says, looking up at the grouchy old man. "But you've got to admit that it's kind of true."

Mel shrugs and walks away. "Anyway," she finishes her thought. "I don't feel so alone."

"Me either," I say, looking into her deep green eyes.

She smiles before dipping a French fry in ketchup.

Who would have thought I'd meet the most charming woman ever right here in the little town of Luchara?

Chapter Eleven

Madison

Lucas is quite ingenuous. He brought a set of sawhorses inside and balanced a piece of plywood over the top of them to make a table.

We pull up the two wooden chairs on either side of the table and get to work on making our Christmas decorations.

"I may have to find somewhere else to sleep," I say.

"Why is that?" Lucas asks as he sorts through the construction paper, pulling out all the Christmas colors, not just red and green, but blue and white and gray.

"Scout has taken over my bed."

"You can't blame him. It's the best seat in the house."

"I guess after you get it renovated, you'll buy some furniture," I say.

"Maybe," he says as he takes the glue out of the package.

"You think the avalanche is going to turn Luchara into a ghost town," I say in response to his noncommittal response.

"I hope not." He looks at me with something akin to horror.

"Sorry. You just seem like you're worried about it."

"I am worried about it. How wide are we going to make the strips?"

"I don't know. I think part of the charm is having them uneven."

"Maybe when we were seven," he says. "I think we should measure them out. Maybe half an inch."

"Okay then. You measure and cut. I'll glue."

He takes a ruler and starts measuring off half inch strips.

"You were serious?"

"We don't want our tree looking like a child decorated it."

I give him a look. "They're paper strips. They aren't going to exactly look like designer décor."

"Good point. Still. I prefer to measure."

"Okay." While he measures, I walk over to the kitchen counter and fill a bowl with popcorn Mel popped for us and bring it to our table.

"I thought that was for decoration," he says as I pick up a handful and start eating it.

"It would be if we had a needle and thread."

"Ah ha," he says. "But I've been thinking about that. I

found some fishing line in a box and there's a fish hook that we can use as a needle."

I drop the uneaten popcorn back into the bowl. "Now you tell me."

"I actually just thought of it," he says with a disarming grin that sends butterflies slamming about in my stomach.

"Are you sure you don't want me to cut some of those?"

"Okay. But I hope you have a steady hand," he says, sliding a piece of red construction paper with precise lines in my direction.

I pick up the scissors and start cutting. "Are you sure you aren't an architect?" I ask.

"I'm sure. That's my brother's thing. So Trenton got a degree in architecture. Jack majored in aviation. And I, believe it or not, majored in psychology."

"Psychology?" I stop cutting and study him. "I would not have guessed that."

"Yeah well. Turns out it's not worth much as an undergraduate degree. Takes advanced degrees to do anything with it."

"You didn't want to get an advanced degree?"

"Nope." He keeps his gaze down, focused on drawing exact lines over a piece of green paper. "My plan was to play football."

"Now that I can see. Did you play in college?"

"I did. It's actually the whole reason I went to college. But I didn't make the pros."

"I'm sorry."

"It's okay. I don't think I would've cared much for the lifestyle."

I go back to cutting strips. "So you decided to become a handyman instead."

"I've been learning construction since I was a kid following my uncle around. It was either that or muck out stalls."

"I'm not sure what that is, but it doesn't sound like something I'd want to do either."

"You wouldn't like it."

I take the cap off the stick of glue and secure two ends of one of the paper strips together.

Holding it up, I frown at it. "I think we're going to have to make these strips smaller."

"You want a small chain?"

"I think it would look better, don't you? Let's try it." I pick up the scissors and snip one of the strips in half then glue the ends. "Better?"

Lucas takes his ruler and draws a mark down the middle of the paper he's currently measuring out. "Done," he says.

"You're funny."

"Yeah. Well. That's what my family keeps saying. But they don't mean it as a compliment."

He keeps his face down, making it hard for me to see his expression, but I don't have to be a psychologist to sense the hurt he's feeling.

"Your family is wrong," I say. They're wrong about him. And right now I'm thinking maybe it's a good thing that I'm the one who gets to spend Christmas with Lucas.

If his family doesn't understand him, then I'm the lucky one.

Chapter Twelve

Lucas

"I THINK we're good for the night," I say, stretching a blanket out onto the floor. "We've got three sleeping areas. With Scout in the middle."

"He snagged the best spot," Madison says.

"That's okay. He's acting chaperone for the evening."

Madison grins. "Funny."

"We've got plenty of firewood and the little heater behind us."

"It's nice and warm. As long as we don't lose power, we should be good. Does the power ever go out up here?"

"I have no idea," I say. "I hope not."

"At least we have a candle and a flashlight."

"So... do you want me to let you sleep in or do you want to get up early and walk to the diner for coffee?"

"Does coffee include breakfast?"

"It can. I don't think Mel ever leaves the diner."

"Then I'm in."

"A breakfast girl. Interesting."

"What? You have something against breakfast?"

"Breakfast is my favorite meal of the day."

"I can't tell if you're being serious." She carefully arranges the paper garland which looks surprisingly good. She calls it ombre, keeping like colors together with an elaborate plan to wrap them artfully around the tree we're going out tomorrow to chop down.

"I would never jest about breakfast," I say.

"Good to know," she says, stifling a yawn.

I add a log to the fireplace and use an iron poker to rearrange the logs.

"We have a big day ahead of us tomorrow," I say.

"Yes. About that. I'd like to walk with you down to the avalanche area."

"Sure. We should see what the weather's doing though before we plan to go very far."

"Okay," she says, obviously disappointed.

"I have an extra pair of boots in the truck," I say. "We can try lacing them up really tight. See if you can walk in them."

"Okay," she says, with a smile. "Just wondering. Does the shower work?"

"It's not much to look at, but it works just fine."

"Good. I'd like to shower before we start our day."

"I'll wake you up early. Walk to the diner to get us coffee while you shower. Then we'll walk back to the diner for breakfast and on to the avalanche area."

"Then we'll go chop down our tree."

"Yes. I suppose we'll go chop down a tree."

"You still have hope that we'll get out of here," she says.

"Even though I know better, yes, I guess I do. I've never missed Christmas with my family."

"Then we need to manifest a miracle," she says.

I don't know about manifesting a miracle, but I do know that we'll find a way out of here. I just haven't figured out exactly what that way will be yet.

Chapter Thirteen

Madison

I HONESTLY HADN'T THOUGHT I'd be able to sleep in a strange place with a stranger sleeping just a few feet away.

But with the distant roar of the rushing river outside and the gentle crackling of the fire in the fireplace and, Scout's soft snoring, I soon find myself drifting off.

Lucas has been nothing less than a perfect gentleman.

And especially now that I know he's practically family, I expect no less. His brother is marrying one of my two best friends. Hannah. I haven't known Hannah nearly as long as I've known Olivia, but Olivia and I just sort of took Hannah into our fold and now she's one of us.

So she's family and that means Lucas is family.

I hate to miss Hannah's wedding, even if she is already technically married to Jack. She thought they were divorced for ten years, but not Jack. Jack waited for her. For ten years.

I wonder just how long he really would have waited. Maybe he knew Hannah would show up one day looking for divorce papers so she could get remarried. It's hard to say.

Whatever he was thinking, his steadfastness to Hannah is like nothing I've ever heard of.

I only met Jack once. Briefly. At a pizza place in Houston. It was months ago. Long enough ago that I don't remember him enough to really compare him to Lucas.

I do remember that he was good looking and Lucas definitely shares that family trait.

Lucas is not only good looking, he's good hearted. He's been going out of his way to make me happy.

He made me hot chocolate, even if it wasn't very good. I'd never tell him. It's the thought that counts and our situation doesn't allow for much.

He set up a table and helped me make Christmas decorations for a tree we don't have yet.

And he's keeping a warm fire going.

I have to admit that I'm quite charmed by him.

Before I know it, I'm drifting off and the next thing I know, I hear Lucas talking to me.

"Good morning, Sunshine," he says. At first I think I must be dreaming, but I pry my eyes open enough to see him kneeling in front of me.

I stretch beneath the warm blankets and try to decide if

it's morning with nothing to go on other than the soft glow of the flames in the hearth.

"I had to take Scout outside," he says. "So I went ahead and picked up coffee."

"Coffee in bed," I say, sitting up. "Doesn't get much better than that."

After he hands me one of the paper cups, I take a sip. "Perfect," I say and I mean it.

"I figured anyone who likes hot chocolate would like a latte."

"You figured right," I say, enjoying the hot coffee.

He sits down on his pallet, but Scout decides he wants to share mine again.

"Good morning, Scout," I say. "Did you have a good walk?"

"He made snow angels."

"You did not," I say, rubbing Scout's head. "Is it still snowing?" I look toward the window, but it's still too dark to tell.

"Not right now, but it's a winter wonderland out there."

"Oh. I can't wait to see it."

"Get your shower and put on some warm clothes. It's not going anywhere anytime soon."

"That bad, huh?"

"I brought these boots in for you to try." He holds up a pair of well-worn, broken-in boots. "If we were in Alpine Falls, I'd know exactly where you could get boots."

"It's okay. After I get showered and dressed, I'll try them. Thank you. For the coffee and the boots."

"Don't mention it. Did you sleep well?"

"I guess I did. I didn't even really know I'd fallen asleep until I heard you talking."

"I hate waking someone up when they're sleeping," he says. "But I'm a man of my word and I told you I'd wake you up."

"What about you? Did you sleep well?"

"I always sleep well here. It's just amazingly quiet and peaceful."

"Coming from the man who grew up in a quaint little small town."

"How do you know it's quaint?"

"Hannah told me."

The hot coffee has me awake and now that I'm awake, I'm ready to get the day started. Lucas and I have a big day planned. For two people stranded in the middle of nowhere, we have a long to-do list.

Chapter Fourteen

Lucas

THE AVALANCHE AREA is worse than I expected. It literally wiped away any signs that the road was ever even there. Instead of a road alongside a mountain, there's nothing there but, well, the side of a mountain with a ton of it, dirt and rocks, mostly lying in a pile at the bottom of the canyon.

The state police is there with a couple of engineers and they won't let us anywhere near the area.

Madison, wearing her white wool coat with a festive scarf in Christmas red, stands next to me, looking quite frankly, a little ill. She has one hand on Scout's collar. I guess so maybe he won't try to dash off into the rubble.

She looks rather cute wearing my boots, way too big for her. Just knowing that she's wearing my boots gives me a warm feeling inside.

"It's going to be okay," I say, feeling the need to comfort even as I knew the words are empty.

The avalanche was bad. If there wasn't a little village on the other side of it, it would easily have become one of those roads that never gets repaired. In fact, it might anyway. They might figure out a way to get everyone out and let it go. Call it a loss.

In the event that happens, some people will never recover financially. My situation isn't good, but I'll recover. My cabin is an investment project, not something I've put my whole life into.

Like Mel. If forced to abandon his diner, what will become of him. Him and the other merchants?

I angle my thoughts around, away from the worst case scenario and try to focus on the positive. There's no sign of anyone being hurt.

Things could have been so very worse.

"What do we do?" Madison asks.

"We do our thing and let them do theirs. They'll let us know when they have it figured out."

"Is there a way for us to hike out of here?" she asks.

"I don't know. But I do know that they'll figure something out. There are too many lives at stake for them not to."

"We should go and call Hannah and Jack," she says. "Let them know we aren't going to make their wedding tomorrow."

"I guess there's no time like the present to get it over with."

"They'll understand," she says. "I know we don't have Internet, but can you take some photos with your phone and send them to me when I get my phone replaced?"

"Sure." I pull my phone out of my pocket and snap some shots of the avalanche area.

"It's so pretty here," she says wistfully.

"Beautiful, but deadly," I say.

The walk back to town isn't long. I'm still surprised no one heard the avalanche. I guess everyone was just going about their business, not paying any attention to the outside world. Probably listening to music or television or talking on their phones. It just went unnoticed.

And small propeller airplane passes overhead, flying low, as we walk back to town.

"Reporters?" Madison asks.

"Maybe. Or someone just out taking a look."

Back at the general store to use the phone, everyone wants to see the photos.

And everyone is talking about what's going to happen next.

The old timers are saying Lachara will become a ghost town after they get everyone out.

The younger people are hopeful that the road can somehow be repaired.

The few tourists just want to get out. They don't care what happens.

Me? I'm a little torn. On the one hand, I really want to

get out of here and get home to my family for Christmas and my brother's wedding.

But on the other hand, I'm enjoying spending time with Madison. Under normal circumstances, she and I would probably never have gotten to know each other like this.

We would have simply been introduced, then we would have gone our separate ways. She would have hung out with her friends, Hannah and Olivia. And I would have minded my own business, whatever that happened to be at the time.

Even in the midst of a disastrous situation, I can't help but think that this avalanche, somehow, was good.

Chapter Fifteen

Madison

Both Hannah and Olivia both get on the phone with me after Lucas tells Jack what happened.

"I'm so glad you're okay," Hannah says to me then she says to Olivia. "I told you we should have checked on her while we were in Houston."

"It's okay," I say. "You wouldn't have found me no matter what you did."

"I just can't believe you ended up in the same place as Lucas," Olivia says. "He wasn't supposed to be there and you weren't supposed to be there. It's just so strange."

"It's fate," Hannah says.

Looking across the room at Lucas, I send him a helpless expression. He just smiles.

He's standing next to a stand of paperbacks, flipping through one book, then another, looking for something to read since I guess I took his book yesterday. Scout is sitting at his feet.

Maybe it is fate. Or coincidence. Or accidental.

Whatever it is, I'm not complaining.

"Look," I say. "I'm on somebody's landline, probably running up a big phone bill for long-distance."

"Is that a thing?" Olivia asks.

"Yes," Hannah says. "Remember where you are."

"I just wanted to let you know I'm okay and I'll be there when I can. If I can. I'm not going to make the wedding and I'm sorry about that."

"It can't be helped," Hannah says. "Just take care of yourself."

"I will. I love you both."

"We love you, too. Merry Christmas!"

I put the receiver down to disconnect the line.

Squaring my shoulders, I walk over to join Lucas.

"How did Jack take the news?" I ask.

"After he got past the part about being confused about me being here, he actually thought it was a little funny. Not the avalanche part. But the part about you ending up here. Staying in my cabin."

"Yeah. The girls kind of had a hard time with that one, too."

We walk outside. "Too early for lunch," he says. "Feel like going to look for a tree?"

"Sure."

"Boots holding up okay?"

"Not bad." I send him a little smile. I like knowing that I'm wearing his boots, even if they are way too big for me. "Olivia said something that struck me as a little odd."

"Yeah. What's that?" he asks as we veer down the path leading to his cabin, freshly fallen snow crunching beneath our boots.

"She said you aren't supposed to be here."

"They didn't know where I was," he says.

"They don't know about the cabin?" I ask carefully.

"They do not."

I wait for him to volunteer more. Scout runs ahead, then disappears into the trees and comes up behind us.

"He likes doing that, doesn't he?" I ask.

"Yes. He's a little crazy sometimes."

"He's cute."

"When I was in college playing football," Lucas says, picking up a stick and tossing it ahead of Scout. "I'd go for weeks without talking to my family. They had no idea where I was or what I was doing."

"You were busy," I say.

"I was actually a little wild. They got used to it." He looks unseeing off into the distance. "They still think of me as being irresponsible and they don't expect much out of me."

Scout brings the stick back and drops it at Lucas's feet. "I didn't know you could do that," Lucas tells him.

"But you are responsible. You're working."

"Sort of," he says. "Wait here while I get the axe."

I wait while he gets an axe out of a tool cabinet in the back of his truck.

As he tosses the axe over his shoulder, we start walking again, behind the cabin now.

"I bought this cabin," he says. "for the purpose of fixing it up and selling it for a profit."

"So you're flipping it?" I'm a bit impressed now and things are starting to make sense. Like his lack of commitment in buying furniture.

"Yeah. No point in keeping it a secret anyone. No one's going to buy a cabin they can't drive to."

"You never know," I say.

"I was planning to sell it and use the money to help out around the ranch. My way of helping out the family," he says.

"Why didn't you tell them?" I ask as we reach the rushing river and walk alongside it.

"Because in the event it didn't work, they'd just see it as me making a bad decision."

"I don't know," I say, carefully stepping onto a boulder at the water's edge. "I think they would appreciate the effort."

"Maybe," he says. "I guess I wasn't willing to take that chance. It's a moot point now."

"There," I say, pointing across the river. "There's our tree."

"I'm sure there are plenty of trees on this side of the river," he says.

"But that one's perfect," I say.

He mutters something about women beneath his breath, but I see the smile on his face.

He doesn't need to know that I did that one purpose. To distract him.

And it worked.

Chapter Sixteen

Lucas

"You really want that tree?" I ask. "The one across the river?"

"It looks perfect from here," Madison says.

I can't tell if she's being difficult on purpose or if she's messing with me.

Doesn't much matter so much. If the tree she wants is across the river, that's the tree I'm going to get for her.

"Come on, then," I say.

"Where are we going?"

"You'll see."

It's an extra quarter mile around, but definitely worth it.

"We're going to walk across this bridge," I say. "then see if we can find that tree again."

"Everything does all kind of start to blend together," she says.

We walk across the little wooden bridge and backtrack to the area where we'd seen the tree.

"Is this it?" I ask, stopping in front of a blue spruce tree.

She looks back across the river. I know she has no idea.

Not with the snow on the ground.

"Yes," she says.

"How do you know?"

She puts a hand over her eyes. "I see our footprints across the river. That's where we turned around."

"Impressive. Very impressive. There's hope for you city girl after all."

She smiles. "Never underestimate a Houston girl."

"You sure this is the one you want?" I ask, walking around it. "It's too tall for the cabin."

"That's okay. You can cut the bottom off of it. Right?"

"Sure," I say. "Why not?"

"How does this work?" she asks.

"You have to take Scout and stand back."

"Okay. How far?"

"Next to the river would be good."

"Come on Scout." She taps her leg and Scout happily follows.

When I deem her far enough away to be safe, I go about the business of chopping down the tree. It crashes to the ground right where I planned.

Now for the hard part. Getting the tree back to the cabin.

Picking up the tree trunk, I start dragging it.

"Can I help?" Madison asks.

"Just lead the way," I say. "I'll follow you."

"And I'll follow Scout."

Scout is ahead of both of us.

"He's just hungry," I say.

"I'm a little hungry, too," she says, walking along beside me.

"It's the fresh mountain air."

"It must be because I don't eat much."

"We'll fix that," I say.

"Until Mel runs out of food."

"Good point. Someone will drop in food. Too many people here for them to ignore."

"What if it was just us?" she asks.

"What do you mean?"

"What would they do if we were the only ones on this side of the avalanche? Would they drop us food?"

"They would probably evacuate us."

"Then why don't they just evacuate everyone?" she asks.

"I guess they have to figure it out."

With me still dragging the tree, we cross the bridge and follow the trail back to the cabin. We walk in silence, each lost in our own thoughts.

Since I can only deal with what I know, I contemplate how I'm going to cut the tree so that it fits inside the cabin.

There's a pitched area of the ceiling in one corner that will add a couple of feet if we put the tree there.

"There's someone at our door," Madison says, slowing down.

Pulling myself out of my thoughts, I look up to see the cabin just coming into view. Sure enough. There are two men standing at the door.

Chapter Seventeen

Madison

I TAMP down my annoyance at having someone disturb my time with Lucas.

I've accepted the fact that I'm going to be spending Christmas here in Luchara with Lucas.

Accepted and now I'm looking forward to it.

Two men waiting for us at the door of our cabin was not in my equation.

Lucas quietly drops the tree, leaving it behind before they see us.

"Do you know them?" I whisper.

"No," he says, keeping his eyes on them.

"Should we be worried?"

"No," he says, squaring his shoulders.

The two guys see us now, so we stop talking. Lucas walks slightly in front of me as though ready to shield me in an instant.

"Can I help you?" he asks.

The two men are dressed in work clothes beneath heavy down coats and carrying clips boards in their hands. They're wearing hard hats over wool caps. They're dressed a lot like the engineers we saw out at the avalanche area to me, but I don't think they're the same people.

"This your place?" the older one asks. Both men are wearing beards and the younger one is wearing glasses.

"It is."

"My name is Ralph and this here is Teddy. We're canvasing the area to get a firm count on how many people are stranded up here."

"How did you get in here?" Lucas asks.

"Parachuted," the younger man says.

"Well, there's just the two of us," Lucas says. "And my dog."

"Can we get your names?" Teddy asks, ready to write on his clipboard.

Lucas hesitates, but then tells them. It's not that they couldn't just ask someone anyway.

"Lucas Thompson and Madison." He looks at me.

"Lane," I say. "Madison Lane."

"And Scout," Lucas says, putting a hand on Scout's collar.

"How many days do you estimate your supplies will last?" Teddy reads the next question off his list.

"Don't have any," Lucas says. "We're using the diner."

The two men look at each other.

"Do you need anything in the immediate future?" Ralph asks, putting a stop to Teddy's list of questions.

"Depends on what you call the immediate future."

"Now," Ralph says. "Looks like you're safe for the moment."

"I'd say we are."

"We'll get out of your hair, then", Ralph says. "Here's my card if you need anything."

"Don't have cell phone service," Lucas says, not moving.

"Well. Right. I'll just leave it here." Ralph sticks the business card into the door jamb. "Take care now."

We watch as they turn and walk away. We watch them until they disappear around a curve in the road.

"You don't trust them," I say.

"Don't know them. They didn't show us any identification."

I don't bother to mention that he didn't ask, but I get what he's saying. There are scammers everywhere. Not just in the city.

"I'll get our tree," he says. "Make sure Scout doesn't run after them."

I wrap my fingers around Scout's collar and wonder how I could keep a dog as big as a horse from doing anything he wanted to do.

Chapter Eighteen

Lucas

APPARENTLY MY OVERCAUTIOUSNESS WAS ILL-FOUNDED. Ralph and Teddy have been making the rounds, getting everyone's information. They're with some state agency or another.

"What do you think they're going to do?" I ask Mel.

It's the middle of the afternoon and we're the only ones left in the diner after a busy lunch time.

Mel slings a dishcloth over his shoulder. "Not a damn thing."

"Well somebody has to do something," I say.

Madison and I are sitting on two barstools at Mel's counter. He doesn't usually keep barstools out, but with the avalanche and everyone coming in to get information and a little food to go along with it, he had to pull out some more seating.

Mel flips over a hamburger patty sizzling on the grill. "They don't care. What they might do is drop off a few supplies."

"Then how do you propose we all get out of here?"

"I guess I'll be staying."

"Mel," I say with a glance at Madison. "You're going to run out of supplies. What are you going to do?"

"If it comes to that, I'll live off the land."

"Is there another road?" Madison asks, hopefully.

"One way in. One way out," Mel says.

"What about a trail?"

"Not unless you can scale the side of a mountain." Mel flips the burger again.

"I guess that answers that question," I say to Madison.

"I guess it does." She sits back looking a little defeated.

"You hungry?" Mel asks.

We both shake our heads. Mel proceeds to put the hamburger together, then sits down in front of us and proceeds to eat. There's a first time for everything.

"Do you have a map?" I ask him.

Mel reaches under the counter and slaps a dogeared paper map onto the counter.

I spread it out in front of us and get my bearings. Lachera is the perfect place for people to escape and get away from it all.

Until it isn't.

Madison looks over my shoulder. "What about that road right there?" she asks.

Mel shakes his head and doesn't even bother to look up.

"I don't think that's a road," I say.

"There really isn't any way out of here is there?" she asks.

"Doesn't look like it."

Mel finishes off his burger and gets up to start cleaning the grill. The man never takes a break.

"I think," I say. "We just need to go back. Decorate our tree and enjoy Christmas as best we can. Nothing's going to happen until after Christmas anyway."

She nods and forces a little smile.

"Hey," I say. "It's what we planned anyway, remember? We do have the perfect tree."

"You're right," she says, straightening. "It'll all work out."

"Of course it will." I put a hand over hers and gently squeeze it.

I get it that she's a little afraid. But we have everything we need for right now.

We may not get out of here in time for Christmas, but we'll get out in due time.

No matter what Mel says, I have faith in that.

Chapter Nineteen

Madison

On the walk home, with Scout leading the way, I find myself thinking about too many things at one time.

"Penny for your thoughts," Lucas says.

"Really? Okay. But promise you won't laugh."

"Why not? Is it funny?"

"No. It's not funny." I elbow him. "If you laugh, I won't tell you anything else."

"I won't laugh. Scout's honor."

I narrow my eyes at him. "Where you a boy scout?"

"Yes."

I look at him sideways.

"Honest. I was."

"Okay. I was wondering what would happen if we never get out of here. What if we're stuck here for the rest of our lives and we grow old here?"

He laughs out loud.

"You promised you wouldn't laugh." I put my hands on my hips and glare at him.

"I'm sorry. But it's funny."

"How is it funny? Seriously? What if we're stuck here?"

"If we're stuck here, then we'll have a passel of beautiful children."

My eyes widen, wondering how he got to that exactly. "Presumptuous much?"

"No. But if we're stuck here, it'll be like being on a deserted island. We'll be forced to… I mean." He smiles a bit rakishly and I have to admit I get a funny feeling in my stomach. "What else are we going to do?"

"Okay. Let's decorate our tree. Enjoy Christmas in the quiet forest. And know that somehow they'll miraculously rebuild the road in no time."

"Exactly. We follow the plan."

"The plan," I say with a little shake of my head.

"What?"

"It's just funny. I have my life planned out on a spreadsheet."

"Now you're purposely trying to be funny."

"I'm not being funny. I really do have a spreadsheet. Mostly career. I was thinking maybe it's time to make some changes. But… this… this is a little off in left field from what I was thinking."

"Being stranded in the mountains?"

"Yes. With no technology. It's hard to make a career change without the Internet."

"Oh. I don't know. There's a lot you could do."

"Like what?" Scout races up behind us.

"Like we could raise puppies and sell them."

That's unsettlingly close to what I do right now. "Who would we sell them to?"

"We'd have to barter them to the other people who are stuck here."

"Okay. Not exactly profitable. What else do you have?"

"You could make origami?"

"And how exactly would that be profitable?" I ask.

"We could box it up and send it out with drones."

I stop walking and just stand there looking at him.

"I think we need to figure a way to hike out of here."

He runs a hand along the side of his truck. "I sure do hate to give up my truck," he says.

"Do you think insurance will cover our vehicles?" I ask, looking at my own car.

"There's probably a clause in there about abandonment."

"You're probably right."

He unlocks the front door to the cabin and I follow Scout inside, flipping on the light as I go. Lucas turns on the little heater and starts laying a fire in the fireplace.

I sit down on my blanket. "All I know is it's good to be home."

Chapter Twenty

Lucas

I GLANCE over my shoulder at Madison. She's lying back on her blanket, her eyes closed.

I don't think she even realized what she just said.

She'd called this little cabin home.

I'd laughed at her being worried about us being stuck here and growing old. I'd laughed because it was funny.

It's not going to happen.

The thing is I can think of worst ways to spend a life than spending it stranded here in the mountains with Madison. Far worse ways.

It won't happen though. I have some ideas. They just aren't fleshed out well enough to share them.

After I get a fire going, I leave Madison napping and go outside to cut the bottom off the tree. I use a hand saw because it's quieter than a chain saw even if it is a whole lot slower.

After I have what I think is a good height for it, I saw off some of the bottom limbs and open the door to drag it inside.

Madison sits up, pushing her hair out of her face, looking all sleepy.

"Good nap?" I ask.

"I wasn't sleeping," she says.

"No? Okay. I might need your help making sure I get this tree standing up straight."

"You already cut the bottom off." She stands up and stretches.

There are definitely worse things than being stuck out her with her. In fact, right now I'm having trouble thinking of anything better.

"We have to get this thing up and decorated," I say. "Tomorrow is Christmas Eve."

"We should go into town," she says. "And buy some presents to wrap up. Put them under the tree."

"That's a good idea," I say. "It's a great idea, actually."

She grins. "We definitely have to get presents for Scout."

"And each other."

"That might be a little more difficult. I think the shelves are going to be bare pretty quickly."

"We'll find something. And if we don't, we'll make something. We still have construction paper and glue."

"I still don't know origami."

"It's okay," I say, tightening the screws that will hold the tree in the stand we'd bought at the general store.

"We don't have lights," she says.

"Not necessary. We're having an old-fashioned Christmas."

"An old-fashioned Christmas. I like that."

"Here goes," I say, standing the tree upright. "How does it look?"

"It looks perfect," she says, clasping her hands together.

I slide one of the wooden chair over and climb up. "Hand me whichever of those paper chains you want to put on top."

She hands me the yellow one. I wrap it around the top of the tree.

"I have a challenge for you," I say.

"What's that? I'm always up for a challenge."

"Figure out what you want to make for a tree topper."

"Like a star?"

"Yes. Like a star. What color goes next?"

She hands me the pale green chain and I wrap it around the tree.

"We're getting somewhere," I say.

"It's going to look good," she says. "No matter what people might say."

"Who could possibly make fun of our tree? It's a lovely blue spruce. And I take offense to any criticism."

"Me too."

She hands me the gray chain next.

"I think this ombre thing is going to work."

"You had doubts?" she asks.

"None to speak of."

"I think that means yes."

"Nah. I trust you." I climb off the chair. "What's next?"

We finish up with dark blue paper chains at the bottom.

"We forgot to do the popcorn," she says.

"I thought we'd make those next."

We settle down at our plywood table, the big bowl of popcorn between us, and I hand her a fishing line with a hook I straightened on the end.

"Have you ever done this before?" I ask.

"Honestly," she says. "No. Actually this thing looks a bit dangerous," she says as she examines the rusty fish hook.

"Maybe I should do that part," I say. "There's no ER in Lachera. You can be in charge of making sure things don't get tangled up."

"I think I can handle it," she says, but she hands me the ugly-looking hook anyway.

"Besides," I say. "You have to work on the tree-topper."

"Right." She glances back at the tree, then slides the stack of construction paper toward her. "What color are you thinking?"

"You're in charge of that part."

"Red," she says. "We have one piece of red left."

"Red it is. We really need a video on how to string up this popcorn."

"How hard can it be? Just stab it through the middle."

"You make things sound so easy."

She smiles and my heart melts.

I know that no matter what it is, if she wants me to do something, I'll do everything I can to make it happen.

Chapter Twenty-One

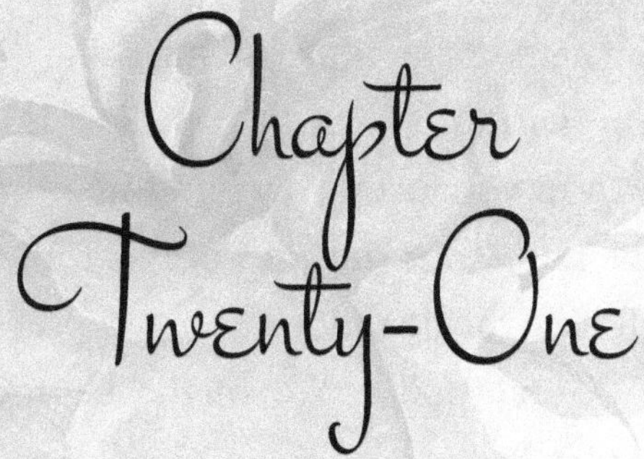

Madison

"It was nice of Mel to let us use his kitchen," I say.

We'd gotten caught up in our tree decorating activities and by the time we got back to the diner, Mel was closing up.

"Yes. It was. Even if all he left us with was a frozen pizza."

"I happen to have a fondness for frozen pizza," I say.

"Okay. Let me see if I can follow directions here," He says as he reads the back of the pizza box.

"I think you just sort of throw it in there."

He looks up. "Wait a minute. The girl who has a spreadsheet outlining her life doesn't follow cooking directions?"

"I pick my battles," I say. "Actually I do read boxes. That's how I know you just throw it in there."

"Okay," he says. "But since we only have one pizza, I'm just going to follow the directions."

I wince. "Good point. We might be rationing food before we know it."

"It's not going to come to that," he says with certainty, keeping his gaze on the back of the pizza box.

"You sound rather sure of that."

"I'm manifesting."

"How does that work exactly?" I take two bottles of water from the refrigerator and set them on the our table.

The shades are drawn and the doors are locked, so we have the diner to ourselves.

Scout ate a bowl of dog food, then curled up in front of the door and went to sleep.

"I wish I knew," he says, finally sliding the pizza into the oven. "I think I could have achieved a lot more."

"I know, right. What do you think Jack and Hannah are doing right now?" I ask.

"Probably watching a movie with Trenton and Olivia."

"Are Trenton and Olivia really a thing?"

"I think they are."

"Don't we think that's odd?"

"I don't think I'm going to answer that right now," he says.

Smiling to myself, I wander back to the kitchen. "He's got a sound system in here."

"Really? I didn't know that."

"You've never been back here in the kitchen, have you?"

"Not even once. How does that thing work?"

"I don't know." I press a button and music starts filling the diner. "I guess it just works like that."

"Eighties music. Mel has good taste."

I smile. "I never would have thought it."

When a familiar slow song starts playing, Lucas holds out a hand. "Care to dance?" he asks.

"Here?"

"Why not?"

"Okay." I put a hand in his and he pulls me close.

He's taller than me. I hadn't quite realized how much. The top of my head reaches just beneath his chin.

"This might be the best Christmas I've ever had," he says.

I look up, my gaze meeting his. "I don't know what to think about that."

I don't know what to think, because I know it's the best Christmas I've ever had.

He suddenly twirls me around and brings me back against him.

"You're good at this," I say. "Did you learn to dance in your wild football days?"

"Something like that."

"I can't tell if that's a yes or a no," I say.

"None of that matters now," he says, looking into my eyes.

"It made you who you are," I say, feeling slightly breathless.

"True. But all that matters is right here. Right now."

The timer on the oven goes off, alerting us that our pizza might be ready.

"I have to get that," he says.

"I know."

He kisses me on the forehead and leaves me to pull our frozen pizza out of the oven.

I drop into the nearest chair and wonder just how much trouble I'm getting myself into.

By such a quirk of chance I ended up here.

A place I wasn't supposed to be with a man who wasn't supposed to be here either.

And we certainly weren't supposed to be together. And yet... And yet we work.

We're good together.

Maybe it's just the clean mountain air.

Or maybe it's the prospect of being stuck here forever in the little town of Luchara.

Whatever it is, I don't quite know what to make of the way I feel about him.

I like him.

And I'm pretty sure I would have liked him no matter where we met.

I just don't know if we would have gotten the chance to know each other if we'd met under different circumstances.

Chapter Twenty-Two

Lucas

AFTER OUR PIZZA and some ice cream we find in Mel's freezer, we put on our coats and walk away from town toward the cabin.

"It's going to snow again," I say, looking up.

"How do you know?" Madison asks, following my gaze.

"The stars. On a clear night, the stars up here are bright and seem impossibly close. But when there are snow clouds, we can only see a few of the stars shining through."

"So you think they're snow clouds?"

"I just feels like snow. Growing up here in the mountains, you start to get a feel for these things."

"I hope it does snow," she says. "It's supposed to snow on Christmas."

"Says the girl from Houston who's never seen real snow."

"Snow at Christmas is on my ideal Christmas list. For someday."

"You might just get your wish this year," I say. If I could make it snow tomorrow, I would do it.

I turn on the flashlight as we leave town with its old-fashioned lamp posts, heading down the trail toward the cabin. A wolf howls somewhere in the distance and a second later, another one not too far away answers with a howl of its own.

Sensing Madison's hesitation, I take her hand.

"We'll be home in a few minutes," I say.

"Not soon enough," she says.

"Sleepy?"

"A little."

I know she is. I can see it in her eyes.

"But," she says. "We have gifts to wrap tomorrow."

"Yes. We do." The weight of the bags with the gifts we'd bought is heavy in my left hand. The one roll of wrapping paper we'd found at the store sticks out of the top of the bag. We each bought some gifts the other one doesn't know about.

It reminds me of when I was a kid and the whole family would pile into the car and drive into Boulder on Christmas Eve. We'd go to the mall and buy last minute gifts for everyone. There had been a lot of slipping around getting surprise gifts for everyone. Nothing big. Just little fun things. Like a box of cookies for Grandma and a fishing lure for Grandpa.

I had fond memories of being part of a big family. We'd been close then and I miss it. And even though we're not close in the same way anymore, I'm going to miss being with my family tomorrow at Christmas.

Reaching the cabin, I unlock the door. Scout races in first, claiming his place in front of the fireplace.

I flip on the lights, chasing away the worst of the darkness and reluctantly let go of Madison's hand.

"I'll take my shopping bag," she says. "Wouldn't want you to accidentally peek inside and ruin your surprise."

"Same here," I say, taking my own bag and stashing it on the kitchen counter to sort through and wrap everything up tomorrow.

It's a nice reminder that even though I'm not with my family, I'm with Madison and she's a different kind of family.

She's the person I can see myself starting a family of my own with.

"I'm going to get ready for bed," she says, heading into the bedroom.

"Take your time," I say.

I open a can of dog food for Scout and set it out for him. As he happily gobbles it up, I change out the water in his bowl.

It feels colder tonight.

I go outside and bring in an armload of wood. Get a fire going in the fireplace.

With that done, I pull a bottle of pinot noir out of my shopping bag. I was going to bring it out tomorrow, but tonight seems like a good time to open it.

Uncorking it, I pour some wine into two plastic wine glasses I'd borrowed from Mel and wait for Madison to come out.

We have a nice romantic fire in the fireplace. Some good wine. It's a nice way to end the evening.

And it really is the turning out to be the best Christmas I've ever had.

Chapter Twenty-Three

Madison

Wearing my pajamas, my face freshly washed, and my hair brushed, I walk out into the living room to find Lucas waiting for me.

"I was going to save this for tomorrow," he says, handing me a glass of wine, but then I realized we might as well have some tonight, too."

"Our Eve of Christmas Eve celebration," I say.

"Exactly."

"To uncertain times," he says, tapping his glass gently to mine.

I sit on my pallet and take a sip of the wine. It's deep with a slight nutty flavor. This is one of those times when I wish I'd taken the time to study wines. Maybe when I revise my spreadsheet, and I will be overhauling it, I'll add learning about wines on there.

"Penny for your thoughts," he says.

"I was just thinking how I'd like to learn about wines."

"Me too," he says. "Maybe that's something we can do together. When we get out of here."

"Okay," I say, forcing myself not to think about just how impossible that is with him living here in the mountains and me living in Houston.

It makes me think more about my life revisions. Not that I have to make those kinds of changes right now. If I had my phone, I'd take some notes. Start organizing my ideas.

Lucas sits on his pallet and Scout stands up, shakes, and goes to sit next to him, putting his head in his lap.

"Oh," Lucas says. "So you've decided to do some sucking up."

"He loves you," I say.

"I know." He scratches his dog's ears. "And I know how hard it is to not be enamored by a pretty girl."

I raise an eyebrow, but don't say anything.

Somewhere outside, a wolf howls, sending an involuntary chill down my spine. I'm glad we're safely inside the warm cabin away from any wildlife dangers.

"We should call Hannah and Jack tomorrow," I say. "Wish them a happy wedding."

"We will. What would you be doing if you weren't here? If you were in Houston?"

"Usually just spending some time with my family. But not this year. This year my parents are on a cruise and my brother is with his girlfriend."

"Oh. I'm sorry."

"No. It's okay." I take a sip of wine and pull one of the blankets over my feet. "My family never really got into Christmas traditions."

"I see. That's why you have an extensive list of things to do on an ideal Christmas."

"I suppose it is. I never really put that together." I study the wine in my glass as it reflects the light from the fire.

"Psychology degree finally came in handy after all these years."

Turning, I look over at Lucas from beneath my lashes. The overhead light is out and I can only see him in the shadows from the firelight. He's stretched out on his own blankets, looking all the world like a man relaxed without a care in the world.

He's stranded here with me, a stranger, for Christmas, missing Christmas with his family and his brother's wedding, and he doesn't seem to be the least bit bothered by it.

"Have you ever thought about going back and getting your masters in psychology?"

"Nah," he says, swirling the wine in his glass.

"Why not? Most people who get advanced degrees in psychology are older."

"How do you know that?" he asks.

"I'm like a sponge," I say. "And I used to be a dog walker for educated, rich people. I listen."

"Maybe you should go back for your masters."

"I don't think so." I look into the flames again. One of the logs fall, sending sparks up the chimney. "I'm ready to do something to make money."

"What's that going to be?" he asks.

"I don't know yet. The pet adoption thing isn't it. I need something else."

"You need to think bigger," he says.

"Yes! Bigger. I just don't know what it is yet."

"You'll figure it out," he says.

"I know. I've learned that if I don't force it, it'll come to me."

"It will."

Chapter Twenty-Four

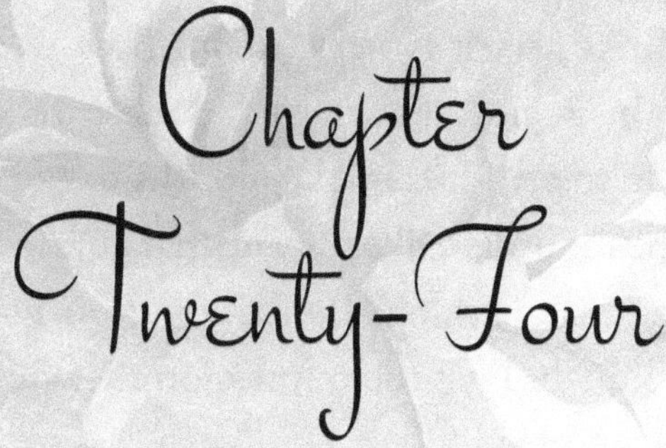

Lucas

SITTING in front of a cozy fire on a cold winter's night with a pretty girl, my dog sleeping next to me, life can't get any better.

We have a huge Christmas tree standing in one corner of the room, decorated with paper chains and popcorn strung on a fishing line and at the very top is a star Madison made out of red and white construction paper. I can imagine just how festive the tree would be if it had lights on it, but even without lights it has an undeniable charm.

She looks relaxed over there on her little pile of blankets, but I can sense the tension beneath the veneer.

She's gotten herself worried about how we're going to get out of here and it's a valid concern. The road is completely destroyed. It can take months to build a road on the side of the mountain like the one that got washed away.

I also sense something deeper going on with her, but that's just a hunch. I get the impression that she's searching for a new direction in life.

I have some ideas about that, but I don't think she's ready to hear them yet. So I keep them to myself.

"What's one of your favorite Christmas memories?" I ask her.

"Oh." She pushes her hair back off her face. "Like I said, we didn't have a lot of traditions."

"Surely you have some fond memories."

"My brother and I used to go outside and light sparklers on Christmas Eve."

"Sparklers. Those are fun."

"We were young. So yeah. And we had this dog. Spot. Spot was so funny. We'd wrap him a little gift and put it under the tree. Not in a box or anything. Just a chew toy. Like a stuffed frog. It could sit there for days and he wouldn't touch it. Then when we started opening presents, he'd go under the tree, get his present and tear off the paper."

"Now you're just making this up."

"Not even a little."

"That's a good memory."

"Yeah. What about you? What's one of your favorite Christmas memories?"

"One year my mom got mad at us. Having three boys, it's understandable. But that year she decided that instead of having Christmas at home doing the normal things, we'd all go into Boulder and spend the day volunteering at the homeless shelter."

"Seriously?"

"Seriously. It was one of the most satisfying Christmases I ever had."

"You liked helping people."

"I did. I felt like I made a difference."

"You only did it that one time?"

"It never came up again. I guess she was satisfied with whatever she was trying to teach us that year. I'd do it again though."

"But you enjoy being with your family."

"As crazy as they are, yes. I've never missed spending a Christmas with them."

"Maybe we'll have a Christmas miracle and you can make it this year."

"It would take a miracle," I say. "But it's okay. I'm content to spend Christmas right here. With you."

She smiles a little and looks away.

Maybe she doesn't believe me or maybe she's thinking practically. About how she lives in Houston and I live in Alpine Falls.

What she doesn't realize is that there's more than one kind of Christmas miracle.

They come in all shapes and sizes.

And she just might need to be open to a miracle of her own.

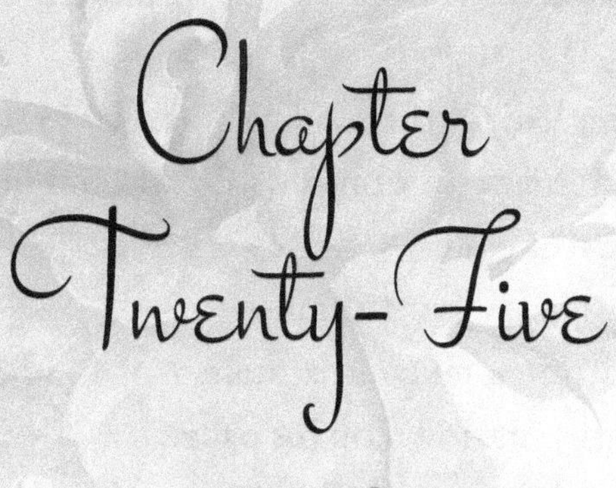

Madison

I WAKE to the sound of Christmas music.

Deciding I must be dreaming, I turn over and pull the blanket over my face.

But then I smell the scent of bacon and eggs.

And coffee.

It's enough to wake me up the rest of the way.

"Good morning, Sunshine," Lucas says.

I sit up and look at him. "Good morning. You've got food. And coffee."

"I woke up early so I went into town and got us breakfast to go. Thought you might like Christmas Eve breakfast in bed."

"I've never had Christmas Eve breakfast in bed."

"I figured if it wasn't on the list it should be." He hands me a to-go cup of coffee.

"It is now," I say, with a smile.

He hands me a takeout container of food and, holding one for himself, sits down on his pallet.

"You seem happy today," I say, opening the lid to find a full meal of bacon, eggs, and two pieces of toast.

"It's Christmas Eve. The most magical day of the year."

"More so than Christmas Day?"

"I think so. When Christmas Day gets here, the magic is winding down."

"I tend to agree with you," I say. "You must have been up for awhile. You built a fire. You walked into town." I glance back at the tree. There are gifts wrapped in festive red and some wrapped in plain brown paper I didn't know we had. "You wrapped your presents."

"I did," he says, grinning. "And you slept through it all."

"I'm sort of a heavy sleeper," I say.

"It's a good trait to have. What do you want to do today?"

"Well. I need to wrap my gifts."

"That won't take long."

"It always takes longer than it should."

"I can help you."

I point my fork at him. "Nice try, big guy."

He grins.

"Considering that they're all for you."

"Aw. You shouldn't have."

"Wait," I say. "Are all those presents under the tree for Scout?"

"One of them. No. Two of them."

"The rest are mine?"

"Who else would they be for?"

I shrug. "I don't know. Maybe you bought presents for Mel and the other merchants in town."

"No. I would consult with you if I did that."

I hide my surprise behind my coffee cup. He would consult with me?

That's new. That's not something I expected him to say.

"This is really good," I say.

"It's the crisp—"

"mountain air." I finish the sentence for him.

Grinning, he looks at me again.

"I have an idea," he says.

"Okay. I like ideas."

"You've got wedding clothes in your car, right?"

"Right."

"Since it's Christmas Eve, why don't we wear our nice clothes? You know. Just to make it special."

"Oh." I give him a little nod. "I like that idea."

"Good. Me too."

"You have your wedding clothes here?"

"Oddly enough. Yes. Don't ask."

"Okay. I won't ask. I'm going to take a shower first though and wrap my gifts."

"Perfect. I saved you some wrapping paper."

I wonder what's gotten into Lucas. Maybe he just woke up with Christmas spirit and I happen to be the lucky recipient of it all.

Not complaining. Not even a little bit.

Chapter Twenty-Six

Lucas

By mid-morning on Christmas Eve, all our gifts are wrapped and under the tree. Scout doesn't go near them. I wonder if dogs somehow have a weird understanding of wrapped Christmas gifts because I know for a fact that there are doggy treats under there that he can smell.

I bring Madison's suitcase in and she disappears into the bedroom. Since I'm already wearing my tux which I'd picked up in Boulder on my way here—some things are just fortuitous that way—I busy myself with some house plan drawings.

I've got my plans for this cabin finished up, so I entertain myself with some rough plans for a house I've been thinking about building for myself.

Maybe I should have gotten that degree in architecture. I could go back, still, and do it. But my brother, Trenton, can help me with any details and finishing touches after I get through playing. I'll probably never even do anything with all the house plans I've sketched out. It's just something I enjoy doing.

After what seems like forever, the bedroom door opens and Madison steps out.

She looks absolutely stunning and I'm speechless.

Her dress is in a dark crimson color, for Christmas, the color of a cardinal. I remember Hannah telling Olivia that her colors were inspired by a Christmas cardinal she'd seen perched on a window when she first got to our house, but I hadn't realized just how stunning the color would be in an evening gown on the prettiest girl I've ever seen.

She did something with her hair, too. It's straight with little curls at the ends. And she's wearing makeup. Her lashes are long and dark. Her eyelids sparkly and her lips glossy.

I just sit there, staring at her.

"Is this okay?" she asks, jarring me out of my daze.

"You're stunning," I say.

And now I have the answer to the question I'd been asking myself.

I'd asked myself if I would have noticed her at the wedding if we hadn't met like we had.

The answer is an absolutely hell yes.

Anyone would notice Madison and I can't look away.

"You look nice, too," she says. "Do you have your phone? Let's take a photo in front of our tree."

Shoving my paper aside, I pull out my phone and meet her in front of our Christmas tree.

I put my arm around her and we lean together, smiling for the camera.

I lower the camera, but neither one of us moves.

Turning slightly, keeping my arm around her, I look into her lovely green eyes.

We don't need lights on the Christmas tree.

We don't need music.

We have everything we need.

I lower my head and kiss her.

She closes her eyes and neither one of us moves as we stand there, our lips pressed together.

This. This is the meaning of life.

Scout stands up and barks once, breaking the moment.

"I think Scout wants to go outside," I say.

"It's time for us to go to lunch anyway."

"I guess it is."

I look down and grin. "I see you're wearing my boots with that dress."

"What can I say? I'm a practical girl."

"I can get behind that."

"Let's get our coats on and go see what Mel's cooking."

Scout barks again and dances around in a little circle.

"Scout agrees with that idea," she says.

"Scout agrees with just about anything."

Except kissing. Unfortunately, he doesn't seem to be too tolerant of kissing.

Chapter Twenty-Seven

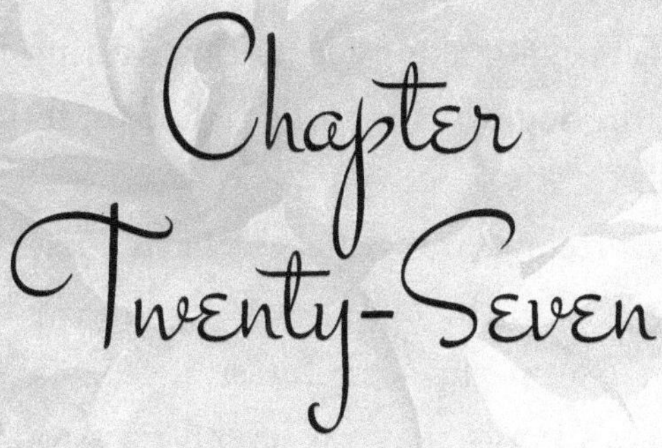

Madison

It should feel a little odd, wearing the dress I was
going to wear to Hannah's wedding to lunch at the Luchara
diner, especially since we have to walk along a curvy mountain trail to get there.

It's so peacefully quiet. Nothing but the sound of the
wind whispering through the trees. The steady roar of the
river, water rushing past us as we walk along the bank for a
time. Little patches of snow, protected from the sun,

beneath the trees. The scent of wood smoke from the various fireplaces, including ours.

And yet, walking alongside Lucas, wearing his tux, my hand in his, his dog trotting along beside us, it doesn't seem strange at all.

Instead of feeling strange, it feels like Christmas and that makes it okay. With the magic of Christmas swirling in the air, it doesn't seem the least bit strange at all. Not even wearing Lucas's boots that are several sizes too big for me beneath my evening gown.

The diner is packed and Mel seems happier than I've seen him in the time I've spent here. The guests, locals and tourists alike, aren't even talking about the avalanche or wondering how we're all going to get out of here.

It's like everyone made a tacit agreement to take a break from talking about it, even if only for just one day.

After lunch, walking back to the cabin, the sun shining, Scout runs through the trees and comes out somewhere behind us only to race past us.

"He's such a funny dog," I say.

"Yeah. I like him."

"He's a good fit for you," I say.

"Is there some hidden meaning there?" he asks.

"I don't know what you mean," I say, smiling over at him.

Walking among the blue spruce trees, holding hands with Lucas feels right.

Impossibly impractical, but at the same time right.

"Should we open our presents tonight?" he asks. "Or tomorrow?"

"Both," I say. "Some tonight. But save some for in the morning."

"Okay. I like that plan."

I slow down as a sound registers.

"What is it?" Lucas asks, slowing down, too.

"Do you hear that?" I ask.

"The helicopter?"

"Yes. That's what it is." It sounds so strange out here in the quiet wilderness. I feel like I haven't heard a car motor or anything modern in forever. "Flying over checking things out?"

"Could be," he says, looking up.

I follow his gaze until I see the helicopter flying this way.

"It's landing." I say, not sure if I'm asking or telling.

But it is landing. Up ahead near the cabin.

"Why is it landing?" I ask.

"Let's go see," he says, squeezing my hand.

By the time we reach the cabin, the helicopter's motor is turned off, leaving just its faint echo lingering in the air.

We round a bend in the trail and there's the helicopter sitting in a clearing that looks all the world like it was make for it, not far from my car and his truck.

Then I see Hannah.

Hannah?

And Olivia. And Jack and another man who must be Trenton.

"They're here?" I ask Lucas.

Lucas is grinning.

"Looks like it," he says.

"You knew they were coming." Not waiting for an answer, I pull my hand free and rush forward to hug my two friends.

"What are you doing here?" I ask.

"We came to get you," Hannah says. "I couldn't get married without you at the wedding. And your dress, Madison. It's beautiful."

"You picked it out."

"I know, but I didn't expect it to look so great."

I glance at my watch. "Your wedding."

"Plenty of time," Olivia says. "Alpine Falls is like a ten minute flight from here."

I look at Jack. "Wait. Jack flies helicopters?"

"Did I not mention that?" Hannah asks innocently. "Jack does so much. It's hard to keep up."

"We've got to get your phone replaced," Olivia says.

Lucas walks up to his brothers.

"Looks like you've got some explaining to do," Jack says.

"Been keeping secrets," Trenton says, nodding toward the stack of wood.

"I'll tell you all about it," Lucas says. "But we've got a wedding to get to."

"Do we have room for some luggage and things?" I ask.

"Plenty of room," Jack says. "What needs to go?"

"I need a few minutes to pack up," I say, heading toward the cabin.

"We'll help you," Olivia says. "Come on, Hannah."

"We've got to get Hannah dressed," I say.

"All in due time," Olivia says.

They follow me into the cabin.

"Lucas has a Christmas tree," Hannah says with obvious surprise.

"Actually we do. We picked it out and decorated it ourselves. Hold on a minute."

I walk back to the door. "Lucas? We're taking our gifts, right?"

"Of course," he says. "I'll bag them up. Don't worry. Just get packed up. We're getting out of here."

"Right." I look over at the tree and feel a wave of sadness wash over me.

I'd gotten so wrapped up in spending Christmas with Lucas that even seeing my friends, even getting to attend Hannah's wedding, even getting out of Luchara doesn't make up for not getting to spend Christmas with Lucas.

I square my shoulders and pull myself up by my innate practicality.

Getting out of here is a good thing.

And we've got a wedding in just hours.

Besides. It's okay because Lucas will be there, too.

Chapter Twenty-Eight

Lucas

I**T HAD TAKEN** everything I had to not tell Madison my secret.

I talked to Jack this morning and we made tentative plans for him to fly over and get us. He hadn't been able to guarantee that it would be today though. Since Jack doesn't own a helicopter, it had taken some work for him to find one that he could borrow. Apparently all the pilots with helicopters that he could call upon were using them until now.

Hannah had insisted that they all come, wedding or no.

I feel a twinge of nostalgia as I pack up the presents beneath our tree. It has been a memorable couple of days to say the least.

Madison and I had created something together. We'd made a good thing out of a bad situation.

I hadn't been exaggerating when I'd said it was the best Christmas I'd ever had.

But just because we're relocating doesn't mean that will change. We're taking the Christmas we created with us.

It'll be good to be with my family, especially since Madison will be there, too.

Having Madison spend Christmas with my family only adds to the perfectness of this year's Christmas, even if it does mean that we have to leave our little haven.

"This is interesting," Trenton says, lifting one of the paper chains.

"Madison and I made those," I say with obvious pride. "We strung the popcorn, too. With fishing line."

Jack and Trenton exchange a look.

"You should get stranded with a pretty girl more often," Jack says. "It suits you."

"Well," I say, reaching under the tree and pulling out gifts. "We thought we were going to be spending Christmas here."

"Not on my watch," Jack says. "If I can help it."

I stand up and put a hand on Jack's shoulder. "You're a good brother." No point in telling him that I was perfectly content to be stranded here with Madison.

"Can I make a suggestion?" Trenton asks.

"Sure."

"While the girls are packing up, we can undecorate this tree. Then use the decorations to put on a tree in your apartment over the barn."

I look blankly at him.

"It would be a nice surprise for Madison," he says. "Don't know when you'll get back up here."

"It's not a bad idea," I say. It's actually a very good idea. "But I'll take them off if you'll pack up my power tools from the truck. Assuming you have room for them."

"We have room," Jack says. "Come on Trenton, let's give Lucas a minute."

"I don't need a minute," I say in a weak protest as they walk off. But looking at the tree, I decide maybe I do.

Madison and I invested a lot in this tree and taking the decorations with us is a good idea. A very good idea. And I think Madison will like it.

If I had time, which I don't, I'd get her something nice for Christmas. Instead, all I have are these little gifts from the General Store.

But maybe it really is the thought that counts.

If it's the thought that counts, then I'm giving her my heart.

Chapter Twenty-Nine

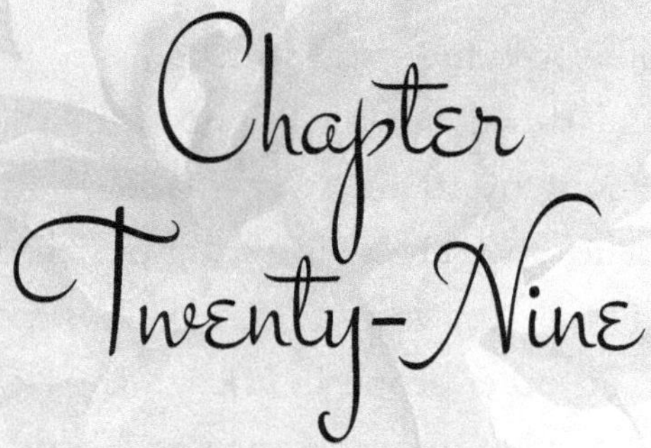

Madison

FLYING AWAY from Luchara in the helicopter, my hand firmly in Lucas's, Scout sitting between us, I watch the little cabin, then the little town, then the destroyed road, vanish below.

I'm happy to be leaving. I really am.

If it hadn't been for Lucas being there, I'm not sure I could have stood it. I'd probably have gone into a full blown panic.

As it is, having him next to me now makes leaving here tolerable.

"We'll come back and visit," he says.

"Maybe." I frown out the window, then look back at him. "What about my car and your truck?"

"Jack said he can get them lifted out by helicopter."

"Oh." I'll have to worry about the cost of that later. "What about the other people in Luchara?"

"The guys... what were their names? Teddy and Ralph? They're working on that."

"But we have inside help."

"Family comes in handy at times," he says.

"As does found family," I say and he squeezes my hand.

"You'll always have a place with us," he says. "No matter what happens."

"Thank you," I say, finding it a rather odd thing for him to say. I can't help looking for his true meaning behind the words. Maybe it's because I'm Hannah's friend and she's marrying his brother.

It just seems like an odd thing for him to say after kissing me. Maybe that kiss had simply been him getting swept up in the moment.

"We're here," he says just as the helicopter starts its descent.

I hold onto his hand in response to the sudden change in direction.

We land behind his parents' house, proving that there are most definitely benefits to a helicopter over even a small private airplane that requires a runway.

We're unloaded in no time and I'm set up in a room with Olivia.

There's no time to dally, though, because we have to turn Hannah into a bride befitting a wedding, even if it is a small wedding.

It takes Olivia five minutes to change into her dress that matches mine perfectly and we're off to Hannah's room. She's already had a shower and is working on drying her hair.

When did my friends get so fast at getting ready? Or maybe I slowed down.

Either way, the three of us go into a flurry of activity, getting Hannah into her wedding gown, doing her hair and makeup.

"What's Lucas like?" Hannah asks as Olivia smears eyeshadow on her lids.

"What do you mean?" I ask, turning on the hair straightener. It seems like such an odd question coming from someone who is practically related to Lucas.

"Just curious," she says. "We don't get to spend much time with him so I don't really know him. You've probably spent more time with him in two days than I have in fifteen years."

"Oh. Well. That's sad." I pick up a brush and run it through my own hair. "He's a very nice guy. A gentleman. Kind. And thoughtful."

"He seems that way," Olivia says. "Likeable."

"Yes. He's likeable."

"Did he mention why he doesn't come around the family much? He lives on the property, you know. He has an apartment over the barn and he's either there taking care of the horses or off somewhere."

Because he doesn't feel appreciated. But it's not my place to tell anyone that. Not even my closest friends. Especially not the friend who's about to marry his brother.

"He's private, I guess. And just does his own thing."

"What's the deal with the cabin?" Olivia asks. "It's obviously under construction. Trenton said he had tools in his truck. I didn't know Lucas did that kind of work."

"I don't know," I say. "All I know is he was nice enough to let me stay there when there weren't any rooms in town."

Olivia clucks her tongue and gets to work on Hannah's eyelashes. "It looked cozy to me."

"It was cozy," I say. "It snowed and we were warm. I'm going downstairs to get us some water."

Turning on my heels, the high heels I'm wearing now, I leave them there. Let them speculate. I don't care.

I know what it's like to be a private person. I've always been the most private person I know.

I hadn't really noticed coming in, but I stop at the bottom of the stairs and admire the deep red poinsettias on every surface. On the little table behind the sectional. On the coffee table. On the mantle.

I wander to the fireplace and find Cupcake, Olivia's little Yorkshire terrier with an adorable caramel colored head and a white body sitting in front of the fire, mesmerized by the flames. It's thanks to her unusual coloring that Olivia gave up on finding someone willing to adopt Cupcake and kept her for her own dog.

I sit down on the ledge next to her.

"Hey Cupcake. You like the fire?" I rub her head, warm from the fire. "Do you like the warmth or the flames?"

Cupcake doesn't answer.

"Both. Me too. Where did the guys get off to? It looks like everything is just about ready for your Aunt Hannah's wedding."

Cupcake barks once.

"Do you want to go outside?"

Cupcake barks again and hops off the ledge, running toward the back door.

"I guess that means yes."

Following her to where she waits at the back door, I find her leash and clip it onto her harness.

With Cupcake leading the way, we step outside onto the back deck and walk down the stairs to the backyard.

Holding the leash with one hand, I hold the banister with the other as I navigate the stairs with high heels I'm not accustomed to wearing. I was much more comfortable wearing Lucas's hiking boots even if they were too big for me.

While Cupcake searches for the perfect spot to do her business, I see the three guys heading my way as they come out of the trees by way of a dirt trail that reminds me of the walkway from the cabin to the diner in Luchara.

"There she is," Jack says.

"And neither one of them is wearing a coat," Trenton says.

I'm shivering and I hadn't even realized it. Cupcake is shivering, too.

"Cupcake has a coat?"

"Absolutely," Trenton says.

"Cupcake," I say sternly. "You didn't tell me you were supposed to wear a coat."

Smiling, Lucas removes his own coat and drapes it over my shoulders.

"Thank you," I say, looking into his blue eyes.

"You're welcome." He takes Cupcake's leash from me and hands her over to Trenton. "Her daddy is a bit overprotective."

"I am not." But he takes her leash and leads her back toward the house.

"Sorry," I say. "I just needed some fresh air and Cupcake needed to come outside."

"It's okay. It takes a minute to get used to needing a coat when you walk outside even for a few minutes."

"I guess it does. It's almost time for the wedding. Everything okay?"

"Yeah. We just had something we had to take care of before Jack jets off on his honeymoon."

"They're flying?"

"Of course. While he has the helicopter, he's taking Hannah somewhere."

"Where are they going?"

"I don't know. He won't tell me."

"A surprise honeymoon. I wonder what Hannah thinks about that."

"I think Hannah probably has a good idea. She would have to. To pack."

"True."

"So. The girls ran you off?"

"No." I sigh. "They kept asking too many questions." I turn sideways as the wind blows hair into my face.

"What kind of questions?"

"They wanted to know about you and the cabin. It wasn't my business to tell them. So I didn't."

He smooths the hair off my face. "I appreciate your loyalty, but I just told Jack and Trenton what I was doing there. So you don't have to keep my secrets anymore."

"Well. Now you tell me."

He grins. "I have something I want to show you. After the wedding."

"After the wedding? Trying to keep me in suspense?"

"Absolutely. It's a Christmas Eve surprise."

"Then it must be good," I say.

"I think you'll like it. Ready to go back inside now? Get those two married off."

"Sure."

"By the way," he says. "Just between you and me. I think Trenton and Olivia are going to be getting married next."

"You really think so?" I ask, as he takes my hand and we walk together up the stairs leading to the back deck.

"I really do."

"Don't you think that's a little odd? Your brother getting married to your other brother's wife's friend? Never mind. It's too complicated."

"I don't happen to think it's strange at all. I think it's quite efficient."

"Efficient."

He opens the door and we walk into the warmth of the house.

"You have to admit the efficiency is a bonus." He takes his coat off my shoulders and hangs it up. "Looks like everyone is here and the wedding is about to start."

"I'm not sure they were going to wait for us," I say.

"Welcome to my world."

"I'm beginning to understand a little better what you were talking about," I say as we take our places.

Chapter Thirty

Lucas

THE WEDDING WAS as it should have been. Simple and sweet.

My brother, Jack, and Hannah were first married over ten years ago. Shortly after the wedding, something happened and there was a divorce. Supposedly a divorce.

Hannah spent ten years believing they were divorced, but Jack knew they were still married. He knew because he never signed the papers.

All that time, he remained faithful to Hannah.

Since she didn't know she was still married, she dated others. In fact, she was engaged to someone else when she showed up in Alpine Falls seeking a copy of divorce papers that didn't exist when she learned she was still married to Jack.

The rest is history. They decided to renew their vows for a fresh start.

Smart idea considering all the water that flowed under that bridge.

Hannah is a beautiful bride. There's no denying that. But Madison is the girl I can't take my eyes off of.

During the ceremony, she looks in my direction and our gazes lock. Her cheeks flush prettily. Fate. Kismet. Whatever label someone chooses, it feels to me like it's meant to be.

Trenton and Olivia will be married next. Now all I have to do is convince Madison to stay here. We can built a house of our own. I don't even care where we live. If she wants to live in Houston, I can do that, too, even though I'd rather stay around here.

Small wedding. Just family. So the reception consists of our dad opening bottles of champagne and everyone getting a glass.

It's obvious that Jack and Hannah are ready to get out of here.

"We have to get going before it gets dark," Jack says.

"You know you can wait until morning to leave," Dad says.

"We know," Jack pulls Hannah close. "But we have reservations."

"Go," Mother says. "Don't be trying to fly that chopper at night.

"Take good care of Bandit," Hannah says, picking up her cat and holding him close against her.

"You know we'll take care of him like he's ours," Olivia says.

"He'll be fine." Madison leans in and gives Hannah a hug. "Enjoy yourself."

We follow them outside and watch as they board the helicopter.

I figure they've got about one good hour of flying before the sun dips below the horizon. That tells me they aren't going far. They don't have to go far to feel like a world away from here. I know that from experience.

Standing next to Madison, we watch the helicopter until it's just a speck on the horizon, then we can't see it anymore.

"We're going inside," Olivia says. "You coming?"

"We'll be along in a bit," I say. "Come on," I tell Madison. "I have something to show you."

Suddenly feeling a little bit nervous, I take her hand and lead her down the path toward the barn where I have a little apartment on the second floor.

"Remember I told you I moved in over the barn to help out after my dad's accident?" I ask.

"Sure. I remember. Is that where we're going?"

"Yes. Promise me you won't be judgy."

"When have I been judgy?" she asks, looking over at me.

"You haven't. That's why you get to see my little apartment."

"I'm honored," she says.

Grinning, I take her hand.
"I'll remind you of that," I say.
She just smiles back.

Chapter Thirty-One

Madison

THE BARN as he called it is more like a stable in my opinion. On the first floor, there are individual stalls for two dozen horses.

"Only fifteen of them are filled," he tells me.

"Still. Fifteen horses." Having never been in a barn or a stable before, I'm a little surprised by the strong scent of hay and animals. Scout, walking along beside us, seems to know exactly where he's going.

Pausing, I peak into one of the stalls and see a large dapple gray horse.

"Pretty," I say.

"Yeah. That's Morgan. She's Jack's horse."

"Where's your horse?"

"I don't have one."

I start to ask why he doesn't have a horse, but decide to wait. It's Christmas Eve and I don't want to make him talk about anything that makes him uncomfortable.

"You're welcome to help me feed them later, if you want."

"Sure. But I don't know about the mucking part."

"I won't make you muck the stalls."

"Thank you."

Reaching a door, about halfway through the first floor of the barn, he opens it up and we go upstairs.

I don't know what I expected, but I did not expect this.

The apartment is more like what I would call a loft or maybe a studio apartment and it still smells like freshly cut wood.

It has a medium sized bed. Nothing too small. Nothing too big. Nicely made as I had suspected from the way he kept the bedding folded at the cabin.

There's a love seat and a little television. A desk with a closed notebook computer on it. A stack of what looks like house plans on one side of the desk.

One wall is all windows looking out over the forest with the snow-capped mountains in the distance. It's the opposite direction from the main house, giving it a very secluded feel.

"This view," I say. "Amazing."

"I know. Doesn't get much better."

"Did you build this space yourself?" I ask, running a hand over the small kitchen table for two. Everything is clean and uncluttered.

"I did most of the work, yes."

"You're really quite handy," I say. "I'm glad you showed me this."

"Me too." He stands back on his heels. "But this isn't what I wanted to show you."

"Oh? There's more?"

"Yes." He grins and moves aside a little tri-fold partition between the window and the desk.

Behind the partition is a real Christmas tree, about five-feet tall. A blue spruce like we'd had in the cabin.

And our paper chains and popcorn strings are looped around it. The little star I'd made from construction paper sits at the top of the tree. And our presents are arranged beneath it.

Turning, I look at him, feeling something catching in my chest.

"It's smaller than our tree," he says. "But it's the best I could do on short notice."

"You recreated our tree," I say, stunned and amazed.

"It didn't seem right to just leave it."

"It's perfect," I say and throw my arms around him.

As he kisses me, Scout barks once, then darts beneath the tree and comes back dragging out one of the gifts in his mouth.

"Look at him," I say. "That's what my dog did."

"That's his present," Lucas says. "His treats."

"He knows."

We watch as Scout uses his mouth to tear the paper off the bag of treats.

Once it's unwrapped enough, Scout looks at us expectantly and Lucas opens the bag and hands him a treat.

"We said we'd open something tonight," Lucas says, reaching down and picking up a gift. "Come sit down and open it."

We sit side by side on the loveseat and I unwrap the gift.

"It's a notebook," I say, not sure what to make of it.

"You like to make lists so I thought you might go old-school. Of course, we were at the cabin at the time." He shrugs.

"I do like to make lists," I say. "And I like to write things down by hand. Thank you."

"You're welcome."

Running a hand along the plain black cover of the note-book, I ask. "Is there anything in particular you were thinking I might want to write down?"

"Yes," he says with a little smile. "As a matter of fact, there is."

"What would that be?" I look into his smiling blue eyes, my heart swelling with happiness.

"I want you to stay," he says.

"Stay? What do you mean?" I have butterflies in my stomach. If he means what I think he means...

"Here. In Alpine Falls. Here." He sweeps a hand back in the direction of the main house. "In the house. With me."

I flip through the blank pages of the notebook. "How long are you thinking I should stay here?"

Scout barks once and jumps onto the sofa, putting his head in my lap.

"Long enough to fill that notebook and a million more like it." Lucas takes my hands. "I want you to stay forever."

I swallow the lump in my throat, but it doesn't go away. "That would take figuring out some details, wouldn't it?"

He taps the notebook. "Hence the notebook."

Biting my lip, I smile. "Hence the notebook. So... I'll live with your parents while you live here?"

"Until we figure things out," he says. "Trenton and Olivia will be getting married next."

I raise an eyebrow, but don't say anything.

"That would give me plenty of time to court you properly."

"You think I need courting?" I ask, unable to resist the smile spreading across my lips.

"A gentleman always courts the woman he plans to marry."

"I see."

Scout licks my hand.

"Scout wants you to stay, too," Lucas says.

"Well. With two handsome boys asking me to stay, how can I resist?"

"Does that mean you'll stay?"

"I have details to work out, but yes. I'll stay."

He leans over and kisses me.

"The best Christmas ever," he whispers against my lips.

"The best," I say.

Epilogue

Madison

One Year Later

"No peeking!" Lucas says.

Holding onto his hand like a lifeline, I keep my other hand over my eyes.

"I'm lost already. Even if I see where I'm going, I won't know where I am."

"You'll ruin the effect," he says. "We're almost there."

I'm wearing my not-quite-broken-in trail boots and a heavy wool coat that's quite suitable for snowy weather.

We've been walking for what I gauge to be about fifteen

minutes, give or take, so we're not too far from their house. Our house. My house.

We've followed the river most of the way, too, so I could find my way home if I had to.

"Is it snowing?" I ask. "It's snowing, isn't it? On Christmas Eve."

"Yes," Lucas says. "It's snowing, but that's not your surprise."

I make a sound that has Scout looking up at me.

"What's that?" Lucas asks.

"I didn't say anything."

He stops. "We're here."

"Finally. Can I look now?"

"Yes. You can look."

I open my eyes and the first thing I see is a delightful snowfall. Little fluffy flakes drifting lightly down all around us, landing on my coat sleeves. My eyelashes.

"What do you think?" Lucas asks.

"The snow is beautiful," I say, mostly because I know that's not what he's asking about.

"Not the snow. The view. The trees. The river. Everything."

Shading my eyes with one gloved hand, I look around. We're standing in what I've learned is called a moraine with the river tumbling along beside us.

And the view is just stunning. The river. The moraine with little winter flowers peeking up through the white layer of snow.

"I don't have words to describe this view," I say.

"It's a view you could look at every day, isn't it?"

"Yes. Actually. It is. Very much so."

"It's ours if we want it."

"What do you mean?" I ask, shifting my gaze to his.

"We can have this piece of land to build a house on. If you want to. If you like it."

"We can live here?"

"Yes."

"It's not far from the house or the stables." I've developed a fondness for horses. "And the river. Perfect for sleeping."

"I've been playing around with some house plans, but I thought we could start from the beginning. Make it ours."

"We can design it from scratch. And make the view work for us. Lots and lots of walls of windows." I put my arms around him. "It's going to be perfect."

"It's going to be ours. So yes. Perfect."

"We'll need lots of extra bedrooms with both Hannah and Olivia expecting. Our nieces and nephews can come visit."

"And they can play with our children."

"Our children?" I ask.

"Yes. Our children. You do want children? Right?"

"Of course I do. We talked about that. With dozens and dozens of dogs and cats for them to play with."

"I thought for minute you were going to say dozens and dozens of children."

"I don't think that's physically possible. How about dozens and dozens of grandchildren?"

"Okay." Lucas puts one arm beneath my knees, picks me up and turns around in a circle. "We'll have dozens and dozens of grandchildren."

I tilt my head back, letting the snow fall on my face.

I'm happy.

I'm never been so very happy.

Sometimes I'm so happy it just hits me like a ton of bricks and I can barely believe just how fortunate I am.

An impulsive road trip with a turn down a random road quite simply led me to my forever home.

The End.

Keep Reading for a preview of *Just Breathe*...

AUTHOR OF OUT OF ASHES
KATHRYN KALEIGH
HE WILL RISK IT ALL TO PROTECT HER
Just
BREATHE
THE GRAVITY OF US SERIES

Just Breathe

PREVIEW

Chapter 1
Audrey
Houston, Texas

I became a widow on a stormy Tuesday evening.

I'd just locked up the art gallery on McKinney Street and pulled out of the parking garage when the sky opened up. Blinding rain hammers the roof of my Toyota Camry, loud and relentless, like the storm had been holding its breath until I left work.

My windshield wipers fight hard, but the downpour blurs everything—the road, the streetlights, the familiar city skyline. Sheets of water pour down the window.

Even through the strong new car scent, I smell the rain. Clean and fresh. Washing away the dust of southern humidity.

Normally, I like the rain. It makes the world feel quieter, softer somehow. But not tonight.

I slow at the intersection, squinting through the blur of headlights and storm. Typical spring in Texas—clear skies one moment, flooded roads the next.

I dread the drive home. Even with a straight shot on Interstate 10, it's still a long drive out to Katy. It's a mystery to me and probably always will be just why Thomas wanted to buy a house out in the suburbs when I worked downtown and he spent most of his time at the airport north of town.

So every day, often even on weekends, I get in my car and head east toward downtown while he gets in his car and heads north toward the airport.

As an airplane pilot, he spends the night away from home at least once a week. In his defense, I guess he thought I would be safer out in the suburbs. But the drive...

I hadn't complained. Not when the three-story house, all stone and glass, with its manicured lawn was so pretty. And new. The new house with its brand new appliances. No one else has ever lived in it before us. Considering it was my first house after living in apartments, I'm pretty happy once I get inside.

The gallery had hosted an event tonight for two very different artists. One of them was known for realistic photographs and the other for abstract watercolors.

Two artists, more different in every way possible,

couldn't have been paired together even if we'd tried. Concurrent hosting is new. Something suggested by the new CEO to increase profits.

My job was easy. My job was to make sure everyone else did their job. The hostess. The caterer. Other than that, I spent most of my time talking to guests.

When the first phone call from a number I don't recognize shows up on my dashboard screen, I let it go to voicemail. After an evening of talking to people, I just want time to decompress. That's how I typically use the drive home. I'd replay the evening. Catalog everything away in my head and make room for a glass of wine and a book.

Thomas is on an overnight trip tonight to Austin, so it's just me. I'm looking forward to getting out of my heels and cocktail dress, grabbing a glass of wine, and curling up on the sofa in front of the fireplace with a romance novel.

Thomas and I usually watch a movie or binge watch some series or another, but when I'm alone, I'm content to just spend the evening quietly reading. My go to evening activity before I met Thomas.

The second time my phone rings, I hit the button and send the caller straight to voicemail. I don't need a distraction from driving right now. Not in this thunderstorm.

As though to support my decision, a flash of lightning splits the sky just as I merge onto the interstate followed by an ear-splitting crash of thunder that makes the air tremble.

The third time my phone rings, I'm nearing the outer loop, still gripping the steering wheel, cringing as every car rushes past, sending an extra spray of water onto the windshield. A quick glance tells me it's the same number calling. A local number.

My family lives in Atlanta, so it's either a wrong number or work. This time of night, just after ten, I'm going with wrong number.

But it could be someone with a problem related to the art gallery and as the manager, I'm responsible. I press the answer button on my steering wheel.

"Hello."

"Ms. Albright?"

"This is Audrey." I didn't take Thomas's last name and it rather annoys me that people always assume that I did.

Not that there's anything wrong with a woman taking her husband's name. I just hadn't. And it seems like people shouldn't make assumptions.

"This is John with the FAA."

"The FAA." My stomach knots. "I think you meant to call Thomas's number."

He's quiet for a moment. "Are you driving?"

"Yes." Thunder crashes again and I grip the steering wheel with both hands. Despite the rain and diminished visibility, cars and big eighteen wheelers fly past me on either side.

I just want to be home.

"I hear the storm," he says. "Can I call you back?"

"Sure. But Thomas isn't available."

"It's okay," he says. "I'll call you back."

"Sure thing," I say and disconnect the line.

How had John from the FAA gotten my phone number and why is he calling Thomas late at night?

It probably has something to do with Thomas's return flight home tomorrow. Probably delayed. Thomas, like all pilots, has a lot of delayed flights. It comes with the territory.

Thomas and I haven't known each other all that long all in all. We'd worked together a short time on the annual staff in college, but he'd been a senior and I'd been a sophomore. Four years after he'd graduated and moved on, he'd walked into my art gallery. That was about a year ago.

Although he'd remembered me, I hadn't recognized him right away.

Six months later we were married.

Thomas always seemed to be in a hurry to do things. He'd been in a hurry to get married. In a hurry to buy a house. He just didn't have much sense of delayed gratification. I'd teased him about it, finding it a bit endearing.

And he was charming enough that he was able to convince me to go along with most things. With me being one of the least impulsive people I knew, he amused me. I rather liked that he pulled me out of my comfort zone on occasion.

I exit off the freeway and head toward my gated neighborhood.

Katy, oddly enough, typically has more traffic than downtown, but this time of night, the roads are pretty much empty.

I drive through the gate, make the five turns required to

get to my house, then pull into the garage. Turn off the motor and open my door to the welcome quiet.

The storm still rages outside, but inside the garage, it's blissfully quiet.

It's usually not so bad going from one garage to the next. Even when it's brutally hot outside. Work to home. The rain, however, makes the drive tricky and tonight was one of the worst storms I've driven through.

But I made it.

I let myself inside and head straight upstairs to the bedroom to change clothes.

Just as I step out of my heels, my phone rings again. I pull it out of my purse and glare at the number.

It's the same number. John from the FAA.

"Hello John," I say. "Do you have my husband's phone number?"

"Yes," he says. "But it's you I need to talk to."

I sit down hard on the little bench in my closet as realization slams into me. Glancing over at Thomas's clothes, neatly hung and organized, I smell his cologne from where he'd gotten dressed earlier in the day.

Thomas always calls when he lands. I'd gotten so busy with the gallery event and then driving in the storm, I only now realized that I hadn't heard from him.

I glance at the time. He should have landed about three hours ago. Three hours.

I'd been so distracted, it hadn't even occurred to me until this minute that he hadn't checked in.

"Why? Has something happened?" I ask, remembering

that I'm on the phone with John with the FAA. "He should be in Austin." I have an overwhelming urge to hang up and dial Thomas's phone number. "The storm…"

"Yes. The storm that's over Houston now came down from the west."

"So Thomas got delayed." That would explain things. He got delayed and he didn't call because he knew I had an important event tonight. But that didn't explain why John from the FAA was on the phone with me.

"He didn't get delayed."

I thought for a minute. Thomas had taken me flying plenty of times. He'd taught me some basics. Flight plans. Weather reports. He was careful.

"A detour then. They had to detour him to another airport." Despite my optimist words, there's a knot forming in the pit of my stomach.

"He radioed in with engine trouble."

"Engine trouble? Emergency landing then." Panic is in my voice now replacing the annoyance. My phone is on speaker, but I'm surprised the phone itself doesn't crack with my herculean grip.

"Audrey. We lost contact with your husband's plane about five pm."

Just Breathe

PREVIEW

Chapter 2
Audrey

Two mornings later, I wander downstairs, wearing sweatpants and a t-shirt, my hair pulled back in a messy ponytail, where my two sisters are in the kitchen.

"Who are these people?" I ask, mostly to myself. I don't expect an answer.

There are people in my house. I don't like people in my house.

I didn't invite them.

Neighbors from the looks of them.

People I've never even met.

Sitting on my sofa. Talking in hushed tones. Light chuckles. Furtive glances in my direction.

We stand behind the island looking out over toward my living room.

Lilah, the youngest, is cutting an apple pie into slices and placing them on plates. Not saying much of anything.

Brianna, a year younger than me, stands next to me, hands on her hips.

"That's Mark and Mary sitting together on the sofa. They live two houses down on the corner. Melissa is sitting on the hearth in front of the fireplace. Her husband Kevin is standing next to her. They live next to you on the other side. And the guy standing at the patio door looking out is Bert. He's the president of your Home Owner's Association."

I look at Brianna, my mouth open in awe. "How do you know this? Never mind." Brianna talks to everybody. She never meets a stranger. But even more important. "How do they even know about Thomas?"

"It was on the news," Lilah says, washing the knife.

"It was on the news?" I ask Brianna.

Their gazes land on me at once—startled, uncertain, as if I've just confessed something unthinkable.

"It's okay," Brianna says, pulling me into a hug. "You're okay."

Lilah puts the knife away and arranges the saucers of pie slices on a tray.

I groan when the doorbell rings. "Why so many people?"

"I'll get it," Brianna says. "Lilah. Give Audrey some pie."

"I'm not hungry," I say, but I sit down at the breakfast table, and take the fork Lilah hands me.

I'm still feeling groggy. Someone, Brianna I think, gave me something to help me sleep last night. I'd slept for... I glance at my watch... twelve hours. I never sleep that long.

After distributing the pie to my guests, which makes absolutely no sense to me, Lilah sits down next to me with her own piece of pie.

"It's good, huh?" Lilah asks as she takes a bite. Lilah never eats sweets. Things must be really bad for Lilah to eat pie.

"Yes." Surprisingly so. "Who made it?"

"HEB I think. I don't know who brought it."

Brianna comes back from answering the front door with a man wearing a suit in tow.

I glance at him out of the corner of my eye, then take another bite of pie. I have a good case of not caring. Learning that one's husband was killed in an airplane crash will do that to a person.

"This is Andrew Harrington," Brianna says, then lowers her voice. "Your attorney."

Alarmed, I look up at Andrew Harrington. "I have an attorney?"

He holds out a hand. "I'm Andrew," he says, kindly.

I set my fork down and put my hand in his.

"Is there someplace we can talk?" he asks. "In private."

"Lilah, get Mr. Harrington some pie, would you?" She turns back to Andrew. "Give me ten minutes and I'll have everyone out of here."

Andrew sits down across from me and dutifully eats the slice of pie Lilah puts in front of him.

Brianna takes the empty tray back into the living room.

"Thank y'all so much for coming," she says in what I recognize as her sweetest voice. "But we're gonna need a bit of privacy now."

Five minutes later she has my five unwanted guests herded out the door.

"We can talk now," she tells Andrew as she sits down at the table.

With Lilah on one side of me and Brianna on the other, I brace myself to hear what the attorney I didn't know I had has to say.

Just Breathe
PREVIEW

Chapter 3
Madison

"I've gone over all the paperwork," Andrew Harrington, Attorney says, taking a pair of wire-rimmed glasses out of his pocket and putting them on.

With the pie cleared away, I sit with my hands in my lap, watching him with heavy eyes.

He seems like a kind man. He has kind eyes and his tone is soft and understanding. Even so, it doesn't do much to keep the lump in my throat at bay.

The single word *widow* keeps swirling through my head. I'm too young to be a widow.

"I'm sorry," Brianna says glancing over at me. "Would you repeat that?"

"Sorry," I say, under my breath. My sister somehow knew my attention had wandered.

"Sure," Andrew says, looking into my eyes.

"Thomas made me executor of your estate, so I consulted with your accountant. I can skip over some of the details for now, but let me just boil it down.

"I'm afraid you're going to have to sell the house."

I blink at him. "Okay." Last night when the thought of living out here in Katy by myself crossed my mind, I'd shut it down. It wasn't something I could wrap my head around. But here he was bringing it up.

"You're okay with that?" Andrew asks.

"She needs to think about it," Brianna says.

"No," I say. "I don't need to think about it. I'm okay with it."

"Good," Andrew says. "That's good."

"So she'll have money, right?" Brianna asks. "From the sale of the house and insurance. She'll have insurance to start over, right?"

Frowning, Andrew rubs a hand over his face and removes his reading glasses.

"I regret to tell you the insurance is already allocated," he says.

"Already allocated?" Brianna says. "For what?"

"Thomas had some debt. Some rather large debts and even larger obligations."

Brianna looks at me. "What kind of debts did Thomas

have?"

"I don't know. I didn't know he had any debts." I look outside at the mimosa tree Thomas had planted. He'd been so proud of himself when he'd dug that hole all by himself and dropped the five-foot tall tree we'd hauled from Home Depot into it.

"What kind of debts?" I ask Andrew.

"He had some pretty significant credit card debt, another mortgage, and—"

"Wait." Brianna holds up a hand. "Another mortgage?"

Andrew glances at me. Sits up a little straighter. "He has a condo in downtown Houston."

"Since when?" I ask. Thomas had never told me about him having another condo. When we'd met, he'd lived in an apartment near the Galleria.

"We can come back to those details."

"No. The condo is a mistake. There's no condo." I feel a little dizzy. A little faint. If there was a condo, I should know about it.

"Five years. It's not a mistake."

I steel myself for the sudden realization that I hardly knew Thomas at all. "Tell me why. Why did Thomas have a condo he never told me about?"

Neither one of my sisters says anything as I wait for Andrew to tell us these things about my husband. Things I hadn't known. Things I should have known.

"The child," Andrew says. "Thomas has a child."

I squeeze my eyes closed and Brianna grips my hand.

Lilah watches us all closely, then turns on Andrew. "You

came all the way out here just to tell her this?" I hear the anger in Lilah's voice.

"It's okay, Lilah," I say, looking at her.

"No. It's not okay." She pins her gaze on Andrew. "If you don't have something good to tell Audrey, you can go. Can't you see she's already devastated?"

"I'm so sorry," Andrew says. "But I do have good news."

All three of us just look at him. A gust of warm Texas wind flutters a branch of the mimosa tree against the window.

"His grandfather left him a cabin. It's just outside a small town in the Colorado mountains."

"Who does that go to?" Brianna asks with obvious ire in her tone.

"It's protected. According to the grandfather's will, in the event that something happens to Thomas, it specifically goes to Thomas's first wife."

"Am I his first wife?" I ask, my voice sounding small. I no longer trust anything I thought I knew about my marriage.

Thomas has a child. A child with someone else. He'd never told me about having a child.

"Yes," Andrew says. "You're his first wife."

"The cabin is free and clear of any debts." He clears his throat. "There's a stipend that comes with it."

"So I own a house in Colorado?"

"Yes. Sort of. It's in a trust. It's yours but you have to live in it. You have to live in the house for one year for it to be yours. As long as you live there, you get the stipend that comes with it. But you can never sell the house."

"Thomas said we'd go to Colorado one day. I thought he meant we'd go there for a vacation."

"Audrey can't just move off to Colorado," Brianna says. "She has a job here. A life. Family."

"The cabin is paid for?" Lilah asks.

"Free and clear. All expenses paid by an executor."

"It must be a dump," Brianna says. "She can't live in a dump."

"It's not a dump," Andrew says.

"You've seen it?" Lilah asks, pinning Andrew with her gaze.

"No. But I've seen photos."

"Who's the executor?" I ask.

"I am," Andrew says.

Brianna sits back and crosses her arms. "It sounds fishy to me."

"What town?" I ask. "What town in Colorado?"

"Whiskey Springs."

Whiskey Springs. I'll think about it. Maybe something will come to me. A conversation. A mention.

But I know it won't. Just like the child. Apparently Andrew was a vault when it came to his personal life.

"How much is the stipend?" Lilah asks.

"The stipend is one million dollars."

"In lieu of millions of dollars in insurance," Brianna says, through gritted teeth. "The wife gets stuck with a cabin in the middle of nowhere and a million dollars. It won't last anytime." She looks at me. "You should contest the will."

"He has a child," I say. I don't even know who's side I'm

on at this point. I'm just numb. Trying to hold all this information in my groggy brain and process it.

"So? He should have told you."

"And he shouldn't have died," I say. What I don't say is I shouldn't be a widow. I should not be a widow at twenty-seven.

"Ladies," Andrew says. "I'm going to leave some papers for you to look over. I'd like to come back in a couple of days after you've had some time to absorb everything."

My sisters glare at him.

"Okay," I say. "I need time to think about everything. And right now I'm very tired."

"I understand. I hate to be the one to drop all this on you. But..." He pulls a stack of papers from the briefcase at his feet. "There's one thing I think I need to clarify."

"Okay."

"The stipend. There's enough money in the account to last all of your lifetimes put together and it's in an account that compounds daily." He leans forward, his gaze locked on mine. "The stipend will be deposited in your account the day you sign the papers. One million dollars. Every year. In perpetuity."

Just Breathe

PREVIEW

Chapter 4
Audrey

"She can't go," Brianna says.

"She can't not go," Lilah says.

The three of us sit in my living room on the big sectional with nothing but the flames from the fireplace for light. The contract papers are scattered in front of us on the coffee table. Already dog-eared and highlighted.

It's dark now. After Andrew had left, I'd gone upstairs to take a nap. It seems like I can't get enough sleep.

Without reading it, I left the paperwork with my sisters

to examine. And they had. I'll read it all later. Tomorrow maybe.

They'd gone through everything line by line. Brianna worked for an attorney for a year so she'd felt qualified to go through the paperwork line by line. Then she and Lilah had discussed it while I slept.

They'd even sent it over to our Uncle Carl. Uncle Carl is an attorney.

After I'd gotten up, they'd had pizza delivered of which I'd eaten all of one slice.

Not content with me eating just one slice of pizza, Lilah had made popcorn and set it out. I grab a handful and nibble on it.

"Audrey doesn't know anything about the mountains."

"How much different can it be than Katy?" Lilah, obviously not a fan of Katy, wrinkles her nose and picks up a bowl of popcorn. She doesn't eat sweets, but she'll eat anything salty. All ninety-five pounds of her.

"Have you ever been in the mountains?"

"She'll be fine. It's not just a cabin. It's a big house and it has maid service."

"I don't trust it." Brianna sits back and crosses her arms.

"You do know I'm right here," I say.

They both turn and look at me. I honestly think they had forgotten I was sitting right here.

"Of course we do," Brianna says.

"Is that in the contract?" I ask. "The maid service?"

"Yes," Lilah says, her face brightening. "We pulled up pictures on the Internet. Do you want to see them?"

"Sure." I shrug. I'm curious. For a lot of reasons. Not the least of which is why Lilah is suddenly fighting against Brianna for me to go to the cabin.

She links her phone to the big screen television—one of Thomas's prized possessions—on the wall over the fireplace and pulls up Google Earth. Types in the address.

"I see a lot of trees." Squinting, I lean forward. "And a rooftop. I can't tell anything about it."

"See," Brianna says. "It's blocked or something."

"It might be blocked," I say, munching on popcorn. "Some private residences are."

"You're both missing the point," Lilah says. "It's big. It's not just a cabin."

"Andrew said he has pictures. Did you ask him to send them over?"

They both look blankly at me. Then they look at each other.

I locate his business card on the coffee table and send him a text asking for pictures.

"Now," I say. "We just wait. He'll send..."

My phone vibrates.

"He must have been waiting."

"You have photos?" Lilah asks. "Put them up on the television."

I have three photographs. The first one is of the outside of the house.

"It looks like a lodge," Brianna says. "Two stories."

"Three if you count the attic." Lilac stands up to move

closer to the television. "Look how pretty it is. It looks a log cabin but with glass. Look at all the windows. "

"We don't know how old the photos are," Brianna says.

Lilah turns on her. "Since when did you become so negative?"

"Since my sister is thinking about moving to the other side of the world to live."

"It's not the other side of the world," I say, keeping my eyes on the photo. Taking in the what is supposed to be a cabin, but looks more like a lodge just as Brianna pointed out.

"Couldn't be much worse than Katy," Lilah grumbles.

I don't say anything, but I tend to agree with Lilah. Something about the place looks so peaceful.

"Thomas never said anything to you about it?" Lilah asks.

I shake my head and lower my gaze to my phone.

"Lilah," Brianna admonishes.

"It's okay. We have to talk about him eventually." I slide to the next photo.

The inside of the cabin looks surprisingly modern with lots of light. An open floorplan much like this house.

"Look at that view," Lilah says. "You can sit in your living room and look out at the mountains."

"If she goes," Brianna says.

"I wonder if it's furnished," I say.

"It is. Fully furnished."

"That might not be the same furniture it has now."

"Brianna. Stop it."

"It doesn't matter," I say. "I don't need a lot. And with the stipend if I don't like it, I can replace it." I slide to the next photo.

"Look at that fireplace," Lilah says. "I think that's real wood."

Brianna bites her tongue.

"I can learn how to light a real fire," I say, knowing what Brianna is thinking. "How hard can it be?"

No one says anything for long enough that I shift my gaze to Lilah, then Brianna.

"You lost," Lilah says to Brianna.

"I know."

"Lost what?"

"The bet. I bet that you would be. Brianna bet that you wouldn't. I won."

"I haven't decided yet."

"You can't not go," Lilah says.

"She can live with me," Brianna offers.

"In your one-bedroom apartment? No thank you."

"Our parents."

I'm already shaking my head. "I'm definitely not moving back to Atlanta."

"By the way," Brianna says. "Our parents will be here in the morning."

"They should have just driven," Lilah says. "They'd be here by now."

"It's too hard on them. They're too old."

"They didn't have to come," I say. But I knew they'd be here for the funeral.

"It'll be good," Brianna says. "They can help pack."

"So they're too old to drive, but not too old to help pack?"

Brianna shrugs.

"Again. No need. I'm going to pack up my personal things and let the rest go with the house." I look up at the photo on the television. "It looks like my next place has everything I need."

Lilah is right.

I'm going.

Moving to Katy hadn't been my idea, but I'd gone along with it.

And Thomas had left everything to a child I hadn't even known he had.

And he might not even have known about it or intended it, but he'd left me a cabin in the mountains. Along with a healthy stipend.

I'm not going to let this opportunity slip by me.

Keep Reading Just Breathe...

ALSO BY KATHRYN KALEIGH

CONTEMPORARY

The Gravity of Us Series

(Reading Order)

Just Breathe

Just Surface

Just Melt

Standalone Suspense

Out of Ashes

Alpine Falls (Maybe Yours) Series

(Reading Order)

Still Yours (Maybe)

Yours for Christmas (Maybe)

Forever Yours (Maybe)

(ALPINE FALLS)

Stranded in Alpine Falls

Belonging in Alpine Falls

The Spirit of Christmas in Alpine Falls

Christmas Wishes in Alpine Falls

Finding True North in Alpine Falls

A Ghost of Christmas Magic in Alpine Falls

Secrets and Second Chances

Honeymoon with a Stranger

Not Our Wedding

(SILVER PINES)

The Way Back to You

Back to Where We Began

When We Were Us

(ONCE UPON FOREVER)

My Forever Guy

Our Forever Love

Forever Vows

Finding Forever

Accidentally Forever

(TRUE NORTH)

Borrowed Until Monday

Still Mine

The Moon and the Stars at Christmas

Perfectly Mismatched

On the Way to Forever

A Merry Little Christmas

On the Way Home to Christmas

It was Always You

(UNBREAK MY HEART)

Begin Again

Love Again

Falling Again

(FOR THE LOVE OF THE FLIGHT)

Just Stay

Just Chance

Just Believe

Just Us

Just Once

Just Happened

Just Maybe

Just Pretend

Just Because

(MAGNETIC NORTH)

Second Chance Kisses

Second Chance Secrets

First Time Charm

Three Broken Rules

Second Chance Destiny

Unexpected Vows

(FALLING FOR CHRISTMAS)

The Heart of Christmas

The Magic of Christmas

In a One Horse Open Sleigh

A Secret Royal Christmas

An Old Fashioned Christmas

(CITY SKYLINE BILLIONAIRES)

Billionaire's Unexpected Landing

Billionaire's Accidental Girlfriend

Billionaire's Fallen Angel

Billionaire's Secret Crush

Billionaire's Barefoot Bride

(TRULY, MADLY, DEEPLY)

The Lady in the Red Dress

On the Edge of Chance

Sealed with a Kiss

Kiss Me at Midnight

The Heart Knows

(STOLEN ECHOES)

When Cupid's Arrow Strikes

Chasing Fireflies

A Chance Encounter

(EDGE OF THE HORIZON)

The Forever Equation

Pretend Boyfriend

All our Tomorrows

Kissing for Keeps

Out of the Blue

The Princess and the Playboy

(RED LIPSTICK KISSES)

Red Lipstick Kisses and Small Town Wishes

Stolen Dances and Big City Chances

Chance Connections and Upside Down Plans

A Christmas Kiss on the Twenty-Fifth

Believe in the Magic of Christmas

Vows of Inheritance Series

(Reading Order)

Vow to Protect

Vow to Redeem

ROMANTASY

(IN THE SPIRIT OF LOVE)

Spirits of the Heart

Out of Dreams and Ashes

Etched Upon the Heart

WESTERN ROMANCE

(LONE STAR HEARTS)

Wanted by a Texas Ranger

Saved by a Texas Ranger

(WHISKEY SPRINGS)

Finding Natalie

Promising Samantha

Falling for Allyson

Saving Savannah

Claiming Charlie

Rescuing Keira

Protecting Gabriella

Courting Isabella

TIME TRAVEL

(INTO THE MIST)

Written in the Wind

Scripted in the Stars

Destined in the Twilight

Promised in the Mist

Trapped in the Melody

(DRAGON'S BLOOD)

Dragon's Blood

Lavender Blue

Champagne Silver

Twilight Frost

Mountbatten Pink

(WHEN HEARTSTRINGS BECKON)

Rescued in Time

Meet me in 1879

(WHEN HEARTSTRINGS ECHO)

Messages Across Time

Falling Through to Forever

Once Upon a Winter's Spell

(BECKONED)

Before the Storm

Twist of Fate

When the Stars Align

Once Upon a Christmas

Once in a Blue Moon

A Wish Upon a Star

(BEGUILED)

When Lightning Strikes

Storm of Time

Midnight Storm

When the Moon Falls

Stormborn Angel

(SPELLED)

Time Tempest

The Heart Remembers

A Moment in Time

Moonlight Shadows

HISTORICAL

(TAPESTRY OF BLUE AND GRAY)

Shadows Beneath Magnolia Blooms

Secrets Among Southern Roses

(IT HAPPENED BY ACCIDENT)

Accidentally Alluring

Accidentally Married

(SOUTHERN BELLE CIVIL WAR)

Beyond Enemy Lines

Love Always

Hearts Under Siege

Hearts Under Fire

Away Down South in Dixie

The Reluctant Bride

Stay with Me

Jasmine Kisses

Magnolia Kisses

Gardenia Kisses

(THE QUINNS)

Wait for Me

Take Me Home

Keep Me Safe

FATED MATES

Riley's Mate

Aiden's Mate

Brayden's Mate

STANDALONE SUSPENSE

Lost and Found

All I Want for Christmas

Serenity

Courting Alley Cat

All of the books in each Series are standalone and can be read out of order. However, some books have characters from the previous stories in them.